I, Death

I, Death

Mark Leslie

METRO VANCOUVER   DOMINION of CANADA

I, Death

Paperback published October 2014
ISBN: 978–1–927609–03–3

Simultaneous publication of eBook October 2014
EPUB ISBN: 978–1–927609–04–0
MOBI ISBN: 978–1–927609–05–7
PDF ISBN: 978–1–927609–06–4

The text in this novel is copyright © 2014, Mark Leslie Lefebvre, who asserts his moral right to be established as the owner of this work.

Cover design by and copyright © 2014, Bret Taylor
www.HowyadoinGraphics.com

Author's photo by John Robbie
www.JoRoPhotography.com

Lyrics used in the chapter "Wednesday February 15, 2012 — 5:14AM" for the song "Welcome to My Life" were written by Pierre Bouvier and Chuck Comeau. It was recorded by Simple Plan on the 2004 album *Still Not Getting Any...* which was released by Lava and Atlantic Records, and is available through most outlets. Please support your local independent musical artists.

Typeset in Warnock and Helvetica

The "Atomic Fez Publishing" logo and the molecular headgear colophon is designed by, and copyright © 2009, Martin Butterworth of The Creative Partnership Pty, London, UK (www.CreativePartnership.co.uk).

PUBLISHER'S NOTE:

This is a work of fiction. All characters in this publication are fictitious and any resemblance to any real places or persons — living or dead — is purely coincidental. Any scenes involving alcohol, drugs, and / or teen-age sex are not in any way an endorsement of these sorts of behaviour by the publisher or the author. Kids: don't do drugs, stay in school, use a condom. Word, yo.

All rights reserved. No part of this book may be used or reproduced in any manner whatsoever without written permission from the authors, except in the case of brief quotations embodied in critical articles or reviews.

ATOMIC FEZ PUBLISHING
№304 – 2065 Triumph Street
Vancouver, British Columbia
V5L 1K7, CANADA
WWW.ATOMICFEZ.COM

Library and Archives Canada Cataloguing in
Publication entry available upon request

10   9   8   7   6   5   4   3   2   1

Table of Contents

Foreword: "Walking the Writer's Road"
    by Steve Vernon   vii

Dedication   xiii

I, Death

    Part I: The Online Journal of Peter O'Mallick   7

    Part II: Brecht's Story   267

    Part III: Sin Eater   305

    Epilogue   363

About the Author   365

Walking the Writer's Road

Foreword

When a fellow walks the writer's road he gets to know an awful lot of people that he never gets to meet.

That is just how it goes sometimes in this crazy racket I am in. I send my stories off to editors whom I never meet and I cheerfully let them pick apart my life's work. I see my stories appearing in magazines and anthologies alongside of people whom I appreciate and respect. Folks whose words command my attention and give me pleasure — in the form of stories and poems and novels they have written — folks whom I never get to meet.

That's the way it is with me and Mark Leslie Lefebvre.

I actually met Mark back about ten years ago when he came to Halifax to read and sign his collection of short fiction, *One Hand Screaming* — although I had stumbled across and admired his work in a couple of magazines and anthologies before that. At the time Mark was working as a Product Manager for the local Chapters outlet in Hamilton.

Now you have to understand that when a writer tells another writer that he works as a manager at a bookstore — right away that writer achieves a sort of psychic promotion from being just a lowly wordsmith into something more along the lines of "godhood".

It goes something like this.

Steve — "So what do you do for a living when you're not writing?"

Mark — "I'm a manager at a Chapters store."

Steve — "I am a worm. I am a lowly wiggly worm. I am truly not worthy."

Mark has pretty well always worked in books. He started as a part-time bookseller at Coles on Sparks Street in Ottawa and then he worked within The Book Company stores at Carlingwood Mall and Bank & Slater. He moved to Hamilton in 1997 and worked at Chapters in Ancaster as a Product Manager. In 1999 he took the role of Database Quality Manager for Chapters Online and spent seven years learning the ins-and-outs of metadata, industry standards and SQL relational database systems.

The man knows his stuff.

In August 2006, Mark retired from Indigo and began working at Titles — McMaster University's bookstore, which turned 75 years old the year he joined — the man had that much effect on the place.

I'm kidding. Mark revolutionized that bookstore by purchasing and installing of one of the first Espresso Book Machines — under the "Titles on Demand" name — and guiding a thriving Print on Demand business. The man has *always* walked on the cutting edge of the publishing business. In October 2011 he took on the position of Director of Self Publishing & Author Relations for Kobo, a global eBook retailer that operates out of Toronto, Ontario. He was the driving force behind *Kobo Writing Life*, a DIY portal for authors and small publishers to get their works published to Kobo's global catalogue.

Just imagine the responsibility and the street cred that comes with those sorts of accomplishments. Mark has doomed himself to stand beneath his own shadow in that tens of thousands of readers and writers have come to think about Mark as "that Kobo guy."

Mark is more than that.

Mark is a heck of a writer and a rock solid editor and a very good friend. He has helped me and hundreds of other writers like me in countless different ways. He is the kind of friend who if I called one night from a pay-phone and said "Mark, I need to move" he'd be there the very next day in a stolen truck.

If I called and said "Mark, I need to move a body" he'd show up with that very same truck, a body bag, and a Bible just in case I wanted someone to say a few words.

In short, the man is reliable.

The man does exactly what he says.

The man delivers.

In 2004, Mark collected some of his previously published works in *One Hand Screaming*. In 2006, he edited *North of Infinity II*, an anthology of speculative stories for Mosaic Press. In 2009 Mark edited *Campus Chills*, a themed anthology featuring horror tales set on colleges and universities across Canada. In 2013, Mark edited *Tesseracts 16: Parnassus Unbound.* He has written three ghost story guides for Dundurn Press: *Haunted Hamilton: The Ghosts of Dundurn Castle & Other Steeltown Shivers* (2012), *Spooky Sudbury: True Tales of the Eerie & Unexplained* (co-authored with Jenny Jelen) (2013), and the upcoming collection *Tomes of Terror: Haunted Bookstores and Libraries.* That's not to

Foreword / **ix**

mention the many indie-published eBooks he has created, as well as that upcoming Canadian werewolf novel

Like I said, the man delivers.

He delivers in this book, *I, Death*, as well.

I, Death is a lively, intriguing and fast-paced easy-to-read story of a young man named Peter O'Mallick who is struggling beneath a death curse. *I, Death* is a death rattle coming of age story; it is a song, and it is the world's funniest dirty joke — all rolled into one. Everyone that Peter O'Mallick knows and loves meets with some dire fate in very short order. The story is told in the form of an actual blog — once again demonstrating Mark Leslie Lefebvre's cutting edge style.

So, whether you know him as "Mark Leslie" or "Mark Lefebvre" or "Mark Leslie Lefebvre", you ought to know this: Mark delivers, every time.

You call him up the next time you got a body to go.

**Yours in storytelling,
Steve Vernon**

Dedication

For Gem, who was there at the beginning of this writing journey.

I, Death

Prologue

The kid was a killer, a mass murderer; that much Bryan Brecht knew for sure.

What he still hadn't been able to figure out, though, was how exactly he was going to get close enough without falling prey to the powerful death curse that had people around the kid dropping like so many dead flies.

Removing his glasses, Brecht rubbed the side of his face, absently scratched at the patch of weeks-old stubble on his chin and started thinking about his options.

Brecht had learned about his existence thanks to the kid's online web log. *Fuckin' idiot*, he'd thought. Throwing his every emotion, his every feeling, all of the events of his pitiful life up on that blog. And it's not that he was entirely stupid about it — at least not until he was well into his almost daily rambling and moaning about his strife. The kid did know that people were reading his online diary, that they were following the macabre events which seemed to spiral around him. He knew there were readers out there — all over the world, in fact — checking in to see how he was doing, and perhaps also to keep track of the latest body count the kid left in his wake.

Another thing Brecht couldn't figure out was why nobody out there had alerted the authorities. Particularly since this

Prologue / 3

kid pretty much admitted to being responsible for no less than the deaths or crippling accidents of a dozen people.

Maybe it was that 'mob mentality' Brecht remembered reading about in a first year Psychology course at University. The fact these deaths were being broadcast and talked about so cavalierly on the internet might have meant every single person who stumbled upon it assumed someone else would alert, or even have already alerted, the police or FBI or the fucking *Ghostbusters* about this.

But another possibility occurred to Brecht.

Perhaps when people read the account of this teenager, this Peter O'Mallick who lived in a remote northern town and described the details of leaving a wake of bodies in his path, they wanted to believe it was a hoax; they wanted to believe this kid was making everything up.

Because to believe in the power this kid professed to have — the ability to kill someone so simply, so ruthlessly, so easily, without even needing to raise a single finger — that might be too much for the average person.

And if Brecht hadn't witnessed, first hand, the fact this kid wasn't actually lying about the evil force that burned within him, perhaps he wouldn't believe it either.

He not only believed, but he recognized the urgency of wanting to put the kid's power to his own use; of trying to control Peter and his supernatural ability to make Brecht more powerful than ever.

Finding the kid would be easy enough. Brecht had enough contacts, had enough means to find almost anyone anywhere.

But figuring out how to control the kid, how to not fall prey to his power, would be more difficult. Brecht knew he had been lucky both times he'd encountered the kid. But he couldn't count on luck to keep him alive. That wasn't how he operated.

Brecht picked up his thick, pop bottle glasses and put them back on.

Though he'd read it a hundred times, he returned to the kid's blog, wanted to read it again.

Wanted to dig into it for any clues he could find that would help him elude the kid's intense death curse.

Part I

The Online Journal of Peter O'Mallick

Wednesday January 18, 2012 — 10:23 PM

It's over. I can't believe it. Sarah won't speak to me. It's as if she blames me for her father's death sentence.

I can't say it's a new feeling, though. It's like all my life death has consumed the people close to me. First my parents, then my best friend, now Sarah's dad.

I've been where Sarah is now, but she won't let me help her — hell, she's not even talking to me.

Ever since her father announced to the family that he had an inoperable cancerous brain tumor so far advanced the doctors were giving him a 50 / 50 chance of living beyond one more month, she stopped talking to me, refused to see me and ignores my phone calls.

It's been four weeks now. Four long, painful, horrible weeks. I think I'm going to die. I wish I was dead, actually, like so many of the people I've cared about.

Our school's guidance counselor suggested that I start this blog in order to try dealing with it.

So here I am, typing, trying to come to terms with it. But I don't want to write about how I feel — I keep stopping and just sit here smashing my fingers down on the keyboard, smashing my fists down on the desk. I want to break something, smash something, throw my computer monitor through the fucking window.

This is bullshit.

I: The Online Journal of Peter O'Mallick

— 3 Comments —

Anonymous — said . . .
I don't know you, but I can tell you that blogging does help. Keep it up.

Anonymous — said . . .
I'm not sure if blogging really helps, or even takes away the pain. My own life has been filled with the death of many people who were close to me. I have blogged about it. I just can't say that it has helped. What might help, though, is for you to know that there are other people out there like you and who feel the same way.

Frank — said . . .
Fuck, dude. Sounds serious. Don't throw your computer out the window, though. How the hell else will you be able to blog about this?

Thursday January 19, 2012 — 9:27 PM

Sarah's still not talking to me.

She wasn't at school today, either.

I must have called her cell half a dozen times just today. Also, her home phone. She has her own private line — I keep leaving messages. But she won't answer.

The bitch.

No, I take that back. She's not a bitch. I love her. She's my soul-mate. That's why this hurts so fucking much, that's why it feels like somebody ripped my heart right out of my chest and started stomping on it.

We're studying Shakespeare in school right now — *Hamlet*, actually. I can't concentrate on much, but this is something that caught my attention. It's the scene that everyone has heard without having seen *Hamlet* — the one where he's standing there talking to himself — it's called a *solil*-something. Sounds like "a solid query" or something like that.

It doesn't matter.

What matters is that our teacher, Miss Hamilton, explained the monologue to us in proper modern English — I normally don't pay all that much attention to the old bird, but this time, I couldn't help but hang on her every word — well, this monologue, it spoke to me.

I: The Online Journal of Peter O'Mallick / **11**

To Be or not to Be.

Wow — what wild crazy shit. I mean, what made him put it into such a bizarre term? Who would have thought that that's what Hamlet meant — that he was considering committing suicide. I find myself reading and re-reading the quote over and over again. I think I have a lot of it memorized now, because I can recite it.

> *To Be or not to Be. That is the question. Whether 'tis nobler in the mind to suffer the slings and arrows of outrageous fortune, or to take arms against a sea of troubles and by opposing end them.*

"And by opposing, end them" — what a wickedly cool statement.

> *To die — to sleep no more. And by a sleep . . . to end the thousand heartaches, the thousand natural shocks that flesh is heir to. To die — to sleep. To sleep, perchance to dream. Aye, there's the rub.*

Ay, yes, "the rub"

> *For in that sleep of death what dreams might come when we have shuffled off this mortal coil.*

I know this Shakespeare dude lived hundreds of years ago — but he knew, man. He knew exactly how I feel. I don't know how, but he does.

Fucking strange.

— 1 Comment —

Frank — said . . .
You sound like you have a real tormented soul. Love is never an easy game to play it seems.

Friday January 20, 2012 — 6:04 PM

Okay, so the guidance counselor was right. I actually slept almost the whole night last night.

Fucking shrink. Who'da thought?

I actually felt better after writing the last blog entry. I even went a whole day without calling Sarah. A whole freakin' day.

It's actually helping, I think.

Saturday January 21, 2012 — 10:02 AM

Just when I thought I was getting over this — that the guidance counselor's therapy was finally working — it all fell apart.

The elated feeling I had yesterday seems to have slipped away, because I fell back into the old pattern again after a day. I woke up this morning with an urge to talk to Sarah. It was like this burning sensation I couldn't control.

I just wanted to talk to her. That's all.

Just talk to her.

Like an itch that you can't reach, I kept trying to scratch it, but it was no use.

All morning I just kept calling, leaving voice messages on her cell and land line (she has her own phone line — have I mentioned that already?) But she never calls back.

She never calls back.

Damn, that whole therapy thing was a temporary fix — it helped me for a very short time. But now, now I'm right back where I started. Or maybe even worse off, because for a day or so there I actually started to feel better.

Damn.

Saturday January 21, 2012 — 3:44 PM

I was considering writing about *Hamlet* and my thoughts about his little monologue and how it made me feel. It actually did help, and I think I need to get back on track like that again.

I think I need to express a bit of my pain. But not just today's pain; the pain that I've lived with my entire life.

I think in order to understand this, to come to terms with what's happened, I need to go right back to the beginning.

Right to the first person that was taken away from me.

To the beginning of this chain of death and misery.

My mother died during my delivery. As the story goes, there were some complications. The umbilical cord had wrapped itself around my neck and nobody had noticed. My mother was told that her baby had died in the womb, but that she had to give birth to it anyway.

She was screaming hysterically — it took everything that my father had just to calm her down, he'd said. The doctors then talked her through delivering her stillborn child. Although she did what they told her, she kept screaming through the whole process.

At one point, in the middle of the final push, she let out a gut wrenching scream, which happened to be her last mortal contribution to this world, and my head finally cleared her cervix in a huge rush of blood. Pushed down on the full flow

I: The Online Journal of Peter O'Mallick / **15**

of blood, the rest of my body came out so fast that the doctor and nurse who'd been ready to receive me didn't catch me. I landed on the floor with a wet slurpy thud and the strangest thing happened next.

I started crying.

The labour room staff were mystified.

Somehow, I'd come back from the dead just as my mother had breathed her last breath.

I'm told that my father didn't even know of my successful birth, even as the staff scrambled to pick me up, cut the umbilical cord, clean my eyes, ears and mouth of the birthing fluid. Despite the loud and unwavering crying I was making, he was completely unaware.

He just held my mother and cried — his own crying much louder than my own.

Welcome to the world, Peter.

— 1 Comment —

Frank — said . . .
That was some introduction to the world, Peter.

Monday January 23, 2012 — 9:10 PM

Damn, I hate the fact that the guidance counselor was right, but I felt even better after getting the first death, my mother's, off of my chest.

Sarah returned to school today and, while I did keep an eye on her whenever possible, surreptitiously glancing at her in class when she didn't realize I was looking at her — I have managed to not stalk her or approach her. And it's been two days since I called her. Sure, last night, before going to bed, I picked up the phone and started punching-in her number, but I put the phone down before I finished.

Who knows? If I keep up this journal type writing, maybe I'll get completely over Sarah.

I guess I should share the second death in this lifelong chain, then.

My father.

He died when I was about seven years old.

I can barely remember the man, but I do have these vague memories that play back to me like an old movie in my mind. One of my favorites is this memory from a time when I think I might have been four or five years old. I'm leaning back against the refrigerator, and my father is standing in the kitchen, talking to me but looking out the window at something outside. And he's reflecting on something, like he's sharing a deeply personal memory or experience with me. I

I: The Online Journal of Peter O'Mallick / 17

can't remember what he's telling me, but I remember being very interested, enraptured by his words. All that comes back is this memory of him talking to me and the musky, ripe scent of his pipe.

To this day, I cannot smell a pipe without thinking about my father and about that early memory. Though most of what I know about him is through stories told to me by relatives, I always have that image of him, standing near the window in the kitchen, talking to me and looking off into the distance, as the main picture in my head of him. And just like I have few memories of my father, I don't have many memories from when I was seven. But I remember that.

Plus this other one. All too clearly.

We were fighting. I was playing cops and robbers with a couple of friends, and my father wanted me to come in because it was time for my bath and I needed to get ready for bed. It was early summer and I remember being so angry that I had to go in when there was so much light outside. I thought I should only have to go in when the sun was down. It just wasn't fair.

I ignored my father, even though he was standing at the top of the steps and I was in the driveway. I remember wishing that he'd just shut up, wishing that he would go away, die, whatever, and just leave me the hell alone.

When he came down the steps, I ran across the street, toy gun in hand, looking toward my buddies who had already crossed the street and were pretending to shoot at each other over and around a hedge. I wanted to be over there with them, in the pretend world of cops and robbers, engaging in the mystery, the fun, not running from my dad.

He followed me across the street.

I didn't even see the car, but I heard it.

My dad must not have seen it either.

The impact instantly killed him.

18 / *I, Death*

— 2 Comments —

Frank — said . . .
Crikey, Peter. That is some burden for a small lad to carry. I don't imagine it is much of a lighter burden as an adult.

Trish — said . . .
Oh my. What a terrible memory to have to carry around!

Tuesday January 24, 2012 — 3:58 AM

I can't fucking sleep now.

I've been tossing and turning for several hours — been thinking about my dad getting hit by that car ever since reliving it a few hours ago. I never realized how guilty I felt about the whole thing. I mean, just moments before he was killed, I'd been wishing that he'd go away and die.

And I suddenly had this memory of standing over his dead body and laughing a bit. Laughing, because when I looked at his dead body I was thinking that this couldn't be my father. He didn't have a pipe sticking out of his breast pocket and I couldn't smell that musky pipe scent on him at all.

So I just stood there laughing. And that's how they found me: Standing over my father's dead body and laughing.

I never realized that I must have repressed the whole thing. I only remembered it after regurgitating the memory of my father getting hit by that car.

Yes. "Repressed" — it's a fun word — the guidance counselor at school has used it a few times when I've been speaking with him. I've been visiting him regularly lately — gee, I think I've been repressing those visits, although I do find them helpful. We don't often talk about Sarah or the whole 'death thing,' he often helps me just by listening to me talk about my day. Occasionally, the conversation will drift

20 / *I, Death*

towards Sarah or the many different people in my life who have died. But mostly it's distracting conversation.

I'd never admit this to him, but it's actually helpful.

I wish that I could talk to him about this feeling of guilt, this repressed feeling that I just uncovered.

But instead I'm stuck with the coping technique he'd suggested — write about it in my journal.

So much happened so quickly after my father died. I was moved away from most of my friends in Sudbury, sent to live with my Uncle Bob and Aunt Shelley in the small town of Levack. They've been raising me ever since — they're really good parents, actually. Maybe they've always been extra nice to me because they couldn't have kids of their own and they felt sorry for what had happened to me. But in any case, it's been good being their son.

Uncle Bob taught me how to fish, how to hunt — we often went out in his boat, on camping trips. Aunt Shelly has always been good to me; loving and supportive, but not at all imposing or restrictive. She's been protective, but also gave me my space when I needed it, let me have my freedom.

Of course, I'd never admit to them how good it's been. It's been years since we've been able to talk to each other, years since Uncle Bob and I have gone on a hunting or fishing trip together.

I miss that closeness, but I find that they annoy me and get on my nerves so easily these days.

Tuesday January 24, 2012 — 10:15 PM

I don't know if it's the lack of sleep from last night, but I finally fell asleep shortly after 4:00 A.M. and had to get up maybe only three hours later — I need to be up early to catch the bus to Sudbury, which is where my high school is. It takes about an hour to get there — but I've been a real wreck today. Made a huge ass of myself, too.

I waited for Sarah in front of her locker. Skipped a bunch of classes to do it, as well; just planted myself there and waited for her. For hours. I think she'd seen me a few times and purposely avoided heading down the hallway. But it was in the early afternoon, when the hallway was busy and I guess she couldn't see me through the crowd when she approached.

She was startled, I think, to see that I was still standing there.

She stopped, just a foot in front of me and stared.

Then she turned, without saying anything, and started walking away.

"Sarah!" I called out after her, my voice breaking, tears flowing freely down my face. "Please, don't ignore me any longer! Please talk to me! Sarah!"

She just walked away and I sank down on my knees, my face in my hands and cried.

22 / *I, Death*

I didn't look up again until the hallways were cleared. I just couldn't face all the people who'd seen me break down like that.

Damn Sarah. Why does it hurt to love her so much?

— 2 Comments —

Frank — said . . .
Peter, your last statement reminds me of a porn movie I once saw. In it, one hooker asks another, "What is love?" The other hooker replies, "I can't tell you what love is, but I do know that it hurts." I can't believe that I can quote a line from a porn movie but yes love hurts.

Franny — said . . .
Peter, maybe it's time to back off of Sarah for a bit? She's probably getting creeped out. No offense, but I am too. Just trying to help.

Wednesday January 25, 2012 — 4:58 PM

Okay, so I can't believe I never noticed this before, but apparently there are people who have been reading my journal entries, and even leaving comments.

I guess I never paid attention to the comment feature — I'm kind of new to the whole blogging thing, so wasn't really sure what I was doing — I just picked a template, loaded an image, filled out a few personal details and got started. I never realized how big this whole blogging community is, or even that there are other people out there doing this very thing.

It's kind of freaky, actually, knowing that there are people out there reading my words and deepest thoughts.

And this Frank guy who has made several comments seems to really get me and what I'm going through. Love *does* hurt. Funny, in his comment to my last post, he mentioned a quote from this old porn movie that he saw once. Have I mentioned that my Uncle Bob is a huge movie buff? I wonder if that extends to porn films. I mean, we've never talked about that genre, but I'm sure there must be classic porn films that are studied and discussed, all while these academic types sit there stroking their goatees (rather than stroking other parts of themselves — HA! HA!)

But this Franny person, the one who commented that I should back off Sarah, that I'm being a creep, well she just doesn't get it — she doesn't get what true love is. She has no

24 / *I, Death*

concept of the passion and love that Sarah and I felt for each other before she stopped talking to me. No fucking clue. How the hell can people go online and judge other people like that without knowing them? Sarah and I are soul-mates, destined to be together. She just can't see that right now.

Comments like that just piss me off.

— 1 Comment —

Trish — said . . .
I know how you feel, Peter. I've gotten a few comments like that myself. I think that most people, Franny included, have good intentions. Hopefully you will find some of their comments insightful. Just ignore the others. :)

Thursday January 26, 2012 — 2:10 AM

Can't get to sleep again. Dammit, it took me several hours to fall asleep because I was tossing and turning, and thinking about that comment this Franny person left about me being a creep. But when I finally did fall asleep I had a damn disturbing dream. So I decided to write about it to see if that helps me sleep. It worked the other night.

I had this vivid dream. An erotic dream. About Sarah.

Damn.

There we were, in my Uncle Bob's truck, like so many times before. Sarah's favorite album by Evanescence was playing, but neither of us was paying any attention to it. We'd just finished talking around the issue of University, neither one of us wanting to admit that after graduation it was possible we'd be heading to two different cities. The frustrated conversation ended the way it always had when we started talking like that: us telling each other that we loved each other and that's all that mattered — we'd be together forever.

And then we completely avoided the whole issue by getting hot and heavy.

Within seconds of our lips and tongues melting together, I'd been able to get her shirt pushed up to her shoulders. As I rolled her bra down, revealing taut firm nipples, I slipped down in the seat to let my tongue swirl around them in small circles. She tasted like candy, and as she moaned beneath

26 / *I, Death*

me, I felt myself strain uncomfortably against the denim of my jeans.

Her hands quickly found my zipper and fumbled with it while I darted back and forth, unable to settle on a single breast, but instead wanting my hands, my lips, my tongue to explore every inch of them.

By the time her hand slipped past my underwear and she took hold of my stiff cock, my lips stayed focused on a single nipple, sucking it in, flicking it with my tongue, swirling around and around. My hands began working her shorts down, my finger poking, exploring the hot moist warmth of her pussy.

It was always a struggle as to who would go down on the other one first, and this time Sarah moved faster than I did.

Knowing she'd won, I laid my head back against the seat, letting her take me in her mouth and just relishing the moment, but still able to reach and rub one breast with my right hand, the nipple stiff against my palm and still damp with my saliva.

She worked my pants midway down my legs as she bobbed her head up and down. She moaned in pleasure, and the sound of her muffled voice, stuffed full of my hard-on, brought a heightened sense of arousal. Every so often she'd stop, look up at me with a devilish glint in her eyes, flap my cock against her cheek and let out a girlish giggle.

She'd alternate between pumping her fist around my aching shaft and taking me full in her mouth, her head bobbing madly, impossibly fast, up and down, up and down.

"I'm going to cum," I gasped and closed my eyes as she switched again from pumping to sucking...

A sudden noise, a throat clearing, startled me. When I opened my eyes a moment later, there stood Sarah's father, silently staring at us through the passenger window.

I: The Online Journal of Peter O'Mallick / **27**

Unable to stop myself, I shot a load of cum deep into her throat as her father looked on.

I woke with a start at that point.

I can't believe I re-lived, through that dream, that horrible night.

Well, it'd been a wonderful night until Sarah's dad showed up.

Man, he'd been pissed.

But he didn't say anything, he just stared at us as Sarah and I scrambled to get our clothes back on properly. When Sarah was dressed, he pulled her out of the truck.

I sat there, stunned. I didn't know what to do. So I followed them to his car which was waiting just a few parking spots away. I can't believe we hadn't seen him pull up — well, I can believe it — we'd been too deep into the moment, hadn't noticed anything around us.

After putting Sarah into the car the way you see cops put suspects into the back of a cruiser, he whirled around and faced me. But instead of yelling at me — accusing me of having my way with his little baby, his little angel, or punching me, kicking me, spitting on me, all things that I'm sure he must have wanted to do — he just stared me down and the words he spoke hurt, struck me harder than any physical or verbal assault could have at the moment.

"I trusted you, Peter" he said. "I trusted you with her."

The words struck me deep. I wanted to tell him how much I loved Sarah, that she was the only girl for me, that we would be together forever, that I wanted to marry her — that there was nothing wrong with what we'd done because we were everything to each other.

But I just stood there, wishing he'd go away, that he'd just die, drop dead on the spot — whatever it took to relieve the guilt and shock that he'd just inflicted.

Wishing that he'd die.

28 / *I, Death*

And now, he's going to die.

I can't help but think that it's my fault.

But who the hell would believe me?

Maybe Sarah would — maybe that's why she's avoiding me. But I never got a chance to speak with her since that night. The next time she spoke to me, it was to tell me about the results of his doctor's appointment — the death sentence he'd been handed.

— 3 Comments —

Frank — said . . .

Peter, I have read your blog with interest since I stumbled on it. I don't recall reading what you will study when you leave school. After this post I got to thinking that you should be a writer; erotica meets *Twilight Zone* type writing.

I know it's probably a little insensitive saying that knowing what you write is a biographical account of your pain. But you should consider it.

Also, don't worry about this Franny person. I think you must just go with your own gut on how to deal with Sarah.

Kelly — said . . .

I don't know, dude! I tend to agree with Franny. Back off on the Sarah stuff for a while. It's still too fresh, man.

Kim — said . . .

There is a saying: if you love something, set it free. If it comes back to you it's yours. If it doesn't, then it was never meant to be.

Sarah's hurting too, Peter. Give her time. Hold onto the good memories until then.

Sunday January 29, 2012 — 9:24 PM

I haven't been sleeping much since that last nightmare a few days ago.

The worst part about it, of course, is the fact that it's not just a nightmare — it's a nightmare in which I relived everything that occurred that night exactly as it happened. That's almost worse, I think.

Every time I close my eyes, I see Sarah's father staring at me; his hurt, painful eyes. Dammit, why couldn't he have just been pissed off with me and taken a swing at me? Why did he have to come off like that? All "I trusted you, Peter" and shit. Man, that's what really gets me.

I also spent a long time reading and re-reading the three comments on my last post. It's funny that Frank should mention me being a writer. That's what Sarah wants to be. And she's going to be a damn fine writer, too.

But that's her. Not me.

At least Frank gets me. Fuck, the guy lives in South Africa (*I followed his comment to his own blog — what a fucking awesome thing this whole blogging thing is*), and he gets me. I don't know how he found my blog, but at least he fucking gets me. Yet people I know, within my own town, they just don't get it.

There are a couple of other comments from Kelly and this Kim chick. Yeah, okay, I see the advice, and I hear you. *Blah,*

30 / *I, Death*

blah, blah, fresh pain, if you love something set it free. Gee, you think I haven't heard these things from my friends?

Well, I guess I *would* have heard these things from my friends if I was hanging around with them. But I haven't been. I've been avoiding them since Sarah dumped me. You know why? Because I don't want to hear all that bullshit from them. And now I'm reading it here. Jesus. You just can't escape people and their unsolicited advice. Even if they're complete strangers and you haven't a fucking clue who they are.

I did let Sarah go, dammit. Do you have any idea how long it's been since I've tried to call her or approached her at all? It's been almost a week. Fuck. What do you want? Want me to move to another town? Do you have any idea how difficult it is to just "back off" anyway? It's not easy — not at all easy.

If only I could fucking sleep. Just a little bit.

— 5 Comments —

Frank — said . . .
Everyone is a pseudo-helpline these days. I just don't think women grasp what they do to us. Here's hoping you catch some sleep, Peter.

Goldilocks — said . . .
It's hard to chill out and sleep when you're worked-up over someone. Things just keep replaying over and over in your mind like a broken record. When I'm this way, I find that Tai chi helps me to chill and finally sleep... you should try it. :)

Kim — said . . .
I realize that the advice given to you on your blog is unsolicited and perhaps a little corny and self-explanatory. However, the reason you are getting advice from people is because your pain has touched them in some way. And that makes them reach out and want to be there for you. They may not

I: The Online Journal of Peter O'Mallick / 31

understand completely what you're going through, but everyone that has loved someone like you love Sarah knows how horrible it feels to have that love ripped away.

If you don't want advice, then tell people to back off. Just keep in mind that you don't have to go through this on your own, if you don't want to.

(and by the way, men can do just as much to women as women can do to men!)

Mantaray Ocean — said . . .

Peter, Goldilocks is right. It is hard to chill out when you are that worked up over someone. I think I know some of what you must be going through, when it comes to Sarah. No matter what anyone says to you, you must follow through with your heart.

Not to give you more unwanted advice, but I find that the thoughts will stay in my head and play over... and over. The only escape I found was words. So, I begin to capture my thoughts, and put them on paper. I continued to write word upon word until all the thoughts that were in my head were now on paper. Then, I slept.

I really believe that your guidance counselor was on the right path in advising you to start a blog.

I hope that you find peace soon.

Trish — said . . .

I applaud you for going a week without calling or approaching Sarah. I know it's not easy. I've been in similar situations, and when you love someone so much, it's not easy to walk away. If only you could have the chance to show them how much you care, maybe things would be different...

Good luck, Peter.

Tuesday January 31, 2012 — 7:40 AM

Couldn't sleep again last night.

Still haven't been able to sleep properly.

I keep having these erotic dreams about fooling around in the truck with Sarah that always end with some horrifying image of Sarah's father dying.

I've been a wreck at school.

Can't concentrate on anything; except Sarah.

When she passes in the hall, I stand there staring at her. Like a big dumb jackass, I guess, standing in one spot, the crowds of students moving all around me, just staring at her, and, after she leaves, at the spot she was last in.

A big dumb, tired, and horny jackass.

And I noticed that I've got more comments, more advice, more people concerned. I don't know. I don't want advice, but it's nice to know that at the very least there are strangers out there who seem concerned enough. At least somebody cares.

I'm so tired, I just want to sit down and fucking cry.

Wednesday February 1, 2012 — 11:47 PM

It's always the same, now.

I know I'd previously said that dreaming of exactly what really happened that night in Uncle Bob's truck was the worst kind of nightmare. But I was wrong, because these new nightmares I've been having the past few days are far worse. I can't get rid of these maddening dreams.

To sleep, perchance to dream. Aye there's the rub.

It doesn't matter what time I fall asleep, whether I stay up late or go to bed really early — it always starts the same — hot, heavy, and frisky, then the blowjob, then Sarah's father shows up all of a sudden.

But it ends differently each time.

One time he's standing there and he starts to fall apart. Chunks of his face start dropping off in bloodless pieces, like some sort of animated 3D puzzle, until there's nothing in front of me but a pile of his pieces all quivering on the ground like some strange new flavour of JELL-O.

Another time, he's staring at me with that hurt look in his eyes. Then his eyeballs start bleeding and his skins starts sweating profusely. Then, slowly — ever so slowly — he starts melting. His flesh starts crawling down the sides of his face like giant beads of sweat or tear-drops, until his head

34 / *I, Death*

caves back in on itself, and he melts like some Dairy Queen cone that has been sitting in the sun.

This last time — the thing that woke me just a few minutes ago — he starts aging in front of me. His hair starts going grey, like some sort of mad time-lapse photography, then his skin starts to crease, wrinkle, and sag. In less than a minute he's standing in front of me like a goddamn zombie, his flesh all dried out, completely devoid of colour and cracked, and I can't look at him. Instead, I look down into the car where Sarah is, and I see *her* zombie face staring back at me, my cum dripping down the side of her face from a huge crack in her cheek.

"Peeeeeter," Sarah says, her voice like the whisper of wind through crusty dried leaves, "I want you in my mouth again." And when she moves her tongue out to lick her lips, a sad pathetic echo of the way she used to do so when she was trying to turn me on, her tongue falls out of her mouth and lands with a sickeningly loud slap in my lap like some piece of thick raw meat landing on a cutting board.

It was the slap of the meat that snapped me out of my sleep a few minutes ago.

I jumped out of bed and started looking around the room, convinced that somewhere in the room, somewhere just out of sight, I'd find Sarah's severed tongue. It took several minutes before I was able to convince myself that it was all just a terrible dream.

About that time I bolted for the bathroom where I puked my guts up.

That was tough, too, since I've hardly eaten anything this week — can barely get anything down.

These dreams are driving me fucking nuts.

— *3 Comments* —

Frank — said . . .
Cripes, Peter. People who interpret dreams would have a field day with these. I really hope it gets better for you and you get some sleep minus all the terrible dreams.

Kim — said . . .
That's kinda gross Peter . . . no wonder you can't sleep. Maybe a sleeping pill will knock you out so you can get some rest.

Monica — said . . .
Wow, those dreams sound scary! The scent of decay permeates the atmosphere of your dreams. No wonder you can't eat. There's got to be a silver lining to this cloud somewhere.

Sunday February 5, 2012 — 11:42 PM

The dreams have stopped.

For now at least.

I dropped into a dead sleep right after lunch and slept for ten solid hours.

Fucking snow. This morning I hated it, but I think it was the snow that helped me finally hit the proper point of mental and physical exhaustion. We got dumped on over-night with somewhere between thirty and forty centimetres of snow. Holy shit. Again. Uncle Bob's snow blower is on the fritz — likely because it's been used so many damn times this winter due to winter storms like the one we just got. At least our friggin' power wasn't out like I heard happened to over 80,000 poor slobs in central Ontario.

Uncle Bob and I went out there and started shoveling the snow around 9:15 this morning, and, without the snow blower, it took the both of us close to four hours to get the snow cleared.

The drifts in the middle of the driveway were almost three and a half feet high in some places, and the two ends of the driveway (we live on a corner lot with a big long wrap-around driveway with entrances on two different intersecting streets) were plowed in at least five feet high by the snowplows. Man, that was the hardest part, that heavy, salt and sand encrusted snow. I thought we would never be finished.

I: The Online Journal of Peter O'Mallick

Anyway, when we came in for lunch, all sweaty and exhausted, Aunt Shelley was pestering me the way she always does about how little I eat. I guess this time she was right, because I haven't been able to eat a solid meal all week. She was pestering me about how little I was eating, and suggested she call the "on-call" doctor so I could get in to see him, when I almost collapsed at the table. From exhaustion, I guess.

I left my plate virtually untouched and went into my bedroom.

Without changing or anything I fell onto my bed and passed out.

I'm pretty sure Uncle Bob convinced Aunt Shelley not to call the doctor, and not to pester me anymore, just to let me sleep the day away, because I woke up in exactly the same position I'd collapsed in, still dressed and everything. Thank God for that.

It was glorious.

Ten freakin' hours of uninterrupted, dark, empty, blissful sleep. I think that's all I really needed.

I've been up for about 10 minutes now, feeling fully awake. Fully rested.

For the first time in what feels like forever.

Don't think I could sleep now if I tried.

— 2 Comments —

Frank — said . . .
Glad you finally got some sleep, Peter. Maybe with some sleep, some of the shit life throws at you may make more sense.

Kim — said . . .
That's awesome news Peter...you know the body tends to heal itself while you sleep!
Hopefully this is the beginning of better times!

Tuesday February 7, 2012 — 10:46 PM

It's amazing what a couple of good night's sleep will get you. Maybe it's all the fresh air and back-breaking snow shoveling I've been doing lately, but something's working right.

I did end up going back to sleep the other night. I dropped off again at maybe half past midnight. Last night, I slept the whole night through as well. And I did dream, but it was normal stuff — none of the nightmarish stuff that's been plaguing me lately.

It's interesting. I saw Sarah today, and, instead of getting all freaked out and staring at her, or wanting to follow her, I just kept walking. Sure, my heart was in my throat and beating a million beats per minute, but I just kept walking, and I think I made it look like things were cool and I was over her. I should be an actor.

Like I said, a couple of full nights' sleep works wonders.

The thought of actually being "over" her and being able to play that part reminded me of something, though. A conversation that Sarah and I had not all that long ago. Back in the fall of 2010, in November, I think, Sarah and I were driving back after seeing the last Harry Potter movie in Sudbury.

I: The Online Journal of Peter O'Mallick / **39**

We were in her father's 76 Impala — a brown beauty of a car with a convertible top. Of course, it was too cool out to have the top down, but man I loved driving that car.

That was the great thing about that car. Sarah loved to drive it, and so did I. It was fun, too, because when she was driving, I'd be undoing her front zipper and slipping a hand under the waist band of her panties, rubbing her with my finger while she drove. And when I was driving, she would either be playing with my nuts or stroking my cock.

That night, she was giving me one of her nimble and expert hand-jobs when the conversation turned to University. Sarah was talking about heading off to Carleton University in Ottawa. She is a brilliant writer and has always wanted to be a journalist. Ever since I've known her, she's always loved to write. I'm pretty sure, in fact, that one of the only reasons I've taken to following the guidance counselor's advice and writing these journal entries is because on some level I've equated writing with Sarah. Maybe somewhere in the back of my mind, writing this stuff gives me the sense of being closer, somehow, to Sarah.

It's funny, too, because this Frank guy who leaves me comments from time to time mentioned that he thought I'd make a good writer. I guess I must have picked up at least a little bit of talent from Sarah and maybe it even shows.

Anyway, Sarah wanted to get in to the journalism program at Carleton, and I wanted to stay here and attend Cambrian College. I've always said that I wanted to take the 'Heating, Ventilation and Air Conditioning' program, but that's just been an excuse to stay here in town and keep doing the things that I'm doing until I can figure everything out.

I'll be fucked if I really know what I want to do. I need a few years of just living and not going to school in order to figure out what that might be.

40 / *I, Death*

They should make that mandatory, you know? I mean, how the hell does anyone who's 18 know what they want to spend the rest of their life doing? College or University should start a few years after high school — give kids a chance to figure out what they want to do. It's all too damned rushed. No wonder our generation is so damn fucked up.

But I wasn't about to admit my reason for wanting to stay around here to anyone — least of all Sarah. There, see how that's working. The guidance counselor would be damn proud of me, I think. I *am* admitting it now, and admitting it to anyone who happens to read this. So it's not like I'm just admitting this to myself. I'm admitting it to the *world*.

Anyway, back to that night, the night we were coming back from the final Harry Potter movie. There was a scene in the movie about the School of Hogwarts that reminded Sarah about something she'd read about Carleton University. Something about the underground tunnels that completely connected all buildings on campus so that you don't need to go outside at all. Apparently, if you lived in residence on campus, you could attend classes in your pajamas and never needed to take a step outside in the snow all winter. She thought that would be the coolest thing, and was hoping that she'd be accepted into residence there.

She started talking about all that, and I immediately became flaccid in her hands.

"Peter," she asked, still trying to work some life back into my now unresponsive cock, "What's wrong?"

I'd been about to say it, about to tell her why I got so tense, so upset when she talked about University, about moving to Ottawa — that I knew what would happen. She would move away, and at first we'd miss each other, call every day, write letters, send e-mails, make trips on the bus back and forth. But then after several weeks, maybe even a month or two, she'd make new friends, begin a new life with new people

I: The Online Journal of Peter O'Mallick / **41**

that had more in common with her. We'd slowly start to drift apart. She'd stop returning my calls.

We'd stop being a couple, two people who knew they were destined for each other, and we'd become friends. Then, maybe after only half a year passed, we'd barely be in contact with each other at all.

The mere thought of it — of being apart from Sarah, of losing her like that — it burned a hole in my heart. Whenever we talked about differing paths after high school, Sarah always reassured me that we'd be together forever and that we were soul-mates and meant for each other. She talked about these future fantasies she had of the two of us, some time off in the distant future, both of us in our thirties, a married couple, and doing fun couple things in our home and on our various vacations.

But I knew the whole thing was inevitable if she moved away. I'd seen it happen to a friend of mine a couple of years ago when his girlfriend's family moved away. It didn't matter how much two people tried, or how much they both wanted it not to happen. It happened: people grow apart.

I'd been about to tell her this when I spotted a pair of eyes low on the road in front of us, two sharp points reflecting the headlight beam. Then a second pair almost above the other. They belonged to two small dark shapes sitting in the middle of the lane immediately ahead. I tried to swerve to miss them, but they started skittering off in the same direction I'd swerved.

The car hit them with a sickening double thump as the tires rolled over them, and Sarah screamed while I adjusted the car back into the proper lane. An oncoming driver who had to brake as I'd swerved laid into his horn, but I barely heard it for the maddening thud of my heartbeat in my eardrums.

42 / *I, Death*

We immediately smelled the unmistakable and putrid scent in the air.

We'd hit a pair of skunks.

"Holy shit," Sarah said. "Did you see what they were doing?" She paused. "I think they were fucking." And then she started laughing. "Man, we're bad news to a skunk's sex life."

I didn't laugh though. I didn't think it was funny. It was disturbing to me. We'd just killed two animals attempting to come together and mate. And it happened at the same time we were talking about our own fate as a couple.

It disturbed me deeply.

But I didn't realize until now just why.

The damn thing was symbolic of the break-up of Sarah and I. It was — what the hell does my uncle like to talk about when discussing movies? It's when the director sets up a scene that alludes to something that is going to occur later in the film — it was *foreshadowing*. Yeah, that's it. The skunk death was foreshadowing things to come for Sarah and me.

This event just mocked me, reminding me that the whole thing was inevitable.

But there was one other thing that disturbed me about that night.

Once I caught my breath and got the car back under control, I realized that my cock was rock solid again. Sarah had removed her hand when she shifted back over in her seat while we were swerving on the road, so she never noticed. But I wonder what she would have thought about that.

Fuck, I'm still not sure what I think about it.

— 3 Comments —

Frank — said . . .
If I was not a believer in omens, this could make me become a believer, Peter. Damn.

I: The Online Journal of Peter O'Mallick / **43**

Rita — said . . .

What a life! I couldn't possibly give you advice; you've been through so much...

As you said, love hurts... (guess that means life hurts as well...) But it seems you're in the right way. By the way, I agree with Frank, you would be a great writer. Wish you all the best!!

Regards, Rita

(yeah, I guess this "blog" thing is really huge! :P)

MacManus — said . . .

It is hard to move on once you leave school. I don't think I actively keep in touch with anyone I was at school with. It's so funny how when we are at school everything that happens there is such a big deal... then when you get out and look back it all seems so petty.

I'm glad you have been sleeping... it helps with the healing, mate. Take care.

Friday February 10, 2012 — 11:23 PM

I walked by Sarah again today in the hall. Again, didn't turn my head, didn't let on how much I still loved her, how much I still missed her.

I was just playing it cool.

And pretty proud of myself, too.

I made it to the end of the hall before I turned to look back.

And saw her laughing with this Chad guy. He's one of those good looking jock types, plays on the volleyball team, is a member of the cross-country running club and can often be found during spares or after school using the weight room. Most of the girls have always had a crush on Chad.

They're both standing at her locker, she's retrieving some books and he's all hanging on her locker door and telling her some sort of amusing story.

The sound of her laughter coming down the hallway is both good to hear and yet slices into my heart like the cold steel of a blade.

Dammit, I was doing so good there for a while, too.

— 2 Comments–

Frank — said . . .
Fuck, Peter. One step forward and two steps back.
Don't you just hate that? I feel for you, buddy

I: The Online Journal of Peter O'Mallick / **45**

Trish — said . . .

Sarah may be avoiding you, but I'm sure she still loves you. Love doesn't just go away. She's upset, but I'm sure the feelings are still there. As for this Chad guy, he's probably someone just to take away the pain for a few minutes with his "amusing" story.

Monday February 13, 2012 — 6:36 PM

Tomorrow is Valentine's Day.

I think it's going to be hard. But I'll get through it. I spent the entire weekend closed up in my room listening to music and playing Xbox, just trying to get the image of Sarah talking with Chad out of my head. I spent hours playing through *Ultimate Spider-Man.* Sure, it's an older game on an older game system but it's a pretty awesome one. You spend part of the game playing as Spidey and the other part playing as Venom.

It's not as good as the *Spider-Man 2* game was, which I still enjoy farting around with, but it's still pretty decent. It has an incredible open environment to roam around in, some good challenges and intense fighting action.

Lord knows I can use the fighting action to let off a little steam.

For the past couple of months I've been pretty good while sitting on the bus. Pretty good about picking a spot where I can't see Sarah and she can't see me.

But this morning, for the first time since we broke up, she was sitting in a seat across the aisle just a few rows ahead. And there was nobody blocking my view. I tried to focus on my Gameboy, then tried to read my magazine, but I couldn't help continually looking up trying to catch another glimpse of her.

I: The Online Journal of Peter O'Mallick / **47**

And I try not to think about what Sarah and I would likely have planned for tomorrow. And with that, of course, wondering if she's going to be doing something with this Chad guy who's been hanging around her a lot lately.

This must be what addicts go through when exposed to that thing — whatever it happens to be for their addiction — that pushes them over the edge. I guess, for me, Sarah is that thing. I'm over her, I'm really trying to be. But when I get close to her, when I see her again, I have to "get over it" all over again.

Tomorrow is not going to be easy.

Fuckin' Valentine's Day. Another seasonal "in your face" reminder of lost love. Yeah, like I need that.

— *3 Comments* —

Frank — said . . .
Like it is any coincidence that Valentine's Day and Venereal Disease have the same initials. Yeah Peter, giving up Sarah is like trying to shake a drug addiction or a disease.

MaliceAD — said . . .
Love, when done correctly, will give you a euphoria similar to being high. Peter, you are going through withdrawal… but you can make it. You must believe.

Trish — said . . .
I feel your pain, buddy. I've had many such Valentine's Days.

Wednesday February 15, 2012 — 5:14 AM

Valentine's Day was harder than I thought it would be. And I'm embarrassed to admit something that helped me get through it.

I don't normally like pop music or top 40 stuff — most of my favourite music tends to be stuff that was released a generation or two back. I do like some new stuff, but they tend to be alternative bands and not the kind of stuff that you'd hear on the average radio station. Maybe that's why I like Q92 so much — they do play new stuff, some top 40 rock and pop songs, but do a great job of mixing it in with a lot of the older things that I like: Led Zeppelin, The Who, Pink Floyd, AC / DC.

Anyway, there's this top 40 song from a few years back they've been playing in a semi-regular rotation on Q92 that speaks to me. It's the song by Simple Plan called "Welcome to My Life"

I love how the song addresses the things I'm going through. It asks if you ever feel like breaking down, if you ever feel out of place, like you don't belong or that nobody understands you.

Sometimes I catch myself singing the song out loud when I'm alone in my room.

"Do you ever wanna runaway? Do you lock yourself in your room?" I sing, usually along to Simple Plan coming

I: The Online Journal of Peter O'Mallick / **49**

out full blast from my speakers so that "no one hears you screaming" as the song goes.

I don't really know much about their music, but this song says it like it is. These guys actually get it. I went and downloaded the song from iTunes and ended up just playing it over and over and over again, and singing the lyrics at the top of my voice.

"To be hurt," I scream the lyrics out. "To feel lost! To be left out in the dark!"

I jump around the room while I sing this, trying my best to let out the pent-up energy and frustration.

"To be kicked," I scream, "when you're down — to feel like you've been pushed around."

All during this singing I certainly feel, as they sing, on the edge of breaking down with nobody there to save you.

Indeed, as their song goes "you don't know what it's like — welcome to my life."

Geez, my buddies, who have similar tastes in harder, edgier rock music would cringe if they knew I was up all night last night, playing this song over and over again with headphones on and screaming those lyrics into my pillow.

But it helps. It really does.

— 5 Comments —

Franny — said . . .
That's a great song. (You had me singing there for a while.) If you have the time, try downloading "Life" by Our Lady Peace. You might like it.

Kim — said . . .
It doesn't matter how you did it, just as long as you make it through. In the end that's all that counts.

50 / *I, Death*

Frank — said . . .
Music can bring me comfort like nothing on earth. You need not care what other people think of your music, as long as it works for you, Peter

Peter O'Mallick — said . . .
I did download that song, like you suggested Franny. And it was pretty cool.

You know what; you're pretty cool, after all.

MaliceAD — said . . .
Have you heard "Never Tomorrow" by Imperative Reaction? Music can bring you great comfort in the most trying of times.

Friday February 17, 2012 — 8:52 PM

I was watching Sarah across the cafeteria today.

I don't know why. Dammit, I was doing so good for a while there, and then along comes this Chad guy, sniffing all around Sarah.

He's one of those good looking jock guys who could pretty much have any girl that he wants. Why is he bothering with Sarah, then?

Why am I so worried about it? And keeping an eye on Sarah now wherever I go?

It's not like Sarah and I are going to get together again. Or that there's a chance that we'll reconcile. I think I've come to terms with that understanding. I mean, I have to give up that possibility, especially since she's not even willing to speak with me.

I mean, the good thing is that I haven't approached her again, haven't gone through my pathetic display of hopelessness. Sure, I'm watching her again. I can't help but pay attention whenever I spot her. But how can I help it?

Sure, a relationship can end, but you can't immediately turn off the feelings that you've had for someone for years.

I can't, at least. Sarah meant too much to me for too long to just be able to forget those feelings so quickly.

So there's Sarah, sitting in the cafeteria, not chatting with her friends, but eating her lunch and writing in a journal.

52 / *I, Death*

She's been doing a lot of that lately. Well, actually, she always wrote in her journal — but she didn't do it in the middle of the day. She usually only wrote in her journal first thing in the morning or at the end of the day.

Anyway, she's writing in her journal and snacking on an apple, and along comes Chad, slips into the seat beside her and starts up a conversation.

I wanted to walk over there, tell him to leave her alone, punch him in the head and then walk off. It took everything in me not to do so. Instead, I just got up from my chair and walked out.

— 4 Comments —

Kim — said . . .
Good for you Peter... I admire your inner strength. Getting it back is a sign of getting better!

FunkyB — said . . .
I just read through this blog from the beginning. It took me a while to get caught up, but I was hanging breathlessly on every word.

Mind your thoughts, Peter. They can take on a life of their own.

Frank — said . . .
I wonder what she journals about these days. Damn it's always a freaking jock they go for.

Trish — said . . .
Damn. Even I'm getting pissed off about this Chad guy!

Wednesday February 22, 2012 — 10:12 PM

I sat on the bus beside Harley today. He's one of the guys in my group of pals. Well, actually, Harley is one of the guys on the edge of the group. I mean, within our group of pals, there have been times when I've been closer buds with Neil or with Jagdish, but I've never felt particularly close to Harley.

Not that I feel close with any of them lately. I've been sticking by myself a lot. It's been so long since I've actually made any effort to hang out with my group of buddies it makes sense that any attempt to get re-acquainted with them would be through Harley; the guy on the periphery. So on the bus ride home today, I sat near Harley. I knew he would start up a conversation almost immediately.

Anyways, Harley was talking about hockey. It's funny to see him all enthusiastic about hockey this year, because a few years ago, during the NHL hockey strike, he was really pissed about the whole thing. He quit hockey that year and for several years after he refused to even put on a pair of skates or even play a quick pick-up game of street hockey. He sort of followed Team Canada in the Olympics, and now he seems a bit more pumped about hockey in general.

Harley said that it's time to have another one of our challenge games with the Sudbury guys and that he's been organizing an outdoor game on Windy Lake — it's to take

54 / *I, Death*

place this coming weekend on the ice near the old Elk's Club Hall.

The Levack guys are challenging the Sudbury guys. See, from our town — actually it's not just Levack, but it's Levack, Onaping and Dowling. Well, that's not really true after all, because several years ago we amalgamated into the Greater City of Sudbury; but we still think of ourselves as a unique town — there's quite a large group of us that take the bus in to school. Anyways, whenever we participate in after school types of events, they always take place in Sudbury, the veritable centre of the universe around here. It's always tough to get any of the students who live in Sudbury to actually show up to anything that takes place out here, even though it's only a 45 minute drive.

One of the only exceptions, of course, is the occasional Levack *vs* Sudbury Hockey challenge. Levack no longer has its own high school, or a hockey team, but the team used to be called the Huskies. So that's what we've named the Levack team. The Sudbury guys call themselves the Wolverines — partly named after the Sudbury Wolves Junior A hockey team and partly an ode to the *X-Men* comic book character.

Harley asked me if I was interested in playing, showed me the sheet of names of players, then said that the Huskies could use a couple of more players. "Whaddya say, Pete?" he asked. "Tired of moping around like a big cry baby and sobbing in your milk over Sarah? Ready to play a man's sport again?"

Harley has this way of saying things in a blunt fashion, not really holding back or worrying about perceptions. This had a tendency to piss people off, but at least you always knew exactly where you stood with him.

But my mind was already too busy to take issue with the way he'd said that, because I'd been looking at the list when

I: The Online Journal of Peter O'Mallick / **55**

he was talking, and spotted Chad's name on the list of the Sudbury team.

I smiled.

Man, it would be a good chance to take my frustrations out on him, maybe a nice cross-check across the forehead, or a body slam right onto the ice.

"Yeah, Harley," I said, a huge grin on my face. "You can count on me. I'll be there."

— 3 Comments —

Frank — said . . .
I guess letting jock boy have it is as good a reason as any for playing. Good luck Peter

Kim — said . . .
Oh crap... Chad better grow eyes in the back of his head!

Good luck with the game... Kick some ass!

Trish — said . . .
LOL Good for you, Peter! Kick Chad's ass!

Sunday February 26, 2012 — 11:40 AM

I don't care what anybody says, revenge is not sweet.

Now I can't be sure — 100% sure — that it's my fault. But given my track record, why the hell else wouldn't I believe it?

Why didn't I just stay away from the hockey game yesterday?

Why didn't I just stay home?

Dammit.

Fuck.

I'm too upset to talk about it right now.

— 4 Comments —

Frank — said . . .
Damn Peter. Sorry that did not work out for you. It seemed like a good idea to me at the time.

Kim — said . . .
Gosh, Peter... I hope you're ok.

MaliceAD — said . . .
Woah... take a deep breath and think things through.

Trish — said . . .
Sorry to hear that things didn't go as planned. Can't wait to hear what happened though...

Wednesday February 29, 2012 — 10:16 PM

The guidance counselor at school wants me to talk about it. Wants everyone who was there to talk about it. Even though it wasn't a school event, there were mostly people from our school there. So he has arranged these sessions with everyone — they started yesterday, and we had another one today.

He wants us to talk about it.

But I don't want to.

It's funny, the only thing that I want to do is to try to find this old movie I remember watching with Uncle Bob several years ago. It was bothering me all week, because what happened reminded me specifically of a scene from a movie.

These past couple of nights I've been rooting through his DVD, BLU-RAYS as well as his VHS tapes. He hasn't completely replaced and updated his original movie collection — shit, he even has a few movies on this format called BETA — he told me that it was all the rage just before VHS players came out — in my mind, VHS players and tapes themselves are ancient. But I haven't yet found the movie I was thinking about. I keep remembering that there's this old guy like whatshisname from that show Aunt Shelly used to love, *The West Wing*: Martin Sheen. Or perhaps it's Jon Voight or maybe that guy who was in *Wedding Crashers*, Christopher Walken. I do know that I saw it a long time ago. So the

58 / *I, Death*

actor must have been quite a bit younger when the movie was made.

But it's the scene I can't get out of my head. Because it's almost as if what happened was right out of that movie.

And I don't think I'll be able to talk about what happened properly until I can see that scene again.

I know it sounds nuts, but I need to do this. And I haven't mentioned this to anyone. Because what would they think of this guy who wants to talk about a movie instead of the real thing that happened?

So I remember this scene from the movie, but there are different images that don't make sense together, almost like a dream. Maybe it's really a few different movies or two different scenes that I'm thinking about and confusing them both in my mind. Who knows? Anyway, it's winter. These kids are playing hockey on the ice of a lake. Then here's where I'm not sure if I'm remembering a single scene from a single movie, or maybe different elements from different movies: there's this guy who's mad at one of the hockey players, or else he has a vision that something bad is going to happen, I can't remember which. Maybe it's both, because it is two different movies I'm remembering. I don't know.

But the next thing you know, the hockey player breaks through the ice and everyone is standing around looking at him. And you can see him through the ice, banging on it, the air escaping from his lips. And everyone is standing on top of the ice, looking down at him, stunned. He can see them, they can see him.

And everyone watches him die.

That's what it was like on Sunday. Sort of.

But I need to know what damn movie, or movies I'm thinking about. I need to watch that scene or those scenes so I can get those images out of my head and then properly talk about what happened.

I: The Online Journal of Peter O'Mallick / **59**

— 3 Comments —

Frank — said . . .
Damn, I also want to know which movie that is from now.

Anonymous — said . . .
Hey dude, it was *Dead Zone* with Christopher Walken.

Bob — said . . . . . .
There is a similar scene in *Omen* (2?)

Friday March 2, 2012 — 7:28 AM

An anonymous commenter and some guy named Bob helped me identify the two movies that I'd been trying to figure out. Man, gotta love this whole blog thing. My uncle did have both *The Dead Zone* and *The Omen 2* in his movie collection.

I ended up watching both movies last night. Well, okay, I didn't actually watch the whole movies, because I did fast forward through most of them and just watched the drowning scenes I'd been thinking about.

Funny how I'd mis-remembered them somehow into a single memory.

But in any case, I've gotten that strange *déjà-vu* feeling out of my mind. I think I can talk about what happened last Saturday now.

We had another session with the guidance counselor yesterday. Sarah was there this time. Until yesterday, she wasn't at school at all this week. She looked like hell, her eyes all bloodshot, her dark hair a frazzled mess.

I just wanted to hold and comfort her, tell her it would all be okay.

But what's the use in that? I'm the one who caused it, after all.

So today more people started talking about what it meant to them. Sarah didn't say anything. When she suddenly left

I: The Online Journal of Peter O'Mallick / **61**

the room crying, I started to get up to follow her and a friend of hers, Julie, held me back.

"Peter, don't" she whispered to me. "She just wants to be left alone."

"But..." I started to protest.

Julie shook her head. "You'll just make it worse."

"Shouldn't you go?" I asked Julie. "I mean, her new boyfriend just died, after all, and..."

She interrupted me. "Sarah hasn't been with anyone since you guys broke up, Peter."

"What?"

"I don't know what you've been hearing, but she hasn't been seeing anyone — certainly not Chad — and she hasn't even been spending time with me or any of her other friends all that much. She just wants to be left alone."

"Are you sure?"

"Definitely,"

Julie had always been one of Sarah's closest friends. We hadn't spoken all that much since Sarah and I broke up. I'd assumed that Julie was still close with Sarah and so had felt uncomfortable around her; I hadn't even spoken with Julie since the break-up.

"But I saw them..." I started to say.

The guidance counselor interrupted me at that point. "Peter, do you have something you would like to share with the group?"

Yeah, your toupee is way too damn obvious I wanted to shout out. But instead, I shook my head and listened to students take turns offering up different versions of the same story. With each rendition I heard, I kept reliving my own experience of that day.

And now that I've heard all those different viewpoints and watched those scenes that had been plaguing my mind, I think I'm ready to talk about it, tell what happened from

62 / *I, Death*

my point of view. But not right now. I've got to start getting ready for school.

Maybe tomorrow.

–2 Comments –

Frank — said . . .
Damn, leave us hanging Peter. Roll on, tomorrow.
   Not seeing Chad. That's a shocker.

Kim — said . . .
Wow, Peter... hang in there.

Sunday March 4, 2012 — 9:28 PM

I never made it back to post about what happened. Instead, what I did yesterday was walk from my home over to Windy Lake, to the spot where it all went down. It took about an hour to make the trek, but it was a beautiful sunny day, not all that cold. And I think I needed that walk just to go over the events in my mind again, get clarity on it all.

When I got to the shoreline, I stood there, looking out over the ice. The crack and hole from last weekend were not even visible from my angle, at least not physically. I couldn't tell if it was because the snow had covered it, or if it had resealed.

Hard to believe, given the massive breaking of the ice that happened in the attempt to retrieve Chad's body. But despite the heavy snowfall and refreezing that had occurred, my eyes easily found the spot.

And I just stood there, staring at it, thinking back to that afternoon a week ago.

It was a cold but clear day, yet relatively warm in the sun if you were dressed right, especially considering the time of year. The teams were on the ice, warming up, getting ready for the game. There were plenty of spectators, from Levack and from Sudbury, standing either on the ice near the shore or on the hill that rose up from the lake's edge. There was a small bonfire near the lake's edge, where a constantly changing group of people were huddled, taking turns getting warm.

Sarah was there, too, not far from that crowd, hot chocolate in hand. I saw Chad skate up to her and start chatting with her, saw her smiling at him in response.

I wanted to skate over there and just haul off and deck him. But I needed to wait until the game began before I'd have my chance.

The game was a good paced one, with a lot of action, and a boatload of tired guys because we didn't have two shifts of players on each side, merely two extra guys on our side and three extra guys on theirs.

Checking wasn't part of this game because we weren't wearing any equipment — no helmets, no skin pads, no jocks, nothing like that, just the extra padding that a sweater and winter jacket provided. But we never played without a little bit of light checking and body contact.

I got a couple of chances to come up behind Chad and give him a seemingly incidental nudge to feel out his balance and strength. He did the same to me. We weren't fifteen minutes into the game when we'd pegged each other for more and more grudge-type playing.

Then at one moment, when I gave him a hit hard enough to knock him over and lose my balance to fall on top of him, we heard something crack. I don't remember worrying about it because in the heat of the moment we were fixated on each other, on getting to our feet. But I certainly remember it now.

It was when we were scrambling to our feet that I turned to him and said. "Stay away from my girlfriend."

"She's not your girlfriend," he grinned at me. Then his face turned serious and he gave me a hit to the shoulder that sent me back on my ass, "and I'll do whatever I damn well please."

The ice must have cracked some more at that point when I fell, but I don't think I heard it. He skated off, back into the action. The fact that he left without our conflict being

I: The Online Journal of Peter O'Mallick / **65**

properly settled riled me. I remember seeing red as I glared at him.

I got up and headed back towards the action, my eyes on Chad the whole time. I remember getting closer into his direction, but the puck and action would shoot off again in another direction, and I'd have to close that distance again.

The entire group skated at least two times over that spot where Chad and I had fallen.

It was the third time — when Chad had the puck on a breakaway for our net, I was the closest person to him, and was rushing at him, rushing to knock him flat on his ass, hit him with all that I had — that it happened.

Another crack broke through the air, more like the overpowering crack of lightning than anything else. It was surprising to us, and we all stopped, almost as if to take cover from a gunshot or something.

Chad was just standing there, puck still on the end of his stick, and I was looking at him and he at me. It was quiet, calm. Nothing but a light wind settled over the ice, evident in the drifting powder of snow visible in the middle of the lake. But it was an eerie calm, especially considering the bizarre and loud explosion of noise that had just occurred.

Everyone around started laughing at their own startled reaction, a huge group release of combined tension. Chad stopped looking at me long enough to wave over at Sarah, then look back at me, a satisfied smirk on his smug jock face. She was looking back at him. My rage intensified and I was about to launch myself in his direction again.

That's when the final, loud, explosive crack echoed through the air, and Chad went down on one knee, or so it seemed at the time because, then, impossibly, he seemed to quickly melt down into the surface of the ice like the Wicked Witch in *The Wizard of Oz* on fast forward.

But he wasn't melting. He was falling through the ice.

66 / *I, Death*

Screams went up; the players on the ice nearest the hole, including myself, throwing themselves flat against the ice — it seems, growing up where we did, and being involved in many frozen lake activities like hockey and ice fishing, we knew our odds on a questionable ice surface were always improved by distributing our body weight over as much space as possible.

I looked over at where Chad had been standing. There was nothing but a fissure in the ice big enough for a person to fall through.

That and the puck he'd been chasing, sitting there as if nothing bizarre had occurred at all.

Plus a small mark of blood on the ice surface where he'd hit his head on the way down to mark his fresh ice cold watery grave. A mark of blood that, one week later, wouldn't even be visible. At least not physically.

— 3 Comments —

Frank — said . . .
Un-fucking-believable Peter. I cannot even begin to imagine how you must be feeling.

Kim — said . . .
Oh my god Peter! It's lucky that only Chad and not the lot of you ended up in the water. No wonder you haven't been able to talk about it. That's hard to come back from.

Take care of yourself.

Trish — said . . .
So sorry to hear about what happened. But, regardless of how you felt about Chad, it wasn't your fault, even if you secretly wished it upon him. Accidents happen.

Tuesday March 6, 2012 — 11:09 PM

I started doing a Google search online a few hours ago. Found some interesting web sites about death, and spent the last couple of hours reading through it all.

Cool stuff.

Freaky stuff.

> *The Death Clock --> www.deathclock.com*
>
> *Death and Dementia --> www.deathndementia. com*
>
> *Death — The Last Taboo --> australianmuseum.net.au/Death-The-Last-Taboo*
>
> *Near-Death Experiences --> www.mindspring. com/~scottr/end.html*
>
> *Death Images --> www.trinity.edu/~mkearl/ death-1.html*

It got me to thinking more about Hamlet's little speech, again. And Death.

I think I want to talk to Miss Hamilton about *Hamlet* again.

Yeah, yeah, I know, Miss Hamilton, our English teacher, is Sarah's favourite teacher and, while Sarah hasn't been spending much time with her friends, she still is hanging around Miss Hamilton a lot.

But that's NOT why I want to chat with her. I want to talk about *Hamlet*, and Shakespeare, and maybe see if she can recommend something else that I can read of his that is just as good. I remember we read *The Merchant of Venice* in Grade 9 and then *The Tempest* in Grade 10 and *King Lear* in Grade 11, but I didn't really like them so much.

There's gotta be something else Shakespeare wrote that's as good as *Hamlet*.

— 4 Comments —

Franny — said . . .
My favorite is *Macbeth*. I think you'd like it too.

Franny — said . . .
Sorry Peter, got my plays mixed up. I meant to suggest *Othello*...

Frank — said . . .
LOL. I was going to agree with Franny, then saw she corrected herself. I thought *Macbeth* was brilliant.

Just been creeping myself out on the death sites you posted.

Kim — said . . .
I personally liked *Julius Caesar*.

Wednesday March 7, 2012 — 10:54 PM

Thanks for the recommendations, Franny and Frank. I will look into those titles. I didn't see your comments, though, until just now. I did end up going to see Miss Hamilton for her advice on other Shakespeare plays to read.

But when I went to talk to Miss Hamilton today, Sarah was with her. It shouldn't have surprised me because I knew that she was always spending a lot of time with her. But I guess I was so focused on wanting to find another good Shakespearean tale that it didn't immediately occur to me.

I walked into Miss Hamilton's class during a spare, seeing her at the front of the room working at her desk through the window on her door. I walked in and started to ask her a question and I froze in mid-sentence and mid-step.

There was Sarah sitting about three rows back writing in a notebook.

"Oh," I said. "I didn't realize that..."

"That's okay, Peter," Miss Hamilton said, getting up from her desk and walking over to me.

"What was it you needed to ask me about?"

"I was interested in..." I began, but I could feel Sarah's eyes on me and just couldn't focus, couldn't think. I suddenly felt embarrassed, not being one of those reader types comfortable with talking about books to a teacher, particularly not in front of someone, and especially not in

70 / *I, Death*

front of such an extremely well-read person like Sarah. Back in the day, I think I would have been excited to share my enthusiasm for Shakespeare with Sarah, and she would have been delighted to recommend something.

But now it was just embarrassing.

And that made me angry.

I stopped, suddenly starting to feel angry. Angry with Sarah, who broke up with me. Angry with Miss Hamilton, who was obviously one of the only people close to Sarah lately.

"Never mind," I managed to say through mostly clenched teeth. And I turned and walked out of the class.

— 1 Comment —

Frank — said . . .
The waves of your emotion must be exhausting. How are you sleeping these days, Peter?

Thursday March 8, 2012 — 8:24 PM

Sarah and Miss Hamilton were in an accident last night. A pretty nasty accident.

Miss Hamilton was driving Sarah home. I guess that they'd both been working after school and Sarah had missed the last bus. So, Miss Hamilton had offered her a ride back to Levack.

It wasn't uncommon for a teacher like Miss Hamilton to do that, particularly not for a student with whom she'd spent so much time. Miss Hamilton lived in Dowling, and so was heading most of the way there anyway.

They were on the highway between Sudbury and Levack. It had been snowing, not heavily, but enough to reduce visibility, I guess. They were just about to cross the bridge over the Vermillion River near Dowling when an oncoming transport trailer crossed the middle line, heading straight toward them.

Miss Hamilton swerved the car, tried to take the ditch, but the snow-covered guard rail near the bridge was so close to the edge of the highway that the car couldn't go far — it simply bounced back off and into the lane. The transport hit the back of the sedan. The sedan flipped up and onto its left side, slid across the middle of the highway, slammed into the guard rail of the bridge and spun around on its roof.

72 / *I, Death*

An oncoming car plowed into the front of their overturned vehicle.

Sarah received some bruises and deep cuts from pieces of the windshield that sliced into her forehead and cheeks. But otherwise, once they cut the vehicle open, she walked away from the accident. That was a huge relief to hear.

Miss Hamilton wasn't so lucky, unfortunately.

Her body was crushed by the oncoming car that had plowed into them, suffering two broken arms and a broken pelvis. She also received severe head injuries in the accident and is currently in the Laurentian General Hospital in a coma.

Could the whole accident have been my fault?

I had been rather angry at the both of them yesterday.

Did that anger spiral into an evil force that caused the accident?

I'm not sure what I'm talking about; not sure what to believe any more.

But it seems as if all it takes is for me to be angry with someone — pissed off with them — and the curse strikes.

It's crazy. Curses don't exist. They're myths.

Superstitions. But it seems to make sense, seems to fit in with what's been happening lately. Lately? It's been happening my whole life! Am I only starting to figure this out now?

Figure what out? I have no idea what's happening to me and to the people around me.

All I know is that Sarah is lucky to have escaped the accident with very few injuries. And I think it'd be best if I completely avoided her, ensure that she stays far away from this curse. I'm too upset with her after all.

If I was the cause of the accident, that is. I mean, if I did cause the accident, and I was the cause of the other deaths, why didn't Miss Hamilton die? Why is she in a coma?

It could just have been that. An accident. Right?

I: The Online Journal of Peter O'Mallick / **73**

I don't know what to believe anymore.

— 3 Comments —

Frank — said . . .

I think you have to believe it was just an accident, Peter, or you may go insane.

It does seem kinda strange though.

MaliceAD — said . . .

Woah, that's awful :(

I hope Miss. Hamilton gets better soon! It's just an unfortunate accident and has nothing to do with you cursing people. Curses do not exist.

Trish — said . . .

I agree with MaliceAD. Death is a natural part of life. You've been surrounded by lots of death through your life, but it's only coincidental. I don't believe that a single one was your fault.

Wednesday March 14, 2012 — 8:05 AM

I'm half-way through the March Break and I can honestly say that this is the worst one, by far. I'm supposed to be out with my buddies, maybe heading out on our snow machines, maybe skiing. But certainly laughing and having fun, knowing that spring is just around the corner. Sure, we had some pretty warm temperatures lately, and even rain, but we're back to snow again.

It's like the cycle of misery that I keep finding myself back in. At least being in school was a bit of a distraction. The only thing I can do for a distraction is browse the 'net, maybe watch some of Uncle Bob's movies. But that's about it. And it doesn't really stop my mind from coming back to Miss Hamilton.

She's still lying in a hospital room in a coma. No change there.

The thing that I find toughest, though, is that I haven't gone to visit her. She was a good teacher. I liked her. She made Shakespeare fun.

But I can't visit her. I'm too afraid that if I show up there, that'll finish her off.

— 2 Comments —

Frank — said . . .

I: The Online Journal of Peter O'Mallick / 75

I cannot even begin to understand your agony right now, Peter.

You have taken angst to a new level.

Kim — said . . .
Send a card, or flowers to show that you care.
You're in my thoughts... take care Peter.

Sunday March 18, 2012 — 11:54 PM

Wow. I can't believe that the March Break is over already. And for the first time in many, many years, I just wasted most of it away. I sat around the house, mostly watching movies and playing video games.

I did take Kim's advice and had some flowers sent to the hospital for Miss Hamilton. I went into town on Saturday with Uncle Bob and Aunt Shelley. When we got to the mall, I went to a florist shop and placed my order to have flowers sent over to her anonymously. I would have done it over the phone, but I don't have a credit card to pay for it. Plus I didn't want my aunt or uncle to know about it.

I'm not sure why. I just don't want anyone to know I sent the flowers.

This week I also watched a series of movies that I was a little bit surprised to see in Uncle Bob's collection. *Final Destination.* All five of them. Although I shouldn't be surprised about it — he does have a pretty wide range of tastes in movies.

I remember seeing the first *Final Destination* half a dozen years ago when some buddies and I rented it from the Mini Mart. So when I came upon it in Uncle Bob's movie collection, I watched it. I was pretty hooked. The whole concept of this unseen death entity stalking the characters down and killing them off one by one intrigued me. Death

I: The Online Journal of Peter O'Mallick

picks them off throughout the movie apparently because it missed its chance to kill them during a plane crash that they avoided at the last minute.

It was an intriguing concept, and made me think a lot about all of the deaths surrounding me and my life. Death takes on many forms and appears in many guises.

No matter how much you run, no matter how hard you try, Death will find you and get what it wants.

Death is the one thing that *will* not and *can* not be denied.

It makes me wonder what is going to eventually kill Miss Hamilton? Do you think it might be a bizarre allergy to one of the flowers in the bunch of wild flowers I had delivered to her room?

Or is the whole series of *Final Destination* movies getting to me?

— 2 Comments —

Kim — said . . .

I suppose anything is possible. Of course if there's no chance that she'll recover, her family could make that decision on their own. Death, like Life, works in strange ways.

Trish — said . . .

I really like the *Final Destination* movies as well. I think *Part 2* is even better than the first, but I haven't seen anything beyond the third yet. It's an interesting concept, but I don't believe that Death really works that way. As I mentioned earlier, you're not to blame for a single death.

Monday March 19, 2012 — 9:49 PM

Despite knowing that Miss Hamilton was not going to be there, I was very much looking forward to going back to school. At the very least school was a huge distraction that often took my mind off of focusing on Death.

All that March Break seemed to be was an opportunity to mope around the house and dwell on dark and disturbing things.

The first part of the day was pretty slow and boring. I kept wishing that Miss Hamilton was still around. But the longer the morning got, and the fact that I never saw her, really brought it home for me.

I did really like that old broad. She was pretty cool. And now she's lying in a hospital bed in a coma that she might never wake up from. And I can't shake the feeling that somehow it's my fault for being so pissed off with her. And that perhaps because of me, Death — who didn't properly get the job done in the first place — is creeping around within the shadows of her room, just waiting for the perfect opportunity to strike.

Like I said, the morning kind of dragged on. But the afternoon was different: a teacher arrived. A new teacher who will be there until the end of the year to take over Miss Hamilton's classes.

Mr. Robinson.

I: The Online Journal of Peter O'Mallick / **79**

I was prepared to hate him. Prepared not to like anyone who tried to step into Miss Hamilton's shoes.

But he wasn't trying to replace Miss Hamilton. He said so himself.

When he first walked into our class complete with this strange little bolo tie, his brown cowboy boots, and the puffy sleeved shirt that reminds me of the pirate shirt on that old *Seinfeld* episode, it was one of the first things he said.

"I'm not Miss Hamilton," he said, "nor will I try to pretend to be her. She was a great teacher. She actually taught me when I was a student here years ago. She was, in fact, one of the finest teachers I ever had. She had this incredible love, this incredible passion for literature, and I loved her dearly. So I'm not here to replace her but, rather, to carry on with the subject with which she showed so much passion. I have my own style of teaching, my own perspective on English class, and my own love for literature. And I owe all those things to Miss Hamilton who was the first teacher to inspire them in me.

"My name is Mr. Robinson. But you can call me 'Robbie' if you like. Just don't Rob me of my love for literature. And if you don't enjoy reading, don't enjoy writing, or don't enjoy talking about great works, I won't hold that against you. I just hope at the very least you do your best to open your mind for the time that we have together here, knowing there's a possibility of seeing something in a way you never saw it before."

Then he said something that blew my mind, and which started to kind of change my opinion of him. He said something that was a direct quote from *Hamlet*. And he spoke it in a deeper voice using a British accent. "There are more things in heaven and earth than are dreamt of in your philosophies, Horatio."

80 / *I, Death*

He paused, just stood there and looked at the class. The classroom was mostly silent. Maybe just a cough here or a sniffle there. I'm sure that I had a huge grin on my face, because I caught the reference immediately. I'm also sure that he cast a knowing smile in my direction, picking up on my awareness. I quickly glanced over at Sarah. It was obvious from the look on her face that she caught the reference, too. A moment later a few of the students who were really into English class clapped their hands together or made strange little grunting noises that seemed to acknowledge that they knew where the reference was from.

But then he seemed to just let it go, as if to allow those of us who understood the reference to bask in the knowledge, and those who didn't to wonder.

"If you get anything out of this class," he continued, walking over to the desk and standing on the chair, one booted foot on the desk, "get this: English literature is a statement — sometimes a statement of truth, sometimes a statement of fantasy — but it's a statement. Writing can be about showing you something about yourself, or showing you something about the world that perhaps you never considered before. A new perspective, a new way of seeing the world.

"Literature is only as limited as a person's imagination. If we let it, it can show us something new, or show us something we thought we knew, but from a unique and distinct perspective." Then he stood up on the desk itself. "Like the perspective of the class that I suddenly have when I'm standing up here. And reading those works, reading that literature, should be as interesting and as memorable as what I'm about to do." He paused, stomped his feet on the desk, smiled at the group of us, then jumped off the front of the desk to the floor with a loud thud.

I: The Online Journal of Peter O'Mallick / **81**

"Okay," he said. "Enough talk. C'mon. Single file, up to the front of the class. Who wants to see English, see literature in this exciting way?"

Everyone just stood there looking at him. Nobody got up. Not even the English keeners.

"That's fine." He said. "Nobody needs to get up. Nobody has to do what I just did. But I'd like you to open your mind to the possibility, to the grand adventure that literature can be. To the perspectives it can open. And I invite you all, at any time during the rest of class time this year, if you need to behold a new perspective, need a sudden paradigm shift, to walk up here, stand on my desk, look around and soak in the new view."

Bobby Shay, one of the Goth guys in our class stood up then. "I'm ready to try," he said. And he walked to the desk, stood on the chair, then stepped up onto the desk, looked around and smiled. Then he jumped off.

The girl who sat directly in front of him — Alicia, I think her name is — smiled, got up and did the same.

Then, one by one, each student took a turn doing so as well.

Mr. Robinson stood silently at the side of the class, smiling a huge smile as each student performed this ritual.

When it was my turn I remember pausing to look around the room, to see the class from an angle I'd never considered before. And I felt strangely liberated. For a moment I was so ecstatic that I forgot about the death, about all the deaths, that had surrounded me. I'd been freed from them. It was a glorious moment. I barely remember jumping back down to the floor. But I remember feeling lighter as I stood there on the desk in front of the class.

Wow.

The whole thing reminded me of a scene from this other movie I remember watching with Uncle Bob about an English

82 / *I, Death*

boarding school for boys. I think the teacher was played by Robin Williams, but I can't remember what the movie was.

— 1 Comment —

Bob — said . . .

Could the movie be *Dead Poets Society*?

I am glad you are feeling better, you need a change of 'tude dude!

Wednesday March 21, 2012 — 9:34 PM

The Ides of March are come.

This morning Mr. Robinson walked into the room, wandered up and down the aisles and just looked at us, a rue smile on his face, without saying anything.

When he completed a full round of the class, he paused in the front of the classroom, and in a very low voice, what he later explained was a 'stage whisper' he said: "Beware the Ides of March. The Ides of March are come."

A couple of the students in the class knew exactly what he'd been referring to, and clapped. Sarah, of course, was one of them.

After another long pause he asked: "What's wrong with what I just said?"

Someone, I'm not sure who, spoke up. "The Ides of March was last week."

Mr Robinson clapped his hands together. "Exactly," he said. Then he went on to explain to the rest of the class that last Wednesday was the 15th or the 'Ides' of March and that he was quoting from *Julius Caesar*. He explained the soothsayer's prophecy, the basic story of *Julius Caesar*, and the fact that, while it would have been cooler to do this lesson on the 15th, that it had been March Break and not at all cool to be in school.

84 / *I, Death*

After telling us a bit about how the 'Ides' referred to the 15th of some months and the 13th of other month, he talked more about Julius Caesar and Shakespeare. Then he had students come up to the front of the class with a shortened script in hand and act out both the soothsayer scene where Caesar is warned and then the scene where he is killed and betrayed, even by his friend Brutus.

He picked me to play the role of Caesar.

I've never acted before, but man did I ever love it.

My favorite part, the very best moment, was when I was pretending to be dying and I grabbed Bobby Shay by the scruff of his shirt, pulled myself up to his face and said. "*Et, tu, Brute*? Then fall, Caesar!"

It was a complete riot. I haven't enjoyed talking about or studying Shakespeare so much as this. I love how Mr. Robinson jumped us into it by explaining what the 'Ides of March' meant and having us act out some of the scenes.

Then he did something completely strange. Once we all settled back down into our seats from Caesar's death scene, he talked about how literature and storytelling in general often was self-reflective and that many newer works often made reference to classic pieces.

He said he would return to this motif often; try to show us how something recently written could be an ode to an older work. So he pulled out this book he said he bought at Chapters at a book signing several years ago. It was by an author who supposedly grew up in the Sudbury area. In Levack, of all places.

The book was called *One Hand Screaming* and the author's name was Mark Leslie. The story Mr. Robinson read to us was called "Ides of March." It was about these snowmen that have come alive, steal a truck and are trying to gather as many other snowmen as they can while driving north, desperately trying to avoid spring.

I: The Online Journal of Peter O'Mallick / **85**

It was a dark, humorous sort of tale, and not something that I thought I would enjoy. But it was okay. Maybe because of the wonderful way that he read the story. Mr. Robinson went on to explain how the author, who he'd chatted with at the book signing, described using the title of the tale to be an allusion to a scene out of literature and incorporated the alluded to warning with the oncoming spring as an ominous element. He explained that this same author had a similar snowman story paired with this one in the very same book and that the author was trying to apply the same theme that Mary Shelly had explored in her novel *Frankenstein*.

Mr. Robinson said that while this particular author wasn't one of the best he had read, it was important to note the author's local stature to illustrate that even modern writing by local authors, or even stories written in so-called 'ghetto' genres, like horror, could be reflective of great classic works.

He asked us to look for such references in things that were available to us in the mass media. Asked for us to come up with comparisons between our favorite television shows and movies or perhaps even commercials and great works of literature.

"And saying the movie *Pride and Prejudice* which is based on a book by Jane Austin, doesn't count." Mr. Robinson said, smiling. "Take whatever TV show that you watch or one of your favorite movies and let's talk about it tomorrow. I'm sure I'll be able to find some sort of allusion or reference or derivative from a classic work."

This guy just continues to blow me away.

— 2 Comments —

Kim — said . . .
Hey! I like Jane Austen!

I'm glad you've found something to life your spirits, Peter. It's always great to find a teacher that inspires you.

Edward — said . . .
I've heard of this Mark Leslie guy your teacher mentioned. He's a blogger, too. His writing sucks, but sometimes his blog is funny, when he's not being all "read my stuff, read my stuff' — he's too pushy about promoting himself.

And the closest I ever came to reading Jane Austen is *Pride & Prejudice and Zombies*. Killer classic!

Thursday March 22, 2012 — 11:08 PM

Man, I thought I was going to stump Mr. Robinson. I thought I'd have him. Because the television show that I raised in class today was *Survivor* — I thought for sure that there was no way that a reality-television show could have allusions to classic literature.

But he completely surprised me, saying "Oh, Peter, that's a real easy one. There are so many works that you could say a survivor-type show are based on, such as what is often considered the first novel of the 20th Century. Joseph Conrad's *The Heart of Darkness*. But there's also *Robinson Crusoe* by Daniel Dafoe or one of a number of other really famous, similarly-themed titles like *Lord of the Flies* by William Golding.

And then he paused, a strange glimmer in his eye, turned, quickly headed to his desk and started riffling through his large packsack until he pulled out a book of short stories. Then he started reading us the story "The Most Dangerous Game" by Richard Connell. It's about this guy who is shipwrecked on this island and meets this rich eccentric guy who owns the island and hunts humans for sport.

It was a spectacular tale. And there's no stumping this guy. Every day in his class is like a new adventure. We seem to shoot off on these tangents. But everyone seems to be

88 / *I, Death*

really enjoying it, and we do end up talking about different novels and stories.

I'm feeling a bit guilty to be enjoying English class so much knowing that Miss Hamilton is in the hospital in a coma. But this Robinson guy is really taking the whole class on this zany fun trip.

— 3 Comments —

Trish — said . . .
I'm so happy that you're enjoying your English class, Peter. What a great way to put aside the negative thoughts that have been plaguing you lately!

Kim — said . . .
Trish is right: focus on the positive!

Peter O'Mallick — said . . .
Thanks, gals. I really am enjoying school and English class again. And it's been a really long time since I've enjoyed anything. That feels really good.

Monday March 26, 2012 — 9:58 PM

I stuck around after class today, wanting to talk to Mr. Robinson, ask him for recommendations for other things to read.

Before he suggested anything, he paused, told me he could tell that I was troubled by something, that I had this huge weight on my shoulders. He asked me if it had anything at all to do with that quiet girl, Sarah, the one who had been in the car with Miss Hamilton when she had the accident.

"How did you know?" I asked.

"I can see the longing in your eyes when you look at her," he said.

"But I hardly ever look at her," I protested.

"You don't need to look at her long for you to reveal your tell."

"Am I that obvious? I must look like this huge geek, drooling all over Sarah."

"No, no, it's not like that at all, Peter," he said, fiddling with his bolo tie. He seemed to wear a slightly different one each day. "It is very subtle. But I'm a writer. And an observer. I spend my entire life looking at the little things, the non-verbal cues that people give off. I doubt that many people who don't know you well have picked up on it."

Then he went on to say that my predicament — having lost my girl, who had been the main focus of the last several

90 / *I, Death*

years of my life during my senior year — reminded him of a character in a book.

"It's by a local author, actually. A Sudbury author. Dr. Sean Costello. I'm not sure if it's even in print anymore, but I have a copy of the book with me, as there was a scene I'd been planning on reading to the class today, but I just ran out of time. But I'd be happy to loan it to you." He then walked over to his bag, dug into it, and produced this pocket book that had a picture of this ugly thin teenager sitting in a wheelchair. The book was called *Captain Quad*.

"The main character had everything, but then he lost it one day after an accident that paralyzed him. The author does a brilliant job of showing the downward spiral of his hatred and anger. Of course, the author then introduces some pretty scary things, not unlike the frightening sort of thing that happens in Stephen King's *Carrie*. It's really well done, and terrifying. The terror hits home not only because the writer has a great talent of bringing the reader into the scene and into the characters, but also because it happens right here in Sudbury.

"Now, I'm not saying that you're like the main character in this book, just that, like him, you've suffered a significant loss. And the key is that maybe by reading his story, by seeing how he falls prey to the anger and the hatred, you might recognize a few of those same things in yourself. And maybe, just maybe, it'll help pull you out of your funk.

"Literature can do that very well. It can be like a mirror that we hold up to ourselves. And the story, the characters can help us see things, detect details about our lives, and examine them."

I thanked him for recommending the book and for lending it to me. And then I walked out of the class, thinking about how he picked up on the whole unspoken thing between me and Sarah.

I: The Online Journal of Peter O'Mallick / **91**

I'd wanted to ask him if perhaps he saw a similar thing in her when she looked at me. But I didn't know how to ask.

— 2 Comments —

Trish — said . . .

I'm sure that it hasn't been easy for Sarah either. I'm sure there's some part of her that wishes things could be different between the two of you. Maybe, hopefully, in time she'll realize that they can be. Good luck, Peter!

Kim — said . . .

I totally agree with Mr. Robinson. Books can open up a lot to those willing to let them. So can keeping a journal; or, in this case, a blog. It seems to be working a little for you, Peter... you're sounding a lot better lately.

And Trish is, again, right. What you two shared isn't something easily cast aside. In time, both of you will heal enough to talk this through. Patience, while annoying, is indeed a virtue.

Let me know how the book is. It sounded interesting and I may have to add it to my list of things to read.

Thursday March 29, 2012 — 2:58 AM

Wow. I just finished that Costello book, the one called *Captain Quad* — I read the whole thing in just two sittings. It was incredible. Blew me away. I couldn't put it down when I started reading it before going to bed.

And now it's quarter to three in the morning, and I haven't slept.

But I don't care.

I'm high with having enjoyed this book so much.

Ever since finishing it, I've been sitting up, reading through some of my previous posts and reading through the many comments people have made for the past few months.

I started wondering why I'm so hung up on Sarah and not willing to move on, especially when there are all these cute girls out there offering kind words of support. Trish and Kim have lately been really lifting my spirits with their comments. It makes me think that if I can stumble upon really nice girls like that on-line so easily I should be able to find someone nice like that around here eventually. Just gotta keep hoping.

I'm not saying that I'm over Sarah. Not really. I think I still love her. I definitely don't want to end up obsessing over her the way the main character in *Captain Quad* obsesses over his lost girlfriend. Man, that was a scary thing. But I do have to face reality. And move on.

I: The Online Journal of Peter O'Mallick / **93**

Oh, what the hell do I know? I'm so fucking tired I feel like I'm just babbling right now. I really should get to bed.

I can't wait to talk to Mr. Robinson about the book, see if this Costello guy has written any more books, and if I can get my hands on them.

— 2 Comments —

Trish — said . . .

Wow, Peter. How flattering to have such kind words about me on your blog! I'm sure that Kim will be very honored as well. :)

I'm glad you enjoyed *Captain Quad*. Perhaps I'll check it out as well.

I'm so happy that things are looking up for you! Have a great night! And you shouldn't be posting on your blog at nearly 3AM. Get some sleep! ;)

Kim — said . . .

Yes, Trish, I am honoured to see such kind words on Peter's blog.

And I'm so glad that you're moving on, Peter. Breaking up is never easy, especially when it involved some heavy emotional circumstances for both of you. Everyone has their transitional periods where they wallow in the remnants of what was and what could have been, but reaching the point where you realize that being hung up on it isn't worth it, is a great spot to be... even if it comes at three in the morning...

So get some sleep...and keep smiling... it looks good on ya!

Thursday March 29, 2012 — 10:21 PM

Mr. Robinson and I, or 'Robbie,' as I now call him, chatted for a long time after class about *Captain Quad* — we didn't talk about my situation, about the bitterness I felt over Sarah having dumped me.

It just felt good to talk about the story, about the scary things that happened, about the creepy feeling I got when reading it.

Maybe the whole reflection piece, the whole moral behind the story is something that just gets planted somewhere in the back of your mind while you enjoy the story itself. In any case, we didn't talk about that; just about how good the book was and the different memorable scenes in it.

And then Mr. Robinson loaned me another book by this Costello guy. This one was called *The Cartoonist* — it looks even better than that first one. It's about this old guy who is a mostly coma-like patient at a hospital and who draws things as if on autopilot. But the things he draws all come true and wreak havoc on one doctor's life through a series of uncanny accidents and mishaps. I'm actually afraid to pick it up and start reading it tonight, afraid that I'm going to get sucked into the book and not get any sleep again.

So I put it on my night side table. I'll start reading it tomorrow because I don't need to get up early on Saturday.

I: The Online Journal of Peter O'Mallick / **95**

— 2 Comments —

Trish — said . . .
The Cartoonist sounds like an odd story indeed! Let us know what you think of it. And don't draw any pictures for me! He-he. Unless, of course, they involve nice things happening to me! :)

Good night, Peter!

Kim — said . . .
I'm impressed by your will power! I know when I get a new book, the first thing I want to do is read read read...

Have fun on Saturday!

Saturday March 31, 2012 — 3:43 AM

I just finished *The Cartoonist* and, tired as I am I just can't sleep.

Dammit, but this Costello guy is a brilliant writer. And he's from Sudbury, no less. Wow, I didn't think I'd like this second book as much as I liked the first, but I liked it even better. *The Cartoonist* was phenomenal. It blew my mind.

Wow.

I can't wait to talk to Robbie about this one, see if there's more stuff that this Costello guy has written.

Sunday April 1, 2012 — 10:42 PM

I did some browsing online, found this Sean Costello guy's website. Found a few online articles about him. I see that his book *Captain Quad* was recently republished. And by a publisher right here in Sudbury.

Cool.

I even found a review of one of his books online written by that Mark Leslie guy that Robbie had talked about in class. Then I linked over to Mark Leslie's site and found a quote that Costello wrote about one of his books.

Costello seems to really like this guy's writing. Maybe I should consider borrowing that book from Robbie too.

I wonder if the two actually know each other. And does that sort of thing — where authors who know each other give each other a praise blurb — happen a lot?

I can't wait to get in to class tomorrow and talk to Robbie about it.

Monday April 2, 2012 — 9:27 PM

Robbie talked about the mystique behind April Fool's Day today.

I'm sure it was interesting, but I wasn't really paying attention. Just when he started in on the origin of the trick rituals of April Fool's Day, I had glanced back towards Sarah. I'd been startled to see that she had been looking at me. She quickly averted her eyes and her eyes never moved back to me.

But I couldn't help obsessing about it and wondering if it had just been a chance glance, the way a person normally looks around the room and their eyes cover everyone in it, or if she had been actually looking at me.

I started to wonder if Sarah had been thinking about last April Fool's. About the trick I had played on her.

That morning, Sarah's friend Julie helped me distract Sarah while I snuck off with her cell phone. I used clear packing tape and taped down the # key, but you couldn't see that the button was depressed. The intention was that every time Sarah went to use her phone, she'd be unable to dial properly. But what happened ended up being more frustrating. Because holding down the # key put Sarah's phone into "lock" mode. And since Sarah had never used the password feature and didn't know the default password, her

I: The Online Journal of Peter O'Mallick / **99**

phone became pretty much useless and it took three days before she could crack the code and use her phone again.

Then I started thinking about what had happened that night. Sarah had been really pissed at Julie and I all afternoon. But we'd originally been planning on renting a movie and watching it at Sarah's house, so that's what we did.

The three of us were in the family room at Sarah's, and the trailers had just started playing, when Sarah went upstairs to make popcorn. A few minutes later, Julie and I heard this loud crash and went running out of the family room to find Sarah sprawled at the bottom of the stairs on her back, her right arm twisted at a funny angle underneath her head, one leg resting on the second step, the other one folded underneath her. The popcorn bowl was overturned on the floor beside her and there was popcorn everywhere.

At the top of the stairs both Sarah's parents were, like Julie and I, standing there, horrified. "My baby," Sarah's mom started to scream and turned to bury her face against Sarah's father's chest.

That brought the horror of what had happened home to me. Sarah could either be unconscious or worse. Broken arm, broken leg, broken neck. I fell to my knees beside Sarah and started wailing her name like some twisted banshee.

That's when Sarah sat up, pointed at Julie and I and said: "Gotcha!"

Apparently, her parents were in on it too. They were pretty cool, that way, often participating in the fun and antics. And of course, I'd completely forgotten the fact that Sarah was double jointed. Once I had seen her reading a paperback held by an arm twisted around behind her head. The double-jointed thing that day freaked me out a bit, but about three hours later, when Sarah and I were rolling around under the sheets together, she showed me some other interesting uses of being double jointed.

100 / *I, Death*

So, I'd been thinking about Sarah and about April Fool's Day last year instead of paying attention in class. It makes me wonder if Robbie could tell I wasn't clued in to his lesson, and it pissed him off.

Because when class was over and I went to talk to him, there was a group of students hanging around to ask questions and talk with him after class. That always happened, but Robbie usually made sure to hang around and talk with me.

So I hung back, like before. But, instead of staying in the classroom as the students slowly dissipated, Robbie started heading down the hall to the staff room, still answering their questions and chatting with them, but in a hurried sort of fashion.

Man, was I stupid. I hope it's something else and not that I pissed Robbie off.

Tuesday April 3, 2012 — 10:58 PM

After Robbie's class today I was able to speak with him, and return the copy of *The Cartoonist* — but it didn't go the way I had hoped.

When I handed him back the book, he thanked me politely and put it in his bag. I thought that he'd ask what I thought, who my favourite secondary character was, any of the usual fun ways he had of getting me to talk about a book I had read. But that was it.

I wanted to talk more, to share the excitement about the book, and about the interesting thing I'd found about the authors Costello and Leslie praising each other's books. So I asked if he had another Costello book that I could borrow.

He told me that he had loaned that book to another student.

He did say that he'd try to bring something else in to class the next day that he thought I would like.

But I kept thinking about the fact that he'd loaned that Costello book to another student. I guess I'd thought that I was the only student he did this with — loaned books to and chatted frankly with.

I'm trying not to get all bent out of shape about it.

And I am looking forward to finding out what book he'll be bringing in tomorrow.

Friday April 6, 2012 — 3:47 AM

Can't get to sleep. My heart is still pumping like crazy from this twisted erotic dream I just had.

After class on Wednesday, Robbie handed over a book called *In the Dark* — it was by an author named Richard Laymon. He told me that Laymon was one of those authors who cut right to the chase and had a way of keeping action and suspense rolling non-stop in a seemly effortless style.

He told me that, while the content of the book — the shocking horrific elements and the seemingly gratuitous sex scenes — might at first seem simplistic and B-MOVIE style, the author had actually invested quite a bit of effort into developing his characters and crafting the story. "He makes it seem simple and effortless" Robbie said. "But the work he put into developing the whole thing is phenomenal."

Robbie explained that he'd read a non-fiction book that the author wrote which documented the story behind his writing. He talked about how the author himself was a voracious reader, often with several books on the go at once, and was well read in multiple genres.

He talked a bit about some of Laymon's favourite authors and the fact that Larry McMurtry was one of them. He'd mentioned that the next book he was going to get me to read was called *Savage* and then after that I was going to read a novel by Larry McMurtry so I could compare the styles.

I: The Online Journal of Peter O'Mallick / **103**

I didn't read the Laymon book the night Robbie gave it to me — it's funny, when he started talking about comparing Laymon to McMurtry it just sounded like the typical crap that English teachers talk about, and I got nervous that I was going to hate Laymon's book.

But, oh man, was I wrong.

Laymon blew my fucking mind.

I started reading *In the Dark* at about 10 o'clock last night. The book was simply riveting, and written in a style that had me begging to just want to turn one more page, just continue on reading for a few more minutes. I thought that I might read for about fifteen minutes, but I read for two solid hours. I wanted to read more, but I was so exhausted that I couldn't keep my eyes open.

At one point I remember finally putting the book down, and struggling with the desire to want to read, slowly peeling off my clothes without getting off the bed, and then turning off the light and sliding under the sheets.

When I first closed my eyes, I couldn't leave the world the author had created for me. Couldn't push aside the heart-stopping plot, the intense and tight timeline for the story, the cliff-hanging suspense of each chapter, the hot and sweaty sex.

I'm pretty sure it was the book that caused the eerie erotic dream that I had.

The dream was, like a few that I've had recently, based on something that really happened. And while erotic and exciting, it was a bit frightening, too.

There Sarah and I were, in the family room. Two of Sarah's friends were there, Monica and Julie, each sitting in an armchair. We were watching a movie, something with Adam Sandler in it. Sarah and I were snuggled up together on the couch with a blanket over us.

During the movie, Sarah's hand moved down and started rubbing me through my jeans. I remember looking quickly at her, then at her friends, a bit anxious at first that we'd be caught, but they didn't seem to know what was going on. I then relaxed against the back of the couch and just enjoyed it.

Sarah's rubbing hand got more vigorous and my erection was straining against the denim, a solid mass of excitement and painful pleasure. This went on for quite some time. Then Sarah reached in with her other hand, pulled down my zipper then pulled out my cock and started pumping it in her fist.

Monica seemed to have heard the zipper, because she glanced over. Julie, sitting in the armchair farther away, must not have noticed, her eyes stayed fixed on the television screen. But Monica looked over, and a wry smile crossed over her face as she figured out what was going on underneath the blanket.

That made me even harder, and I could feel myself pulse within the firm grip of Sarah's palm. Monica didn't turn her eyes back on the television screen, she just looked over at us, a huge grin on her face, and when she saw that I had noticed her watching, she winked at me.

Then she pursed her lips as if to blow a mock kiss at me and ran her tongue across her top lip.

That's when I exploded without warning. A huge eruption of cum that coated the blanket, Sarah's hand, my jeans. Of course, neither of us moved for the duration of the movie. When the movie ended, Sarah and I remained under the blanket, saying goodbye to Monica and Julie without getting up. I remember Monica's knowing smirk — she must have realized what had happened.

But that's where the dream diverted from the memory of reality. In the dream, Sarah is giving me a hand job and Monica is watching, and when Monica licks her lips, Sarah notices her and says "Enjoying the show?"

I: The Online Journal of Peter O'Mallick / **105**

In the dream, suddenly Julie isn't there at all, and Monica's clothes have disappeared, and she is suddenly completely naked. Brushing aside her long black locks to rub a breast with one hand she slides the other hand down and starts fingering herself.

"Why don't you join us?" Sarah purrs, as she removes the blanket. I discover that Sarah and I are also naked beneath the blanket.

Monica lets out a gasp and walks over. I can see that she's so hot and wet that there's actually damp dripping down the inside of her thigh. Sarah's hand pumps furiously. When Monica gets to us, Sarah and I each take one of her succulent breasts in our mouths. Sarah smiles playfully at me as her tongue flicks at Monica's nipple — all the while her hand never stops its rapid stroking.

I reach around, pull up on Monica's buttocks, and she steps onto the couch, then, with both hands on the cheeks of her ass, I pull her in to me, eager to lap up all of the hot wetness that is flowing from her. Still jacking me off, faster and faster, Sarah moves around, kisses my hands and the sweet cheeks of Monica's ass as if they are one, and I can tell from the sudden startled "Oh!" of pleasure that Sarah has stuck her tongue in Monica's ass.

That's when I can't take it any longer. My face still buried in Monica's dark muff, I try to say, "I want to fuck you both so bad it burns," but the words come out muffled, the way they sometimes do in those dreams where you try to cry for help but can barely speak.

And similarly, I can't move either. I want to pull Monica down onto my rigid and aching shaft. But I can't move.

Monica steps back and both of the girls are playing with my cock now, one hand each, occasionally leaning forward and darting a tongue at its swollen head, then quickly kissing each other before again attending to the swollen head of my

106 / *I, Death*

cock. I marvel how this is so much like most guys dreams, and despite the fact that I desperately want to take both Monica and Sarah yet can't move, I try to just lay back and enjoy it.

"Okay," Sarah says. "It's time for the grand finalé."

Sarah flips her raven black hair over to one side, leans over my crotch, takes me full in her mouth, and bites. Hard.

Pain like I've never felt before shoots through my legs, up my spine as her teeth come together through the meat of my cock. She sits back up and she looks at me with that sexy playful glimmer in her eye, all the while chewing a large mouthful of gristly crunchy flesh.

I shriek in pain, in horror, in shock as I feel myself explode in a hot and sticky eruption. Only it's not cum, it's blood. My crotch is shooting up a hot geyser of blood. And Monica is leaning down to try to catch it in her mouth.

Sarah, finished chewing, leans back down to join her, and both girls laugh madly as they playfully fight for mouthfuls of my hot spurting blood.

I woke up at that point, my sheets completely soaked in sweat and cum. I laid there for several minutes, afraid to pull the sheets back, afraid to look down, afraid that I'd see dark red blood instead of white schmeg coating my stomach, legs and the sheets.

— 2 Comments —

Kim — said . . .
Holy shit!
    pauses to think of more to say
    yep...
    Holy shit!

MaliceAD — said . . .
OMG!!!! *shock* *gasp* *shock*

Friday April 6, 2012 — 11:28 PM

It's so funny that I dreamed of Monica, one of Sarah's friends that I'd mentioned the other night. The one from my erotic dream.

Monica's not in any of my classes, so now that Sarah and I have broken up, I barely see her anymore. But I saw her in the hall today and my heart skipped a beat.

I was on my way in to Mr. Robinson's class and she was walking out, with a thin paperback in her hands. I remember glancing at the book in her hands, my mind suddenly as excited to see what people are reading as I used to be to see if I could catch a glimpse of a girl's bra strap peeking out from beneath her clothes.

And I saw the name "Costello" on the spine of the book in her hand.

Ah ha, I thought. *She's one of the other students who Robbie has hooked on these great writers.*

She smiled at me and said 'hi' as we passed each other. I saw her in a completely different light this time, though. I looked at her gorgeous black silky hair and her stunning brown-green eyes and I remembered the dream of her walking naked towards me, offering her breast to my eager lips and tongue.

I turned to admire her ass as she walked past, and I kept staring at her, thinking about the dream (at least the way the

108 / *I, Death*

dream was before it turned nightmarish) and feeling myself getting hard.

I was tempted to go and talk with her, but I couldn't build up my nerve. I couldn't even remember if she'd been dating anyone anyway.

I'm suddenly seeing her in this new light. But I wonder if it's just the dream doing that. Still, I can't seem to get her out of my mind tonight. I just keep thinking about her.

And lusting after her.

Geez, is it possible that I'm starting to get over Sarah? Finally.

— 1 Comment —

Kim — said . . .
Be careful, Peter... friends of the ex rarely turn out to be good ideas... the consequences can be harsh....

I: The Online Journal of Peter O'Mallick / **109**

Sunday April 8, 2012 — 11:14 PM

School tomorrow, and I'm as excited to chat with Robbie about the latest Laymon novel that he loaned me on Friday and that I finished (this one was called *One Rainy Night* and was an incredible non-stop roller coaster ride of mayhem, action, and unadulterated bloodshed) as I was at the chance to talk with Monica.

It took me the whole weekend of dwelling on her to realize that I suddenly had an easy 'in' with her for a conversation. All I needed to do was find out from Robbie what Costello books she had already read, and see if I'd read them as well. Or if she'd read one that I hadn't and I'd read another, at least we could still compare notes.

It'd be a great conversation starter at least.

I feel like a kid in grade nine again, steeling up the courage to ask a girl to dance with me. It's this queasy, uneasy, yet enjoyable feeling.

— 2 Comments —

MaliceAD — said . . .
You should really take this one slow and always remember that she's one of Sarah's friends. Who knows what Sarah has told her about you?

Benny — said . . .
That's a good point MaliceAD...girls talk... A LOT!!!

Tuesday April 10, 2012 — 10:51 PM

So I didn't even see her at all yesterday, but I had a chance to talk to Monica today. But instead of saying anything, I just stood there, my mouth hanging open while she walked by.

She did smile at me. She did say 'hello.' And I was fully prepared to say 'hello' back to her, then mention that I'd seen her with a Sean Costello novel the other day and I was wondering if she'd read it yet and what she thought of it.

But I just stood there, my mouth an open hanger, a veritable fly-trap.

I can't believe this. I'm completely tongue-tied around her.

I wonder if it's because I can't stop picturing her naked — can't stop having this picture of her from my dream as she is walking towards me, her thighs damp with the heat and excitement from fingering herself while watching Sarah giving me a hand job. Can't stop remembering the vivid taste of that wetness on my lips and tongue.

Or is it just because I haven't approached a girl for years? I mean, Sarah and I were together for so long that I practically forget what it's like to ask a girl out.

And the comments that people have been leaving about Monica being a friend of Sarah's — maybe those are eating away at the back of my mind — as in, "Is this really a good idea?"

I: The Online Journal of Peter O'Mallick /

Oh man. I haven't hung around any of my buddies all that much lately. Can't remember the last time I sat down in the lunch room with them. I think I need to find my buddy Neil, ask him for some advice. He was always pretty suave with the ladies. I'm sure he'll be able to help.

Wednesday April 11, 2012 — 11:52 PM

I didn't go sit with my old buddies in the cafeteria today. I don't know why. I mean, it's been so long since I've hung out with them, and I don't know why that is either. Actually it's funny, because when I was going out with Sarah, I would sometimes sit with them and sometimes I wouldn't. It was no big deal either way.

But lately, since our breakup, I haven't made much of an effort to reacquaint myself with the group. Sure, I've still hung out and chatted a bit with Neil, Jagdish or Harley, but I can't remember the last time we all went out as a group, saw a movie, got loaded, whatever.

In any case, instead of just sitting with the old gang, I waited around for Neil after one of his classes.

When he saw me waiting for him, the first thing he said was, "Oh oh. Does this mean that you're ready to come out of your cave, Mr. Hermit?" Now, I've seen this with Sarah and her friends, but it's a rare thing for guys to get snippy with each other for not calling or not hanging out. But Neil is one of those rare guys who can get away with it. I suppose it's the same way that Harley can get away with being an asshole with some of the things he says and does, and we just roll with it. Or maybe the way that Jagdish can play stupid, and, even though we all know he's probably smarter than the rest of us combined, we play along.

I: The Online Journal of Peter O'Mallick / **113**

That's the great thing about friends. Yeah, I've been absent, not hanging around much, and, like Harley said a few weeks ago "moping and sobbing over Sarah" — but I know that when I'm ready to get back to normal and settle in with my buddies, that it'll all be good like it used to be.

I didn't end up asking Neil about what to do about Monica. We ended-up shooting the shit. He started talking about that craziness going on in the local news — a recent murder and that lead to other world news — one of Neil's favourite topics. We ended up making loose plans to go see a movie tomorrow night.

So, no, I didn't end up asking Neil about the situation with Monica, but I did enjoy catching up with him. Besides, I'll likely have a chance to work it into the conversation tomorrow.

— 1 Comment —

Kim — said . . .
It's a start... and it sounds like your friends will be straight up with you in their advice. That's always important.

Saturday April 14, 2012 — 4:30 AM

I didn't end up going to the movies with Neil on Thursday night. We went last night instead. We got in about an hour early and played a game of air hockey and chatted a bit to pass the time.

It felt good — I haven't hung out much with any of my buddies all that much for several months now.

Neil wasn't all lecturing and stuff, but he told me, in no uncertain terms, that he thought it wouldn't be a good idea if I asked Monica out. He cited some of the things I saw posted in comments here, and then we moved on to other things.

It wasn't until just before the movie started, when we were sitting in the darkened theatre, that he turned to me and said "I always thought that you and Sarah made a pretty decent couple. Do you think there's a chance you guys might patch things up?" I didn't respond because the first trailer had started. A new science-fiction thriller starring Bruce Willis. It looked good, and instead of thinking about it or responding, I just watched the trailer. I didn't know what to say to that.

About midway through the movie, I got up to go to the snack stand. This was one of those movies that had its funny moments, but I wouldn't be missing anything while I was gone.

I bumped into Monica who was getting popcorn. I asked her about that Costello novel I'd seen her with the other day,

I: The Online Journal of Peter O'Mallick / **115**

and she started raving about it. We chatted about Costello, and Laymon and about how cool Robbie was for introducing us to them. I told her about Costello and Leslie offering "praise blurbs" for each other's work, and she told me she had found an anthology from a Sudbury publisher that includes a story from Costello and one from Leslie. It was called *Bluffs* — I thought it was so cool that she had made a similar connection between the two.

It felt good.

Then I went and blew it all by tossing out this clumsy little question about whether or not she would be interested in going out with me some time.

She paused. Her face went white, and I knew immediately that it had been a mistake. "You're kidding, right?" she said. "I'm, like, Sarah's friend. That would be so, like, weird." She didn't say anything else at that point, just walked off, leaving me standing there with a bag of Nibs in my hand, feeling like a complete loser. I almost didn't go back into the theatre.

For the first time since Sarah and I broke up, I was having fun just chatting with a beautiful girl. And I blew it. Not only that, I blew it by doing something that Neil and some online friends warned me against.

I'm such an idiot.

I didn't tell Neil about what had happened. I know that he wouldn't have said "I told you so," but just the same I didn't want him to know how much of a fool I'd been.

— 1 Comment —

Kim — said . . .
Well Peter... it could have been worse... you guys could have started something, got neck deep and then realized it didn't work.

You're not an idiot... you're (and no offence here) just a guy!

Wednesday April 18, 2012 — 6:12 AM

I've been sitting up most of the night. Just sitting in bed and staring into the darkness. I was afraid to fall back asleep, afraid of what I'd dream. Afraid I'd dream the same thing which woke me up in the first place.

I didn't really realize what I was doing until I started to see bits of light from the morning sun creeping into my room. That was about when I decided I would sit down and try to write about it.

It all started yesterday at school. I didn't see Monica at school on Tuesday. But I ended up overhearing two girls talking about her. Talking about the rumours about her. The rumours that she had been raped on the weekend. Raped and beaten.

I talked to a few people about it. Neil mentioned that he'd heard the same rumours. That was the frustrating thing about rumours in our school and home town: they spread quickly, and much faster than the truth.

Later in the day, wondering why Monica wasn't at school and still making inquiries about her, I got nowhere. When I'd asked him what he knew, Harley made a comment about her deserving what she got because of all the dirty talk she often used and the way she flirted with everyone. I shouldn't have been surprised at Harley's response.

I: The Online Journal of Peter O'Mallick

Our friend Jagdish hadn't even heard the rumours at all, and then got into an argument with Harley that nobody, not even a hooker, deserves that. When they started their heated discussion, I just walked away.

It was when I got to Robbie's class that I knew I could find out if they were rumours or not. I mean, adults, teachers, they don't take rumours at face value, do they? They get to the truth behind the stories. They find out what's really going on, and they have the means to do it.

That's how I know it must have been true. Robbie seemed to not be himself at all. He seemed less full of energy; less alive and into the class. He seemed to just walk through the class the way I've seen so many other teachers do over the years: simple, tired repetition of the same lesson taught year after year. And why shouldn't he be like that? After all, despite the fact that I was jealous of it, Robbie shared a similar passion for reading and books with Monica that he shared with me. So why wouldn't he be disheartened over learning what had happened to her?

I wanted so badly to talk to Robbie about it after class, to hang around and talk about it, talk about my feelings of guilt over what had happened to her. But I was afraid to bring it up, afraid that by talking about it, it would make that darkness, that depressed and melancholy state he seemed to be in, even worse. That and he never made eye contact with me once during the entire class.

When I got home from school, I scanned through *The Sudbury Star* and there was a short article saying a young woman had been beaten and raped in an alley behind City Centre on the weekend and was being treated in hospital.

I started phoning the different Sudbury hospitals and on my second try, at the General, when I asked to be connected to Monica's room, they put me through.

I hung up. What could I possibly say to her?

118 / *I, Death*

Having confirmed the rumours, that Monica had been the victim mentioned in the paper, I simply started to cry.

I couldn't have possibly brought this on to her, could I? Could this be yet more evidence that there's a curse surrounding me? I tried to think back to how I felt the other night when she rejected me; tried to focus in on the embarrassment, the anger, and any resentment that I'd felt.

Of course, I couldn't deny having felt those things. Which meant it must be true. I must have been the cause of what happened to Monica.

I moped around most of the night, tried listening to music, playing video games, anything to keep my mind off of it. But nothing worked. I actually went in to Uncle Bob's liquor cabinet and nipped a bit of his rum, a bit of his rye and a bit of his gin. An old trick I learned about swiping booze is never to let the bottle drop by any visible amount. But I needed something to numb my mind and help me sleep.

Combining all three in a single glass, I drank it all down in three horrid mouthfuls. It tasted awful. When I drink for fun, I never drink it straight. I prefer mixing rum and Coke. But straight up? *Blech.* Drinking all three mixed like that was pretty nasty.

But it did do the trick. I fell asleep pretty quickly.

But that's when I dreamed. God knows, I would have loved to have had that same dream I'd had before: the one with Sarah and Monica. Yes, even the fact that at the end of that one they'd bitten off my cock. I'd rather dream that dream every time, than the one I dreamt last night.

In the dream, Monica and I were standing at the concession stand at the movie theatre. We were talking about the books we had read, and started talking about Laymon. Monica started admitting that the scene in *In the Dark* where the librarian is looking in the window and watching his girlfriend and another guy getting it on made her all hot.

I: The Online Journal of Peter O'Mallick / **119**

I responded by asking Monica if she'd remembered that one time at Sarah's when she'd spotted Sarah giving me a hand job under the blanket and the way she'd winked and licked her lips. I told her how it was that look she gave that made me blow my load. I told her how lately I'd been able to think about nothing other than her, about how her lips might taste, how they might feel on my cock.

She responded by saying, "Why wonder any longer?" and suddenly we weren't in the movie theatre, we were outside, in an alley. Monica was polishing my knob and I was enjoying it, both hands resting on the top of her bobbing head, my fingers gently playing with her hair. Suddenly Robbie was there, watching us, and Harley was standing there beside him. They were watching us and talking to some other figure, some guy dressed in black, who was standing in the shadows. They were saying something to him, but I couldn't hear what it was.

I started to fill with an inexplicable rage and I pulled hard on Monica's hair and threw her backwards. She smacked her head against the bricks, then fell onto the ground. I started kicking her and punching her and screaming at the top of my lungs.

She didn't move, she didn't get up, she just recoiled with every kick, every punch I landed on her, and I kept screaming, yelling, pleading with her to go away and leave me alone. Then I dropped down on my knees and started to pull her pants off, telling her she deserved what she was getting because she was hanging around me.

"Stay away from me! It's my fault! I caused this to happen to you! Stay the fuck away from me! Stay the fuck away!" I woke up screaming those words. I'm surprised, actually, that Aunt Shelley or Uncle Bob didn't wake up, but maybe the screaming was louder in my dream.

120 / *I, Death*

I've never even raised a hand in anger against a girl. Not even when I was really young and roughhousing with other kids in the playground. If a girl hit me, I just took it, and never hit back.

But the dream I just had kind of says it all, kind of puts it in perspective. No, I wasn't the one who raped and beat her. But given my track record, all the horrible things that have happened to people I've been angry with, and the fact that I was angry at her, I might as well have been the one.

And that's what was going through my mind these past few hours as I stared into the dark, afraid to close my eyes and sleep, afraid I'd dream of hurting Monica.

— 1 Comment —

Anonymous — said . . .
Hey, buddy, maybe it's not a dream. What were *you* doing the night Monica was beaten and raped???

Wednesday April 18, 2012 — 10:14 PM

Monica still wasn't at school today.

Of course.

She's not going to be back for a while. Who knows when.

I pretty much muddled my way through the day. Sure, the rumours about Monica being raped and beaten half-to-death kept flying around, but they seemed to have more details in them. How she was attacked by three guys at knifepoint. How she'd been stabbed. One of the rumours was that she had lost an eye.

All rumours, of course. Nobody knows the *real* story.

I ended up cutting my afternoon classes completely. I'm going to catch hell for it, but I don't really give a shit right now. There's too much on my mind.

Plus, when I got home from school today and saw the comment that someone left — speculating that perhaps I had done this to her while in my sleep — well, that just freaks me out.

I was thinking that maybe a curse around me did this to her. But what if I was the person who did it? What if the dream was somehow a memory of something that I'd done while sleepwalking or something?

Besides, how could I have gotten from Levack in to Sudbury to do this to her in my sleep?

It boggles the fucking mind.

Thursday April 19, 2012 — 10:19 PM

Again, Monica wasn't at school. I shouldn't be surprised, but I keep hoping that the rumours weren't true, that it really wasn't her that it happened to.

Robbie turned things around a bit for me today in English class. He always seems to have a knack for knowing the right thing to say, the topics he covers always seem to hit home perfectly.

"There's a lot of talk around the school about something that happened to one of our students this past weekend," he said. "I'd like to read you a scene from a novel that might help us talk about it.

"The book I'm about to read from not only has to do with the Sudbury area, but is written by a man known as the Dean of Canadian Science Fiction. He has won the Hugo, the top international science fiction award; the Nebula, the "Academy Award" of the SCI-FI genre; is the only writer in history to win the top SF awards in the United States, Japan, France, and Spain; has one of the most extensive and content-rich science fiction web sites available; has made countless media appearances over the years, had an ABC television show made which was based on one of his novels; and is known far and wide as an all-around great guy.

"I'm talking about Toronto writer Robert J. Sawyer.

I: The Online Journal of Peter O'Mallick / **123**

"For those of you looking for a connection between Sawyer and one of the other authors we have discussed in class, Sawyer, the generous person that he is, is one of the authors who gave Mark Leslie a very positive blurb for Leslie's short story collection *One Hand Screaming*. And for those of you who have read that collection, you might notice that in the notes, Leslie mentions losing an Aurora Award nomination to Sawyer for 'Best Short Story (English)', but that he couldn't have lost to a nicer guy. And for those of you who like their connections in threes, an additional connection between the two is that Sawyer wrote the introduction for a horror anthology called *Campus Chills* that Mark Leslie edited a few years ago.

"Now for Sawyer's connection to the Sudbury area. Sawyer wrote a trilogy of books called *The Neanderthal Parallax*. While preparing to write the first book in the series he came to Sudbury, stayed for a few weeks and did research at the Sudbury Neutrino Observatory. The science in this trilogy explores the concept of a parallel world in which Neanderthals survived and Homo sapiens died off, and what happens when a portal opens between those worlds and a Neanderthal appears in the Neutrino Observatory. Sawyer also received an honorary Doctorate at Laurentian University.

"Sawyer has a strong proven track record for using grand 'What if...?' concepts in his writing, often based on cutting edge advances and discoveries in the scientific world. He is not a scientist — his background is in media — but he thoroughly researches his books, and that work shows through in his stories. And if you want to understand the scientific principles he explores in greater detail, I suggest you get Mr. Nelly or Mr. Gravante to bring them up in your science classes with them.

"Because in my mind, the real strength, the true beauty in Sawyer's writing stems not so much from the scientific concepts he explores, but from the characters and character struggles that occur.

"Case in point: Mary Vaughan, one of the main characters from *The Neanderthal Parallax*, becomes a rape victim in Chapter 6, within one of the very first scenes that we meet her in the first book in the trilogy, *Hominids*. I'd like to read you a scene from that chapter and talk a bit about it."

Robbie went on to read the scene to the class. Wow. It was disturbing and terrifying, and it really hit home to a lot of students. A few of them actually started to cry. And I don't just mean the girls. I was one of the guys who had tears in his eyes.

When he finished the reading, Robbie talked a bit about the concept of rape. Asked the class questions like *was rape about sex, or about power?* He explored the reaction that Mary, an intelligent and professional woman, a professor at a Canadian University, had to being a victim of rape. We tried to understand her state of mind after such a brutal attack and explored the reasons why she didn't want to go to the police. We talked about whether or not the scene itself was gratuitous. Then we discussed the idea of the rapist as behaving in a stereotypical Neanderthal way. He asked several males in the class how the scene made them feel — about themselves, as well as about males in society in general.

The class was so involved and moved and eagerly participating in the discussion, that Robbie had to wrap up the class without the whole thing seeming to finish. Several of the students requested more, wanting to keep talking about it. Robbie handed out pamphlets with a toll-free number to a 'kids-line help group' in case anyone wanted to speak in detail about how this incident made them feel.

And he gave us another one of his cool homework assignments. He wrote the link to Sawyer's website on the

I: The Online Journal of Peter O'Mallick / **125**

blackboard (www.sfwriter.com) and asked us to do some research there. Some of the research questions he threw out were: *How was Sawyer able to write a rape scene from a woman's point of view? Where does a science fiction writer get his ideas? If a story is about characters, how important is the actual research into the science?*

I'm only realizing this after the fact, of course, but Robbie has accomplished two things with today's lesson: he not only addressed a frightening and difficult to broach issue and gave us the means to talk about it openly, but he also put a spin to it that has allowed us to enjoy the writing of yet another phenomenal author, and issued a task that will help keep us occupied, interested and learning; not just dwelling on the horrors of what happened to Monica.

I still feel terrible about what happened to Miss Hamilton. But I can't imagine this class anymore without Mr. Robinson teaching it.

— 1 Comment —

Kim — said . . .
Imagination is a wonderful thing... but when we don't always know all the details about something that's really happened, it can run away with us... lead us to places that don't really exist... lead us to scary places.

And some minds shouldn't be allowed to wander on their own!

Friday April 20, 2012 — 10:35 PM

I spent a bit of time last night after posting on my blog browsing through Robert J. Sawyer's website. Wow, Robbie wasn't kidding. There's lots of great stuff there.

Way back when I first started this online journal, someone left a comment, I think it was that guy named Frank, telling me that I should consider writing as a career. I'm still not decided, but I started thinking about that a bit after visiting Sawyer's website, and he also has some articles posted there about the art of writing. Pretty cool stuff.

Many of my classmates were on his site today, and we spent half of the class talking about Sawyer and his writing. Robbie suggested that we start with something like Hominids, which was set in Sudbury, and then read the next two books in the series. But he suggested, for those of us who weren't into reading a whole three books, that we go with one of his earlier works. He'd mentioned that *The Terminal Experiment*, Sawyer's Nebula Award winning book, was a favourite of many, and that an alien being tried in the courtroom in *Illegal Alien* was also an enjoyable one, particularly for anyone who liked courtroom thrillers or was a *Law & Order* fan.

I stayed after class to talk to Robbie and tell him about some of the things I found on Sawyer's site. I'd mentioned

I: The Online Journal of Peter O'Mallick / **127**

how Sawyer did really seem like a nice guy, often responding to comments that fans left on his blog.

Robbie suggested that I take the time to comment on his blog, to tell him I liked his writing, that it moved me. Then he loaned me a copy of *Illegal Alien*, which I took home and am eager to start reading. I was going to ask to borrow *Hominids*, but I've never read science fiction all that much before, so I think I'd like to start with the alien one. An alien on trial for murder in a U.S. court sounds like it could be fun. (Maybe I also didn't want to read that rape scene — listening to Robbie read it was emotional enough for me right now, thank you very much)

Robbie did something when we were chatting that surprised me a bit. He confided something to me. Apparently, when our guidance counselor got wind of the discussion we'd had in Robbie's class yesterday, he'd complained to the principal that Robbie was stepping into his territory.

At a meeting they had in the principal's office, Robbie defended his position, telling them that if the guidance counselor was going to address the issue of a student who had been raped, he certainly had a funny way of doing it by not doing anything. Then he went on to explain that the best way to introduce literature was to make it relevant to topics that were pertinent to students.

He said that the guidance counselor said something like: "Literature. Humph. I've heard what you've been reading and talking to students about. Science Fiction. Cave men. Aliens. Hack and slash horror. That's not literature. That's crap. Mind-wasting rubbish."

Robbie said that he didn't have to listen to that from someone who was not only ill-read and thought only in stereotypes but could barely manage to do his own job, never mind tread on the job of the English teacher. He invited the

128 / *I, Death*

counselor to take over his class so he could see how fast he could put the students to sleep.

The principal put a stop to the argument between the two, taking the side of the guidance counselor, and warning Robbie to not discuss delicate issues without first consulting either him or the guidance counselor.

Robbie told me that he loved being a teacher, loved connecting with students and helping open their eyes to the vast landscape of literature, but that he was tired of working with "close-minded jerk-ass literary snobs." The same kinds of people who praise Dickens today, but if they were around when Dickens was writing, they'd have dismissed his work as commercial tripe that pandered to the masses.

I've never heard a teacher talk about another teacher like that. I almost pissed myself laughing.

— 1 Comment —

Kim — said . . .
It's great that you have connected with such a great teacher. It's teachers like that that make high school survivable.

Monday April 23, 2012 — 11:37 PM

This is so cool. Following Robbie's advice, I decided to leave a comment for Robert Sawyer on his website blog. I told him how much I enjoyed the section of the book that my teacher read to our class and asked for his advice on which of his stand-alone books he would recommend I read.

He responded — pretty quickly too — that his novels *Factoring Humanity, Frameshift* or *Calculating God* were the three stand-alone novels he was proudest of. I thought that it was really cool, how he thanked me for my comment and then answered my questions.

I wonder how many authors do that type of thing?

So then I started scrolling through Sawyer's blog archives and found a "book tag" thing he responded to. Apparently he was tagged by Mark Leslie. It's interesting how there are all these connections somehow. Anyways, I followed the link back to Leslie's site and found that he mentioned Sawyer's *Frameshift* as a book that inspired him in a life-altering way. He didn't mention what it was, but I wonder if maybe that's the book that inspired him to become a writer.

He says to email him and he'll reveal what it was about the book that inspired him. But just knowing it inspired him, and that he's originally from this area — well, that's enough for me to want to read *Frameshift* and perhaps discover what that might be on my own.

130 / *I, Death*

Today in class, Robbie went on about 'Canada Book Day' (which, apparently, was today). He talked about how it had been inspired by 'International Book & Copyright Day', and that at one time a big deal was made about it. He said that April 23rd was chosen as an important 'book day' because a bunch of different authors were either born or had died on this day. He mentioned a bunch of them, but the only one I remember was Shakespeare. Although Robbie wasn't clear if April 23rd was his birthday or the day he died. Maybe it was both.

He said that he wanted to share different authors with us, particularly Canadian authors, and that, since on Friday he'd mentioned Robert J. Sawyer, he thought he would mention an author who was a friend of Sawyer's and has been referred to as Canada's answer to Stephen King. The fellow's name is Edo van Belkom. Robbie said that van Belkom, an author from the Toronto area, not only won the Bram Stroker Award (the highest honour in horror), but has published more than two dozen books, hundreds of short stories and for a short time was even the host of a late night horror movie show on the specialty horror channel Scream.

Apparently van Belkom was also known by Sawyer, and Robbie showed us van Belkom's book *Death Drives a Semi*, which was a collection of van Belkom's short fiction. The introduction to the book was written by, you guessed it — Robert J. Sawyer, and Robbie read to us from the book. He read a story about a superhero stricken with the one enemy he couldn't fight: Cancer.

Wow. Powerful stuff. Robbie went on to read the essay that followed this tale — it was the story on how van Belkom wrote the story on a laptop borrowed from his friend Sawyer while he sat in the hospital room where his wife was recovering from a cancer surgery.

*I: The Online Journal of Peter O'Mallick / **131***

It was great to see behind the scenes into the author's mind and how he came up with the tale. Robbie went on to say that he'd been to a reading that van Belkom gave when his book had first come out, and that van Belkom was one of the best readers he'd ever listened to.

He mentioned that he thought this particular book was now out of print, and that van Belkom had also published a book called *Scream Queen* that poked fun at the reality television trend (something else we'd covered in class a few weeks ago), as well as a series of very popular werewolf books for young adults that were just as enjoyable for adults to read.

At the end of class, I was so excited to learn more about this van Belkom fellow that I almost forgot to ask Robbie if he had a copy of *Frameshift* that I could borrow.

He said he did own *Frameshift*, that he owned every single copy of the books Sawyer had written, and that he'd have to think about whether or not he would lend me his copy of van Belkom's *Death Drives a Semi*. He said that the copy he owned had been signed by van Belkom and since it was out of print, he was worried about losing it.

He then turned to me and asked whether or not I had finished reading the book he had loaned me over the weekend, Sawyer's *Illegal Alien*. I'd completely forgotten about it, because I was so into browsing Sawyer's website and then so excited that he had responded to my question on his blog.

I was a bit disappointed. I mean, I would have thought that by now Robbie would have trusted me with loaning me his books. I've returned all of them in good condition. But it also feels like I let him down by asking for another book without having read the first one. I've just gotten so excited over discovering so many new authors lately.

I can be so stupid sometimes.

— *1 Comment* —

132 / *I, Death*

Kim — said . . .

Hey, don't worry... some people who really like books (like myself) tend to get a little anal about books we lend out, especially when we don't hear about them after awhile.

I too LOVE Edo van Belkom. I hosted a book signing event of his when I worked at a bookstore... his reading made me buy the book (*Death Drives a Semi* actually)... he's definitely worth the read!

Maybe all this reading is the kind of therapy you need?

Friday April 27, 2012 — 7:11 AM

I don't know what hit me.

I went to bed Monday night, and when I woke up Tuesday morning, I could barely get out of bed and my throat felt like it was full of sandpaper, closed up tight. Just swallowing air felt like I was trying to choke down a mouthful of broken glass. I was running a pretty nasty fever as well, my sheets were completely soaked.

Needless to say I didn't go in to school on Tuesday. Aunt Shelley made me a doctor's appointment. Turns out I have strep throat. I barely had the energy to get out of bed while she changed my sheets; barely had the energy to get dressed and get to the doctor's office.

The rest of Tuesday is pretty much a blur. I spent the rest of the day Tuesday falling in and out of feverish dreams. There were pretty vivid, I know that, but I can't recall what was happening in them or who was in them. The only thing that sticks with me is this freaky laughing skull that occasionally flashed into my peripheral vision. And the name "Jimmy" was whispered in my left ear whenever I saw that image.

I have no idea what that means. But that's all I can remember about these dreams. Pretty freaky.

I was feeling better enough on Wednesday that I wasn't just a groggy lump. I mostly stayed in bed and when I was up to it, I read. I finished reading *Illegal Alien* that Robbie had loaned to me. It was really good.

But now I'm torn. I want to read another Sawyer book, I want to read that collection by van Belkom. I also want to read more stuff by Laymon.

But I didn't have any of those books with me to read. So I went back to reading *Hamlet* again. It's funny, I enjoyed *Hamlet* even more when in a semi-feverish state. The two kind of went well together. And I don't know, but reading about Hamlet strutting about and fretting about his peril reminded me of the things going through my mind: the guilt, the grief, the frustrated anger. It made me feel good in a sad sort of way. What's that saying? *Misery loves company*?

I felt good enough yesterday to get out of bed. My fever was still there and my throat still had that sandpaper quality to it, but swallowing was getting a bit easier. I sat up and spent most of the day watching movies from Uncle Bob's DVD collection. I ended up watching two different versions of *Hamlet*: one with Mel Gibson and the other with Ethan Hawke, which was like a modernized version. Except in the new one, something is rotten in the state of Denmark Corporation in Manhattan. Interesting.

Last night Harley called me. It was good to touch base with what I was missing in school. Not that I really cared all that much about what was going on in classes, except, of course for Robbie's English class. Apparently, Robbie spent most of the week talking about books that discussed native issues in Canada, and they spent two full classes setting up mock Parliamentary debates over how to deal with a situation that's been going on in Southern Ontario for years now. Apparently there are a group of natives protesting a housing development and they had this highway and section of land that was sold or taken away from them blocked off, preventing the houses from being finished. It has apparently stirred up

I: The Online Journal of Peter O'Mallick / **135**

a lot of controversy over the years, including a book written by a journalist who took a harsh view of the natives' actions.

It sounds like I missed some fun stuff. Of course, Harley's take on the situation was pretty much a one-sided view of *a bunch of lazy welfare slobs with nothing better to do than prevent other people from making a living.* Big surprise there. I honestly don't know how I feel about the situation. From what I've read about it on the 'net, there are a lot of upset townspeople who couldn't get in to their newly bought homes, and are prevented from getting to work and school. But the native people do have rights; I mean, we pretty much stole Canada from them, and pushed them off onto these reserves, corrupted their lifestyle. I kind of feel sorry for both sides. I don't know how I would have argued in those class debates.

That's one of the things I like about the way Robbie teaches his class. He really makes you start to think.

After that Harley told me that Monica was back in school on Thursday. He said that she didn't look good; that her face was all swollen, her cheeks puffy. She had a pretty nasty black eye, a fat lip, and her right arm was in a sling. He said that she wasn't speaking to anyone except for a few close friends. I didn't ask if Sarah was one of the people she was talking to.

I know this sounds like I'm a chicken, but I was glad that I wasn't there and didn't see her.

I still have this odd feeling about her, like I might be responsible for what happened. I've tried to block that nasty dream where I'm the one hurting her, where I'm the one in the alley with her, trying to tell her to get away from me, and at the same time raining blows down on her. But I can't entirely push it away.

I'm actually feeling better this morning, possibly good enough to go in to school. But I faked it, pretended I felt

136 / *I, Death*

worse than I really do. I need a few more days before I face Monica again.

— 1 Comment —

Mantaray Ocean — said . . .
Now that you have been watching various versions of *Hamlet*, do you think that he was truly mad... or just allowing others to think he was?

I think that *Hamlet* in certain ways is closer to real life in the here and now... than we allow ourselves to realize.

Tuesday May 1, 2012 — 11:58 PM

I didn't see Monica at school at all yesterday. The day was mostly just a big blur, it was like my ears were stuffed with cotton and I was seeing everything through a smoky haze. My heart kept racing every time a girl passed me because I thought it might be her.

But I saw her today. She was far down the hall, and I don't think she saw me. But I saw her, and my heart burned, it ached, and I wept. I wept to see this once strong and confident girl, sexy, bright and cheery, slowly slink down the hallway, her head down-turned. Walking tight to the lockers, she moved down the hall with these little brisk steps like she was afraid someone was going to step on her.

It broke my heart. This wasn't Monica. No, not anymore. There was barely nothing left of the Monica that I knew as I watched this meek person scuttle down the hall.

And the guilt returned to me full force.

I wonder if that's how Hamlet felt when he came upon the grave being dug for Ophelia. It's funny, someone left a comment about whether or not Hamlet was mad or if he was just allowing others to think he was. Honestly? I actually think it was a bit of both. I'm sure that he played up his madness because it made others uneasy, but I also think that there was some truth to his affliction. He was filled with anger, confusion, guilt.

138 / *I, Death*

And, of course, I think back to my own situation, my own anger, my own confusion, my own guilt. There was that horrid dream, that awful nightmare of hurting Monica. I feel guilty for having it, but not because I believe I actually hurt her. No, I think that was my unconscious mind telling me I was responsible for her getting hurt. That she was hurt because of me, because of this curse surrounding me.

I just can't get the image of her slinking down the hall like a fearful mouse out of my mind.

Saturday May 5, 2012 — 2:48 PM

Damn. I've been trying to log onto this blogger account for three days now, and not able to get past the login screen. It's just been hanging there.

I thought, at first, that I'd forgotten my password or something. But that wasn't it. Not sure if it was my connection to the internet or maybe one of the servers at Blogger. Whatever it was, it drove me to start writing my thoughts and stuff in written form, because I've had so many things to sort out lately. When the guidance counselor first told me to start writing down my thoughts and emotions I thought he was nuts. But it's funny that that seems to be the first thing I do now whenever I need to sort stuff out.

I'm going to copy those thoughts I wrote down onto this online journal. Is it just for the sake of continuity? Because I have to admit, I've gone back and re-read the stuff that I've written several times now. That has been just as therapeutic as writing it down. So I will post that handwritten stuff here, but I'm not sure when.

As it is, I don't even know if this is going to publish or not. Here goes nothing...

— 1 Comment —

Kim — said . . .

140 / *I, Death*

I've been journaling for years. It's helped me get through the hardest of times as well as the best of times.

Good luck.

Tuesday May 8, 2012 — 1:19 AM

Okay, so that last post did work. And, unlike my previous attempts it didn't disappear. I waited a full day because I wanted to make sure it didn't delete after the fact. I know this sounds like I'm being paranoid, but the first few times I'd tried to post last week, I ended up losing the work. Maybe I wasn't paying attention properly and missed a key step. But I'm sure I did it right, and Blogger just hung there, not resolving. And when I came back to it, the post was gone, missing, like I'd never written it.

That's why I wrote the following entries down. By hand. And now that things are up and working again, I'm going to re-type them below.

Thursday May 3ʳᵈ, 2012

At the end of English class today, Robbie asked me to hang back a bit because there was something he wanted to ask me. I was terrified. I thought that maybe he knew something about what happened to Monica, that maybe he was going to point a finger at me and tell me he knew it was me — that somehow, in my sleep, I'd gone and beat and raped her. Or that maybe Monica had been talking to him and told him this herself.

142 / *I, Death*

I actually tried to sneak out of the class, tried to just mix into the flow of students out of the room. But he reached right out and grabbed my arm. He grabbed my arm and pulled me back through the crowd. He'd done it so quickly, so forcefully, that I'd thought for sure that he was going to lay blame on me for what happened to Monica.

He held my arm, preventing me from getting away while smiling and making quick small talk with the remaining students filtering out of the class. When the last student left, he let go of my arm and closed the door.

"What's going on, Peter?" he asked, the concern showing on his face as he leaned on a desk at the front of the classroom. "You've been acting really strange ever since you returned to school and Monica is back."

As I rubbed my arm where he'd grabbed and held me, I didn't know how to respond. "W-what do you mean?"

His eyes softened even more. He pursed his lips and looked me in the eye. "You're feeling guilty about Monica, aren't you?"

I didn't answer, but turned my head down and looked at the floor.

"C'mon, Peter," he said. "You can talk to me, man. I think I know what you're going through."

My eyes started to tear up, I tried to hold back the sobs, but my voice repeatedly broke when I responded. "How could you... possibly... know... what I'm going through?"

"Because I've been there too." A strange look came over his face just then and he took a deep

I: The Online Journal of Peter O'Mallick / **143**

breath. "When I was a teenager, my girlfriend was raped at a house party. We went in together, the two of us, and then as we each starting hanging around with different groups of friends, I ended up heading off in a car with a few buddies to pick up some munchies. We did it all the time, go to a party together, split up, do our own thing, then get back together.

"Only this time, this time something happened while I was gone. These guys from another high school showed up. Nobody knew who they were, they just showed up, about ten of them, and crashed the party. A few of them picked a couple of fights with a few of the guys, and three of them ended up pushing their way into the bathroom where Sandy — that was her name — where Sandy was. She'd had a bit too much to drink and was in there being sick to her stomach."

At that point, Robbie paced to the far side of the classroom and looked out the window facing away from me. "The three of them had her way with her. They, they pushed her to the floor, then two of them held her down while the third guy ripped off her clothes and raped her. Then they switched, and another guy took over. Then the third.

"It didn't matter that she'd been sick to her stomach while they were raping her... it didn't matter that she was retching and throwing up and almost choking on her vomit. Two of them held her down so she was unable to resist while the third one raped her.

144 / *I, Death*

"They left her lying on the bathroom floor and that's where the next person going in to use the washroom found her.

"By the time the person going in to use the washroom had figured out what had happened, the entire gang of guys from that other school, even the ones who had started a few different fights, had left. Sandy spent a long time sitting on the bathroom floor, naked and bleeding and covered in her own vomit. Any time anybody tried to comfort her, to help her get cleaned up and dressed, she pushed them off, not saying anything.

"When I got back to the party the whole thing was long over and a few of her closer friends had been able to get her dressed, despite her protests and struggle, and were walking her to a car to bring her home.

"The only thing that anybody can remember her saying was when she looked up and spotted me getting out of my buddy Henry's car. She stood straight up, pointed a finger in my direction and said: 'Thanks for leaving me alone.' Then she got into the car.

"Those were the last words she spoke to me. They might have been the last words she ever spoke to anybody. Her friends had brought her home and that night she'd swallowed an entire bottle of her mother's tranquilizers. She never woke up from it."

Okay, so I stopped writing at that point. I just couldn't continue. I was exhausted and my hand hurt from writing. Retyping this whole thing feels a little silly, but I'm glad that I'm doing it. I've stopped often while keying it in to just

I: The Online Journal of Peter O'Mallick / **145**

read and re-read it again, and realize the effect the whole conversation had on me.

I didn't write in my journal again until the next night, and in it I tried to continue from where I'd left off.

Friday May 4th, 2012

Robbie stood at the window for a long time before he turned back and faced me. When he did turn I could see the moisture welling in his eyes. At that point, an announcement came on the PA system, calling him to the office.

"I've got to go, Peter," he said, "but I've told you my story. So, yes, I think I can understand the guilt that you feel. And I really do think that this is something you should talk about. If not to me, then to someone else, anyone else."

He walked towards the door and just before he stepped out he turned and said. "I really do think you need to talk this out. And I'd really like to help you through this, if I can."

I ended up going to see Robbie at the end of the school day. He just stood there, looking at me, without saying a single thing. And I broke down, started to sob and sob, and told him about the dream I'd had about Monica, about the guilt that I felt about it, and about the fact that I realized that while I'd been intrigued with Monica and interested in starting a relationship with her, that all I'd been really feeling had been a kind of intense infatuation, a kind of misplaced lust, and that fact made me feel all the more guilty about what happened to her.

I'd made her out to be an object of lust and sex and desire, and then someone had raped her.

146 / *I, Death*

The guilt had continued to grow and eat away inside of me.

Robbie explained that rape wasn't about sex — and I had a sudden memory of that topic coming up in our class discussion from a few weeks ago, but for some reason it didn't really stick then. He explained that rape was about power, about dominance, about control over another person.

He talked about my feeling of guilt and my holding Monica in my mind's eye as an object of desire as being typical of teenage infatuation, but that it had nothing to do with what actually happened to Monica. My feelings of lust for her did not lead to her getting raped, and I had nothing to feel guilty about.

We kept talking around and around the issue, and I have to admit that the release I felt to be able to communicate the things I've been feeling for this past while — to communicate them openly and verbally, was overwhelmingly powerful.

I started sobbing uncontrollably at that point, not just out of the guilty and grief, but out of the simple emotion of relief.

That's when Robbie stepped forward and put his arms around me and just held me while I cried.

And that was the point where my hand-written second journal entry ended. It feels strange re-reading it and typing it in. I know that my buddy Harley would say something to the effect that it was a real homo scene with Robbie giving me a hug. But I needed that hug more than anything, and

I: The Online Journal of Peter O'Mallick / **147**

honestly, truly, it felt good just to have someone, anyone be willing to offer me that gesture of compassion.

It's funny. Robbie and I had another after class chat yesterday, but neither one of us has brought up the shared stories — the ones of his guilt over what happened to his girlfriend or my guilt of what happened to Monica.

Instead, we just talked about books. It was great. It was glorious. He loaned me another book. Back to the first author he'd introduced me to: Sean Costello. This one was called *Finders Keepers* and was about what happens to a group of people who come across a lottery ticket worth 10 million dollars.

Robbie said that I'd like the thriller aspect of the story, and that the dark humour employed in the tale would be good to get my mind off of everything. I haven't read it yet, but do plan on starting it tomorrow.

Right now, I should really get to bed.

Thursday May 10, 2012 — 2:04 AM

I've actually felt pretty good since last Friday. The weekend was low key. I ended up cutting the lawn and playing video games on Saturday and then just chilling and watching a movie with my Uncle Bob Sunday afternoon — some old black and white film that I don't know the name of. I wasn't really paying attention. I was pretty much sleeping with my eyes open. Maybe that's why the movie was more like a dream that I had and could only remember in fleeting memories of sight and sound.

I felt relaxed and barely thought back to Monica or Sarah or any of the guilt that I'd recently been focused on over Chad, Miss Hamilton or Sarah's father. Robbie helped me turn that around, that's for sure. Having gone back and typed in my hand-written journal entries reminded me of just how important that was.

Robbie was sick and not teaching on Monday and Tuesday of this week. I was a bit worried about him. But he was back in class today, and in full form.

He was going through a lesson on Wednesday, read us a few scenes from a book called *The Handless Maiden*. It was by a Loraine Brown. It was her first novel, and after he read a few scenes from it he explained how the author of this very powerful story had worked at it over the course of something like ten years. He held it up as an example of something he

I: The Online Journal of Peter O'Mallick / **149**

remembered hearing W.O. Mitchell saying during a reading he'd done in Sudbury almost thirty years ago. It was a statement to the effect that any novel that took less than four years to write wasn't any good.

The class debated the issue back and forth, and I'm sure it was interesting. But I wasn't paying all that much attention at that point. I couldn't help reflecting back on one of the scenes Robbie had read to the class and how it reminded me of Monica.

The heroine in *The Handless Maiden* is a talented pianist who loses her hand in the events surrounding her rape. In her I sensed this feeling of utter loss, the loss of her ability to create beautiful music — I compared that with the loss I sense whenever I look into Monica's eyes. I started to wonder if I had imagined that — if perhaps I was reading something in to her look that I expected.

After all, I really wonder if I could ever truly understand what it is like to be raped. Yes, despite the guilt that I feel, as if my curse is what caused this to happen to her, despite the dark feelings and the grief, I'm still nothing more than an outsider looking in. I'll likely never truly understand.

At the end of class, Robbie and I chatted for a bit. He mentioned to me that this weekend there would some sort of launch event from a Sudbury publisher with a few different authors which included a teaser for Sean Costello's forthcoming novel *Let it Ride*. He said it was taking place on Sunday May 14th starting at 1:30 in the afternoon and he was wondering if I was interested in joining him in attending the event.

Wow. That was really cool. I can't wait to attend the event. When I got home I started reading the latest book Robbie had loaned me. Costello's *Finders Keepers*.

It still hasn't helped keep my mind off of the upcoming event this weekend. I just can't wait.

Saturday May 12, 2012 — 7:04 PM

Holy shit. Did I ever have a lot of fun at the book event today. Right now I'm logged on using the "internet café" computers at the Chapters book store. Robbie is in line at Starbucks getting us a couple of coffees.

We had an amazing time at the book launch. The readings, the entertainment, everything was just awesome. Robbie bought me a copy of Sean Costello's updated version of *Captain Quad*. It was the 20th anniversary edition of the book, this one published by Scrivener Press, a small Sudbury area publisher. I can't believe that I finally met him. He seems like this normal, friendly guy. You'd never know that he wrote these frightening, creepy tales of nasty people doing awful things to one another. This is the first time that I've ever met an author whose book that I read or had a book signed by anyone. It's awesome.

Robbie brought in all of the Costello books that he owned to have signed.

Anyways, Robbie and I had a great time hanging out, mixing and mingling with all the people there. I just don't want today to end. We're going to hang around here at Chapters and browse for a bit, then we're likely heading over to the Kelsey's across the way for something to eat.

Oh. Here he comes. Gotta post this and go.

Sunday May 13, 2012 — 3:14 PM

Why can't things just go right for me? Why can't they just be normal?

I'm pretty fucked up right now over what happened.

And I don't know if I'll ever be able to write about it.

All I know for sure is that I can't write about it right now.

Why, Robbie? Why?

— 3 Comments —

Kim — said . . .
Oh no…

Franny — said . . .
Writing will help you, I think. Though, so will professional help…

MaliceAD — said . . .
OMG! OMG!! OK… You gotta like calm down and assess the situation. It will help you wrap your mind around the issue so you can write.

Friday May 25, 2012 — 1:04 AM

Over ten days have passed since my last post, but it feels as if it's merely been an hour since the tragic events that happened back on the early hours of May 14th.

I've gone over the details again and again in my head, my heart and mind swimming, practically drowning in the emotions. And it has mostly all stayed in my head, no matter how much people have tried to make me talk about it.

But I think I'm ready to talk about it now.

I have to ease into it though, take it slow.

So let me start with the thing that is paining me to talk about, the thing that has wrenched my heart from my chest. Maybe if I get that out of the way I can move on with trying to come to terms with what happened and properly relay the events that occurred that have put me here.

Robbie is dead.

It kills me to write those words, hurts me to acknowledge it — almost as if by typing in those words I'm making it real. But it is. It is real. I avoided going to his funeral, refused to talk to anyone about his death for over a week now. But I have to face the fact. He is dead.

Okay, so I finally got that out. It may not seem like much, but to me that's a huge release, a giant step. Now I can begin

I: The Online Journal of Peter O'Mallick / **153**

to talk a bit about how we got from hanging out at Chapters to how he came die in such a horrific way.

But not tonight. It's taken a lot out of me just to admit this much. I'm going to leave it at that, regroup my thoughts and emotions, and on my next post talk a little bit about the wonderful evening that so quickly and strangely turned into a nightmare.

— 4 Comments —

Kim — said . . .
I'm so sorry about Robbie, Peter. Don't know what else to say.

Franny — said . . .
So sorry.

MaliceAD — said . . .
My thoughts are with you, Peter.

Frank — said . . .
Condolences, Peter. I know how much Robbie meant to you. What happened?

Monday May 28, 2012 — 11:17 PM

I've tried several times to write about this, to explain the events of the evening, but every time I try, I keep tripping on the words and keep getting ahead of myself.

I've decided to make an effort not to rush the events of the evening but to try to go through them in the manner in which they happened — because every time I get ahead of myself, I trip up and it's a big ball of madness in my head and not a clean, straightforward narrative that I'm trying to map out for myself, to properly deal with it.

So here's what happened, right from my last post during the early evening of May 13th.

Robbie came around the corner of a pillar near Starbucks and was heading toward me with two cups of coffee. I can't remember if they're called *Verte* or *Grande* or *Lardass* or whatever the hell Starbucks calls them, just that they were the large size.

He handed one over to me just as I was pushing the "publish" button for this blog on the Internet Café computer. I tried blocking the screen with my body as much as possible, as if I was preventing Robbie from seeing porn or something on the screen. (Although I'm sure that a public computer like this or maybe even one at the library wouldn't allow people to browse through porn on it)

"What are you doing?" Robbie asked.

I: The Online Journal of Peter O'Mallick / **155**

"Ah, just checking some email," I said, thumbing the computer monitor off and then hitting the reset button that shut down the computer and ended my session. I thought back to the time he'd told me how he was an expert at reading people and wondered if the bemused look on his face meant that he knew I was lying.

"What next?" I said, sipping the coffee. It had an Irish cream taste to it.

Robbie smiled. "I had them add a shot of Irish Cream flavour to the coffee. But then I also added a nip of Irish Cream to it as well." He lifted the flap off the laptop bag that he carried around on his shoulder everywhere, revealing the neck of a bottle of Bailey's. He took a sip from his own coffee and then added: "Okay, maybe more than just a little nip."

I laughed. "This is awesome, I'm having a great time."

We then spent the next hour or so browsing through the store, Robbie pointing out countless titles to me that he'd read and loved.

By that time, we'd finished our coffees, and Robbie had found a quiet spot where nobody could see what he was doing to top up our coffee cups with Baileys. As we drank down the creamy alcohol, he started telling me about this one time when he was a kid and almost got locked in a Canadian Tire store overnight. He had crawled inside one of the pup tent displays and had fallen asleep, not waking up until after the store had closed.

We were laughing about how Robbie's father had been searching all over for him, thinking he'd run away from home due to a fight they'd had earlier in the day when this creepy looking man approached Robbie from behind. I remember the odd leering look on the man's face, (it specifically reminded me of the look on the face of the original *Nosferatu* in that old black and white German film) and the way in which he'd started walking towards us purposefully. And then, just as

156 / *I, Death*

Robbie turned in a retelling of the fight between him and his father over the desired purchase of a Canadian Tire basketball, the man quickly shifted, ducked behind some tall shelves, and was gone from view.

If I'd known the trouble this man was going to cause, I would have tried to get us out of the store sooner, before he came back.

But of course, I had no idea, back then, what was going to happen.

Okay, I'm starting to get ahead of myself. But rather than just delete this and trying to start over, like I've done so many times, I'm going to stop here, take a break and get the rest of my thoughts together.

Wednesday May 30, 2012 — 11:09 PM

So there Robbie and I were, in the store, finishing off the bottle of Bailey's, and he was just finishing the retelling of the time he fell asleep in a tent at a Canadian Tire, when his eye caught a table display of books. One of them included a movie-tie in cover; you know, the ones that have the movie poster cover on them.

"That's the wonder of movies," Robbie said. "When done properly, a good movie adaption can add new elements that can be revealed in a manner less subtle than in the book, but still powerful and rich."

That statement he made reminded me so much of my Uncle Bob. It's funny, because, since Robbie was a father figure in my life (yes, I only realize that now), it made sense that I found something in him that reminded him of the man I'd known as my central father figure since the day my own father had been hit by the car and died.

It was shortly after this revelation that the creepy looking man I'd seen earlier reappeared from behind a tall set of bookshelves. This time I think that Robbie must have seen him because, in mid-sentence he put down his coffee cup and said: "Okay, Peter. Time for us to go."

When I didn't move, Robbie grabbed me by the arm and starting walking us quickly toward the exit, completely

158 / *I, Death*

abandoning the small pile of books we'd accumulated, intending to purchase.

He didn't say a word as we moved out to the car, but I could tell that he was stepping more quickly as soon as we left the bright lights of the store and were crossing the dark parking lot. I remember thinking how late it was and that we must have spent a longer time in the store than I'd originally thought. Sure enough, my watch showed that it was already 9:30.

As he was starting the car I finally asked. "What's going on, Robbie? Who was that man?"

After putting the car in gear he turned to look at me. "Peter, I have a confession to make. But the first order of business is we need to get the hell out of here, now," he takes his foot off the brake, slams it down on the gas, the tires issuing a high pitched squeal as we peel out of the parking lot.

I remember looking back, seeing a few different figures heading out the store entrance, one of them tall like the creepy man I'd seen in the store. An unexplainable shiver ran down my spine.

We drove in silence as Robbie raced the car down the Kingsway toward downtown. We raced down the street next to city hall, then made a quick right, then a left, darted around a seemingly random route through the downtown core area of town before Robbie raced onto Paris Street and then turned off again to the parking area near Science North.

He shut off the car and we sat there for a moment, just listening. I couldn't hear anything other than the ticking and clicking of the engine as it cooled down, but the look on Robbie's face suggested he was either listening to the traffic turning off Paris or perhaps to voices from the past, talking to him about the confession he was about to make.

"Robbie," I said. "I'm a little concerned, here."

I: The Online Journal of Peter O'Mallick / **159**

He lifted a single finger into the air, saying nothing, and continued to sit quietly and just listen.

After what must have been ten or fifteen minutes, Robbie said, "I've got to get something. Just a minute." And he got out of the car, opened the trunk, then returned to the driver's seat with a mickey in each hand. One of rye and the other vodka. "Name your poison," he said, reaching past me into the glove compartment where he fished out two plastic cups.

"Me? I'm starting with the rye," he said, pouring some for himself. I said that I'd have that too and he poured me a cupful.

He took a long, slow drink from his cup, then refilled it before he turned to me and said: "It's very probable you're not going to like me much after I tell you this story."

Thursday May 31, 2012 — 11:31 PM

So there Robbie and I were, sitting in his car, drinking rye. It had otherwise been like some skytop sort of epic fantastical dream, hanging out with the coolest teacher I'd ever known, going to a book event, hanging out at a book store, drinking coffee spiked with Baileys then racing a car through downtown streets and then sitting back and drinking some rye from a parking spot that I realized gave a beautiful view of a moonlit Lake Ramsey.

But the tone in Robbie's voice had a nightmarish quality to it. I'd never heard it from him before, and it frightened me.

"Peter," he said. "That man, the man in the store. He's my dealer."

"Oh," I said. Most teachers are supposed to tell you *not* to smoke, *not* to drink, *not* to do drugs. Of those, Robbie hadn't pulled out a pack of cigarettes, but so far he'd helped break all those. I know teachers are human like the rest of us, but it was certainly refreshing to see that evidence first hand. And so what, my English teacher smoked pot. Big fucking deal. Who hasn't?

"So. What's the big deal?" I asked.

"I owe him a shitload of money," Robbie said. "But there's more. And I know I can confide in you, but I don't know how to tell you the rest."

"The rest? Of what?"

I: The Online Journal of Peter O'Mallick / **161**

"The rest of my confession." He drained his cup again in another single gulp and poured himself another drink. I think that was his third in as many minutes.

For the first time in our relationship, it didn't feel like he was my teacher. He was suddenly just another friend, and a friend with a problem. "Just start from the beginning."

"Fair enough. And I'll actually start with a smaller confession. I've been reading your blog."

"You have?"

"Yes. Since about the second day of class. I discovered it one night. Actually, a lot of teachers I know have started doing Google searches of their own names as a means to see if students are blogging or posting comments about them and their class. I spotted yours almost immediately, and went back to the beginning."

"So you know all about Sarah?"

"Yes,"

"And the other deaths?"

"Yes,"

"And about Miss Hamilton's accident?"

"Yes. And also about Monica."

Monica. Oh man, this was so embarrassing. Robbie had been reading my words. But what could I expect, really? There were tons of strangers out there, people I'd never met who were reading my online journal and making comments on it. Why did I think that people I knew wouldn't find it and read it too?

I tried to think back to all the things I'd said about Robbie on my blog, and was slightly embarrassed about how much I talked about him, gushed about him. But it wasn't quite so bad — this was Robbie, after all, and to know that he'd had these insights about me almost from the beginning, yet he still wanted to be my friend, hang out with me — well that was pretty darn cool.

162 / *I, Death*

"I don't know what to say, Robbie." I said. "I feel guilty about what happened to Monica. As if I could have prevented it."

"Oh, Peter," Robbie said, and tears started to roll down his eyes. "You have nothing to feel guilty about with Monica. What happened to her is actually my fault."

"Your fault?" I said, completely perplexed. "How could what happened to Monica be your fault?"

"I know you had feelings for her, Peter. I know you were interested in her. That's what makes this so difficult; so difficult to tell you." He paused, put his head in his hands, then wiped the tears away. "I'm such a fool. I never should have done what I did. But I got caught up in the moment, carried away by emotions. I'd fallen in love with her from the first day that I met her.

"Peter, Monica and I were having an affair."

Friday June 1, 2012 — 11:58 PM

I had to stop that last post all of a sudden. I'm trying really hard to get this story out, but it's hard to convey. And of course, every time I get to a part like that last one, like when I found out that Robbie and Monica were sleeping together, I get a bit overwhelmed with it all. Rather than start going on about how it makes me feel, I stop myself.

After all, I'm trying to get this story out, and get it out in the proper sequence of what happened. Because a hell of a lot went down that night. I found out a lot of things about Robbie, about Monica. And I need to write this out in proper order, so I can keep these details straight in my head.

When Robbie told me that he and Monica were fucking, it was like someone punched me, hard, in the gut, then took hold of my stomach with a steel-tight, ice cold grip, and squeezed. I couldn't respond to what Robbie had told me, it was such a large piece of information that I was still trying to digest it.

"There's more," Robbie said, "that I have to tell you."

My own eyes had welled up, tears of rage were streaming down my face even before my mind started to piece the different bits together and I seemed to make the conscious realization. "*Y-you* raped Monica?" I remember seeing red, ready to strike out at Robbie, to tear his eyes right out of his head.

164 / *I, Death*

"No, Peter. No! I loved Monica; cared for her very deeply. I would never hurt her, rape her. Please let me explain. Please."

The anger started to subside. I sat back in my seat, drank down my own glass of rye and then asked him to refill it for me. "Go on." I finally said.

"Monica stayed after class that first day to talk to me. She was so beautiful, looked so much like a woman I'd loved back in University — Lynda, the woman whom I thought I was going to marry and spend the rest of my life with. And when she started talking excitedly about *The Dead Poet's Society* and how she thought it was so cool that I'd taken a scene from that movie and tried it out in the class, her personality, her spark, reminded me of Lynda again.

"We talked for a good half an hour after that first class. And I loaned her a book of poetry by Keats. The look on her face was priceless, wonderful, when she looked at it. She told me Keats was her favorite poet. And when I saw that sparkle in her eyes when they fell upon the book, I knew I was falling in love with her. I know it sounds strange, but that's exactly how I felt.

"Monica came to visit me after class yet again the next day. And the day after that. And the next. A week or so later when you started hanging out after class, Monica stayed off to the side, slipped out with the crowd. I remember enjoying chatting with you Peter, because by then I'd been following your online journal and feeling a real connection with you. But I was also a bit sad to miss out on my one on one time with Monica.

"She was waiting at my car at the end of the school day. We ended up sitting in the car and talking for hours, about books, about movies, about music, about life, about dreams.

"And almost every single day after that she was there at my car and we did the same. By then I knew it was too late,

I: The Online Journal of Peter O'Mallick / **165**

that I'd already fallen so madly, so deeply in love with her, that there was no going back.

"One Friday, she asked if we could go somewhere, get a coffee or a drink, and keep talking. She put her hand on my leg and told me that she didn't want the evening to end.

"So we went out for coffee, and then to a restaurant and ordered dinner. We stayed there, talked until the waiters were putting chairs up on the tables signaling that it was time to go home. Too wrapped up in each other and the conversation, we headed back to my place without discussing what we were doing. I put on some coffee when we got there and we sat there on the couch, talking into the early morning hours. We ended up making love on that same couch, just as the sun was coming up, still talking, still sharing, our bodies finally as intimate as our souls had been the entire night.

"I did love her Peter. I loved her deeply. I still love her, but she won't have anything to do with me any longer. And I can't say I blame her."

"What happened, Robbie?" I asked. "You said that you're to blame for her getting beaten and raped? How? What happened?"

I remember sitting there looking at Robbie and feeling jealous. Not just jealous because Robbie had been sleeping with Monica — actually that didn't bother me all that much, to be honest. It surprised me, sure, shocked me, stunned me, was like an ice cold splash of water in my face; but I wasn't jealous. While I knew that I had liked Monica, had thought that she was pretty cool, a lot of fun, was a like-minded lover of reading and damn sexy, I didn't actually love her.

As I had figured out before, it had been mostly lust I'd been feeling for her; misplaced lust derived from a strange erotic dream and perhaps the fact that I was lonely and just wanted someone. That someone, of course, was still Sarah,

166 / *I, Death*

but I had to move on, and so likely transferred the intense feelings in Monica's direction.

So yes, I was a bit jealous that Robbie had been sleeping with Monica while I'd been lusting after her, but I was actually jealous of the fact that Monica had gotten so close to Robbie, and of course, of the fact that they had each other while I was still on my own. Since Sarah dumped me, I've been mostly alone, on the sidelines, looking in. This revelation by Robbie about his relationship with Monica was just more salt in that wound.

"Peter, do you remember that night when you bumped into Monica in the movie theatre?"

"Yeah," *Rejection night. How could I forget?*

"Monica was there at the theatre with me. I stayed out of sight when we spotted you. Of course, it was risky for me to be there with her in the first place, but we were just a student and teacher out at the movies, nothing wrong with that. But having read your blog I knew you'd been interested in Monica and would perhaps be jealous of the fact that we were there together."

"Yeah, I would have been," I said quietly.

"It was that night, after the movie, when Monica and I went for a ride. We went up to that spot on Big Nickel Mine Road where you can watch them dump the slag from the side of the road.

"We were sitting there, just chatting, and snorting coke. Yes, the addict that I was, I ended up getting Monica started on my drug of choice. No, I'm not proud of it, but it happened.

"Speaking of drugs, that's where my dealer comes into this. I'd owed him a large sum of money and he'd been carrying me for weeks. I hadn't been able to pay but still kept going back to him for more — I don't know if you'll ever understand an addict's mindset, but there's this belief that with just one more fix you'll be fine and can move on. Only

I: The Online Journal of Peter O'Mallick / **167**

that 'one more' is always in your future, never in your past. You simply can't.

"Anyway, I could talk for hours about the demons I've been facing with respect to my dependencies on drugs and alcohol, but the key thing here is that I'd pissed off someone who held a lot of power over me.

"And that's who showed up that night when Monica and I were sitting in the car. The moment he pulled in behind us, his headlights bright in my rear-view mirror, I knew who it was and told Monica to get out of the car immediately, just leave."

Robbie stopped, drank down yet another full glass of rye and filled his cup again. "She wouldn't leave. She joked that she'd give him a blow job and maybe that'd tide him over. I got angry, told her *this wasn't funny*, that I wanted her out of harm's way. But she refused. And when the dealer approached the car, taking leisurely, slow steps, he did it from her side. I'm sure he not only knew there was someone in the passenger seat, but that he'd been following us all night. He leaned in the window, grinning that sick twisted grin of his, and asked me if I knew why he was there."

Putting down the rye and kneading his hands into his forehead, Robbie whispered, "Dammit, why couldn't I just have convinced Monica to get out of the car and leave? Why?"

I put a hand on Robbie's shoulder. "It's okay, Robbie. Keep talking. It's helping." I for one, should know the recuperative powers of just getting the grief out.

"So Monica starts flirting with the guy, starts saying suggestive things, like maybe we could all talk about this, and maybe there was something she could do to please him, make him forget about money. She was trying to protect me, to help me, and I just sat there like a fucking idiot as she unbuttoned her shirt and started parting it, sat there watching as this bastard reached in and cupped one of

168 / *I, Death*

her breasts. I sat there just watching as Monica whispered something in his ear, and he opened her door, pulling down his zipper. Sat there watching her suck his dick. And all the while knowing that the woman I loved was doing this to protect me, to keep me from harm. And I was too much of a fucking chicken to do anything but sit there and watch it. And the whole time, the sick fucker was staring at me with a huge grin on his face.

"When the scumbag finally blew his load, he laughed, called out 'It's time', pulled Monica out of the car, produced a switch-blade and held it to her throat. That's when two of his cronies appeared on my side of the car and hauled me out.

" 'Now listen up and listen good,' the dealer said. 'I was planning on hurting you to show that I mean business and I want my fucking cash soon. But your lady friend here has given me a much better idea.'

"And that's when he started using the knife to peel off Monica's clothes as he dragged her to his car. I tried to break free of the two thugs holding me, tried to step forward, but there was nothing I could do.

" 'This lady friend of yours is going to hurt in new ways,' he said, shoving her into the back seat of the car then turning toward me again and pointing the knife at me. 'Let's just say she'll be sorry she ever made your acquaintance. And maybe, just maybe, you'll think twice about trying to stiff me out of a payment.'

"Then he nodded, and I felt something connect with the side of my head. That's the last thing I remember before blacking out.

"I woke up after what must have been several minutes. Their vehicle, with Monica in it, was gone."

Saturday June 2, 2012 — 10:51 PM

Robbie stopped telling the story, put his head against the steering wheel and started sobbing uncontrollably. "I didn't do anything to stop them," he said. "They drove off with Monica and they beat her and raped her... and it was entirely my fault."

I looked at Robbie, not saying anything. Of course it was his fault. His drug habit is what put Monica in that predicament. I know that I was supposed to tell him that it wasn't his fault, but I couldn't. He's the reason why Monica was badly injured both physically and emotionally. The reason I saw that hurt animal look in her eyes. Him, not me.

"You talked about her rape in class that week," I said, accusingly. "You used it as class material, as something to help us deal with something that had happened to a fellow student."

"It was also helping me deal with it, too," Robbie said, still not looking at me.

"And that story you told me about your girlfriend in high school. You made that up, didn't you? Wait a minute, you fucker! You'd been reading my blog, so you knew about the dreams I'd had about Monica, about the guilt I'd felt over it. And you let me feel that. You could have fucking told me about this back then."

"How could I?" Robbie said. "How... could... I?

170 / *I, Death*

"I've needed to talk about this with someone, but who could I talk to, and how could I bring it up in the hallway between classes? My girlfriend, that high school party I'd told you about, that happened Peter. It *really did*. That's what makes it that much more painful, that much more difficult, that another girl I loved was raped, and again I could have prevented it, but I didn't.

"I fully expected Monica to tell the police the story, but she refused to talk about it with anyone. I want those guys to pay for what they did to her, want to kill them with my bare hands. But I can't come forward and tell the police what I know. My career as a teacher would be over. Besides, I don't even know the fucking dealer's name. He goes by 'Dillon', but I know that's not his name. I have a cell phone for him and that's all. Who knows if it would even help them find him, if they could even hold him in jail. What evidence is there now?

"Oh God, Monica," he whispered. "I'm so, so sorry."

We sat there in silence. I sipped at my rye, but it wasn't going down well at all. After several minutes, he spoke up again.

"I tried talking to her, tried calling her on her cell phone, slipping her a note, talking with her in the hallways at school. But she won't even respond to me, won't even talk with me. Won't let me apologize."

"What the fuck do you expect?" I said. "Serves you fucking right." But inside, I was feeling sorry for him because he was in the same situation I had been in with Sarah. I guess the difference with Sarah is that I didn't put her in a situation where she'd been raped and beaten. No, in our case, my curse caused her father's cancer, but she couldn't possibly know that. In our case, I couldn't have prevented what happened. But I could still feel for what Robbie was going through, despite the fact that I was angry with him for the situation he'd led Monica into.

I: The Online Journal of Peter O'Mallick / **171**

Fuck. I liked Robbie, respected him, looked up to him so much. And, despite how angry I was with him, I still wanted to comfort him, tell him there wasn't anything he could do.

But I never got that chance. I never got to tell him that, while I was pissed off with him, I still looked up to him, still wanted to make our friendship work.

I never got the chance, because there was suddenly a bright flash of headlights from behind us.

"Holy fuck." Robbie said. "Dillon has found us."

Monday June 4, 2012 — 11:13 PM

My head was swimming with the fresh knowledge of the events that had led up to Monica's rape and beating. A wonderful mentor and father figure had been destroyed by admitting his involvement in the whole deal. And the alcohol was flowing through my veins, clouding my perception.

So when Dillon appeared at the driver side door, his switch-blade already out, it was very much like a dream. He reached in the open window with his other hand and hauled Robbie out by the neck without opening the door. He'd looked tall and lanky in the store, but he was a strong son of a bitch, that was plainly obvious.

He kicked Robbie in the face then leaned into the car door and said. "Oh, so what do we have here? Get out of the car, now." I complied. He stood there and smiled at me across the top of the car. "You fucking him, too, Robinson?"

"Hurt me, kill me, do what you want," Robbie said struggling to his feet. "Just don't hurt the boy."

"Oh I plan on doing more than that," Dillon said, a huge grin on face. "I don't do the 'Hershey highway' stuff, but let's see how good he is at giving me a blow job, and if it's good, I'll kill him quickly. If it's not good, he'll be *begging* for me to kill him before I'm done with him." He pointed the knife at me. "Over here and on your knees, boy." He said to me.

I: The Online Journal of Peter O'Mallick / **173**

"No!" Robbie said, and reached forward. Dillon thrust his blade out, sinking the tip of the blade into Robbie's shoulder.

"I'm coming," I said, starting to walk around the front of the car.

"No," Robbie gasped, stumbling back, grabbing at the gash on his shoulder. "Leave him alone. He didn't do anything. T-take me. L-leave him. Dillon, listen..."

"No, you listen, you dumb fuck. I thought you'd learned your lesson last time, but you obviously need to be taught a more serious lesson now." He grabbed Robbie's shoulder, the one he'd just stabbed, and squeezed, pulling Robbie forward. "Get moving. We're heading down to the water." He turned back toward me. "You lead now, pretty boy," he said to me. "Keep those fucking hands on the top of your head and no funny moves or your lover here gets the knife through his jugular. *Capiche?*"

"Y-yeah," I said, starting to walk through the parking lot toward the waterfront.

He steered us through the dark, down some steps, around a few corners. The whole time I listened to their footfalls behind me, Robbie's heavy breathing, wondering how badly he was stabbed, how much he was bleeding. But I didn't dare look back at all.

When we got to the dock, Dillon told me to stop. He stepped closer, his left hand on Robbie's shoulder, still squeezing it, the blood seeping between his fingers, Robbie wincing under the grasp. Then Dillon placed the hand with the knife in it on my shoulder so that the blade touched my neck.

"On your fucking knees, boy," he said to me.

I froze, just stared at him, feeling the tip of the blade against the side of my neck. I didn't move.

Dillon kneed me hard between the legs and I doubled over, seeing bright spots of light in my vision. He pushed

174 / *I, Death*

down on my back and I folded to my knees, still hunched over, gasping for air.

I couldn't look up, but did vaguely hear Dillon saying something in a laughing tone, and the distinct sound of his zipper coming down.

Things started to happen really slowly at that point. I remember hearing Robbie's voice, a strangled, frustrated cry saying. "No. Not again. No more. No more."

I started to look up at that point and saw Robbie grabbing Dillon by the throat with one hand and wrestling the knife hand with his other. Caught completely by surprise, Dillon was stumbling back. It was only then that I realized Robbie had succeeded in stabbing him. Dillon held a hand to the blood seeping out from a puncture wound in his stomach.

Robbie lunged at him, the knife extended, and the blade glanced off his chest as Dillon flung himself back. In a single, fluid motion, Dillon hit the dock, rolled, pulled a small handgun from a holster beneath his jacket and let off a single shot.

It was Robbie's turn to stumble backwards, holding onto his own stomach, looking down at the blood which started to pour from where he'd been shot.

I still could barely breathe as I watched this scene unfold from my knees. But even if I hadn't been kneed in the nuts, I'm not sure if I would have moved. The whole moment still had that strange, murky, dream-like quality to it as I watched. I'm not sure if I would have actually been able to pull myself out of that state and do something.

Robbie looked at Dillon who by then had the gun trained on me as he was getting to his feet. I remember noticing the gun pointed in my direction, but not actually registering what it meant. It was like I was watching some foreign language film and not completely understanding what was going on.

I: The Online Journal of Peter O'Mallick / **175**

Robbie let out a hoarse cry and rushed at Dillon, the blade extended. Dillon turned the gun back towards Robbie and it went off as Robbie tackled him. I didn't see where that second bullet went, but I did see Robbie manage to sink the blade deep into Dillon's neck before the two of them fell backwards off the dock and splashed into the water.

When I finally managed to drag myself to my feet and walk over to the edge of the dock there were barely ripples visible in the moonlight.

I'm not sure how long I stood there, looking down at the water before I realized that neither one of them was going to surface. I remember whispering for Robbie, wondering if he was okay and just hiding somewhere, under the dock, or treading water quietly, just out of my line of sight.

"Robbie," I called a bit louder. "Robbie," and I started to break down and cry, huge, hiccoughing sobs, as I realized that he was gone and I'd never see him again. I thought back to that first day in class, when he made us stand on his desk to see the class from a different viewpoint. I thought of all the new viewpoints he'd afforded me, all the hope he'd given me. Now gone. And I cried.

I finally got up and moved when I heard sirens in the distance.

I ran off down the boardwalk that led to Bell Park, and from there crossed Paris Street near the hospital, walked through that neighbourhood, then meandered through side streets mostly on my way back to the downtown area and started walking along the highway that Elm Street turned into, on my way towards Highway 144 and Levack.

Thursday June 7, 2012 — 10:32 PM

I can't believe how utterly exhausting it was to write about what happened the night that Robbie died. I never would have thought that it would take me such a long time to actually tell the story. But reliving it as I wrote was extremely difficult. I needed to take a break, let the painful and disturbing memories kick around in my head a bit so I could get everything straight.

So many times I just wanted to get it all out at once, let it flow. Maybe I could have done that if I were speaking to someone, telling them the story. But I wasn't, I was writing it down. The fact that I had to slow down made it more difficult to do in longer pieces.

In any case, sure, it almost took me an entire month to go through it, but at least I've been able to. And I'm tempted to say that I feel better, but I still feel like a walking sack of shit. But just typing the story out, getting it out of my head, that actually has helped.

So much has been going on lately that I don't even know where to begin to get caught up. For the most part, since Robbie died, I've just been going through the motions, getting up, going to school, coming home, watching TV, and going to bed. And that's been enough. It's been hard enough just doing that.

I: The Online Journal of Peter O'Mallick / **177**

At school, our guidance counselor started up sessions again with groups of students, much like he had when Chad broke through the ice. It was different this time, though, at least for some of us.

Robbie was well loved by many of the students. Sure, both Monica and I had had a special, personal relationship with him, so maybe we felt the loss differently than most. But we were in different group sessions, so I never heard how she spoke in the group, or even *if* she spoke in the group. I wonder if, like me, she just played along pretending to just be another student and not someone who shared a special link to this man.

Sarah was actually in the same group session as I was. And she did speak a lot. About feeling guilty over Robbie, but also feeling guilty about Miss Hamilton and the accident. It seemed like she had a lot to get off her chest, and I remember losing myself in Sarah's words, as if it were just her and I and it was the way it had been before, the two of us together.

I remember listening to Sarah and then picking up on something that seemed to lie between and beneath her words. Sure, she was expressing grief and feelings of guilt about the loss of two much cherished teachers. But there was more grief, more guilt beneath that surface. The guidance counselor didn't push with her, as if he knew not to go there. But I could tell. I'd heard enough psycho-babble lately to understand that Sarah was transferring the guilt and grief she felt about her father's cancer death-sentence onto the loss of these teachers. It was almost as if she was trying to pre-grieve her father's loss.

I openly cried while Sarah spoke, and I remember her noticing when she looked over at me once. I could tell she noticed because her eyes didn't just pass over me but lingered a moment longer. I looked back at her, not wiping the tears, just looking at her. I wanted to get up, walk across the circle

178 / *I, Death*

our chairs had been placed in and just hold her; tell her it would all be okay if she just let it out.

But she averted her eyes again quickly, and I knew that I was reaching beyond my grasp again.

Saturday June 9, 2012 — 10:06 PM

The group sessions ended on Friday, and they've been good. It still hurts, still fucks with my mind — and nobody has a clue, of course, of my involvement, that I'd witnessed Robbie's death.

All they know is that Robbie was found dead, his body entangled with that of a known drug dealer in Sudbury.

The police hadn't even showed up the night that I fled the scene. The car I heard must have been heading out on another call. Or I guess it could have even been an ambulance.

Robbie's body was found the next morning by a jogger; and less than an hour later, Dillon's body was discovered floating just around the other side of the bay. There was an investigation, but I was never even questioned. The evidence seemed obvious: a drug deal gone bad.

Could I have stepped forward and given the authorities details about what had happened that night? I suppose I could have. But what was the point? Robbie was dead, the bad guy was dead — there wasn't really anything to tell.

Except where it came to Monica. I mean, sure, if Dillon or whatever the drug dealer's name was — I think it was in the papers when they found his body, but they only used his real name once (I suppose the media rather enjoyed the nickname "Dillon" maybe because it sounded like an outlaw's name) — if he were still alive, then sure, I could perhaps

180 / *I, Death*

give the authorities details on what I knew about him. But he wasn't. And besides, it wasn't really my place to bring something that Monica herself wasn't comfortable bringing forth to the surface.

Yes, I cared about her, but it didn't happen to me, so how could I possibly know the right thing to do for her?

There's only one thing that comes to mind, and I think I'll do it.

Tuesday June 12, 2012 — 10:10 PM

I slipped a note into Monica's locker. I thought she had the right to know.

It simply read as follows:

Robbie loved you dearly and was regretful for what happened, that you ever got hurt because of him. He died trying to avenge his wrongs, and ensured that nobody else will ever be hurt by that evil man again. Robbie died a hero.

Don't worry, I'm not a stalker, I'm just someone who thought you would like to know.

Signed;
A Friend

I know it was a risky and silly thing to do, but it was the least I could do to let Monica know how deeply Robbie had cared for her, how truly sorry he'd been about what happened to her.

I think Robbie would have appreciated that.

Thursday June 14, 2012 — 9:28 PM

I've been watching Monica these past few days, trying to judge if she got my note by any difference in her. I haven't spotted anything yet. Maybe the note fell out of her locker onto the floor.

Oh shit: what if someone found it? What if someone found it, realizes what it's related to and knows there was a witness that night.

Holy fuck. What'll I do?

— 1 Comment —

Kim — said . . .
Maybe she did get and doesn't want to deal with it yet. She's been through a lot.

Don't panic. Not yet.

Monday June 18, 2012 — 9:56 PM

There was a note in my locker this morning. Nothing on it, other than the words:

Thank you

Not signed. No indication who it was from. And while I wouldn't recognize her handwriting I know the note was from her.

She passed me in the hall this afternoon and didn't even give me a second look. I understand that she doesn't want to talk about it, doesn't want to acknowledge what we both know.

I can appreciate that, the fact she wanted to thank me but wasn't ready to speak about the things that had happened. And I respect that

It also made me feel good to know that by writing that note to let Monica know that her secret was safe with me, and that Robbie's love for her was true, it was appreciated in the spirit I'd intended.

That and the fact that Monica did get the note and it didn't fall into anyone else's hands.

— 1 Comment —

Kim — said . . .
Whew!

Thursday June 21, 2012 — 9:03 PM

I was sitting in the cafeteria today with Harley, Neil and Jagdish. Man, I missed those guys.

I've been sitting on my own, or just wandering around like a space cadet for so long, I never got caught up with my friends. Sure, I hung around with them for the occasional event, chatted with them in the hallways and sometimes sat with them during lunch or spares.

But today was different.

It was like old times, back before things between Sarah and I fell apart.

I hadn't felt normal, like one of my old pals since before Christmas. But they welcomed me right back into the fold.

We were talking about old man Cottman and his fuckin' end of year pop quizzes. We ended up getting all razzed about that morning's pop quiz surprise and the fact that none of us passed this one. We started worrying about the upcoming History exam that Cottman would present us with, when Harley made an announcement.

"We should fucking party tonight!" he said.

"What?" Jagdish looked at him, stunned. "It's a school night."

"Fu... Screw that," Harley said, quickly changing the first word of his sentence because a teacher was walking by. "We all flunked this pop quiz, we're likely going to flunk Cottman's

I: The Online Journal of Peter O'Mallick / **185**

exam. Why don't we take a moment to just say 'to Hell with this' and party it up?"

"Not a bad idea with all of the bizarre shit that's been going on around here lately," Neil said. "Both a teacher and a student died just this semester; never mind the accident that nearly took out Miss Hamilton and Sarah." Neil paused very briefly to look at me when he said this, sensitive to my reaction to her name. "We could use the release. Besides, this is our last year in high school. Next year — who knows? We should make the most of our time together."

I started laughing. "Hey, Neil, that's awfully sentimental of you."

Jagdish leaned toward him. "C'mon, Neil. Give us a hug."

"Yeah, you fairy." Harley said. "Let's have a group hug and a cry. What are you, like Oprah?"

"Lay off, Harley," Neil said. "I was agreeing with you, okay?"

The group was quiet for a minute when Jagdish spoke up. "Where?" he asked.

We all looked at him.

"So, we know we're going to do this. So *where*? The pit?"

"Fuckin' A, Jag." Harley said.

The rest of us immediately agreed as well. The pit was an abandoned dump that was just off the highway. There was easy access to it, but the deep pit allowed us to have a bonfire and make a lot of noise without anyone being able to see or hear any of it from the road.

Plans were made as to when we were going to meet, who was going to bring what, and it was all settled by the time the bell rang announcing our lunch period was over.

Man, was that ever a good thing. It's been way too long since I've felt that good. I'm so looking forward to getting drunk with my buddies later tonight. Going to pretend to go to bed early then sneak out. Can't wait.

Friday June 22, 2012 — 5:54 PM

Oh fuck.
It's happened again.
Jagdish is dead.
It's my fault.

Oh shit — Uncle Bob's knocking at my bedroom door — probably wants "to talk" to me again about everything. Dammit.

— 7 Comments —

Anonymous — said . . .
Please tell us what happened Peter. We are listening.

Rainy — said . . .
I just discovered this blog. What is it? Is this a story? Is this real? And why hasn't there been a post in several weeks?

Kim — said . . .
It's real, Rainy.
Peter is real.
And I'm worried about him.

Mantaray Ocean — said . . .
I'm worried, too.

I: The Online Journal of Peter O'Mallick / **187**

Peter? Are you okay? We're still here. It's okay, talk to us. Let us know you're okay.

Kim — said . . .
C'mon, Peter. It has been over a month now and we haven't heard a single word from you.

There are people who care about you.

Please let us know you're okay.

Frank — said . . .
Peter. You were doing so well writing about everything. It was helping to sort things out, helping put things into perspective. You can do that again. You can find help and support through writing about it. Remember the words of advice from your guidance counselor. He was right: writing helps.

Kim — said . . .
Writing does help, Peter. My own journal helped me through some really rough times.

Tuesday July 24, 2012 — 11:37 AM

Stil grounnded not sur if thiss cell phne txt mesage will get thru to my blg feeel so out of toouch fukck

Tuesday August 14, 2012 — 12:17 AM

Christ. That was a long three weeks. Uncle Bob and Aunt Shelly took away all of my privileges, including television and internet access.

Fuck.

How the hell is a guy supposed to do his "self-searching" therapy? I haven't even worked out the whole situation that caused the death of my buddy Jagdish yet, never mind try to deal with the rest of the bullshit that's happened between then and now.

Got way too fucking much to say and I don't know where to begin.

I'm tired. Just want to get back to sleep now. I'll be back.

— 1 Comment —

Anonymous — said . . .

I'm listening

Here's a blog you might find interesting and helpful somehow.

http://PostSecret.blogspot.com/

Tuesday August 14, 2012 — 11:20 PM

I noticed that some anonymous person posted a comment with a link to a site that they thought might help me.

I checked it out. It didn't help me, but I can see why someone suggested it. It's some sort of site where people mail-in secrets and confessions. Some of it was a little disturbing to read, but it didn't make me feel any better. These entries of mine aren't confessions; they're just me trying to deal with all the people around me who are dying.

I didn't do anything wrong. It's not my fault.

Is it?

— 4 Comments —

Kim — said . . .

It's not your fault
> You tend to always blame yourself
> But you can't do that, Peter
> You can't.
> It's good to have you back, BTW. Great to finally
hear from you again

MaliceAD — said . . .

Nice to have you back, Peter.

Frank — said . . .

Was worried about you, Peter. Good to see you're back. Keep writing. You're good at it.

I: The Online Journal of Peter O'Mallick / **191**

Mantaray Ocean — said . . .
So relieved you're okay, Peter. We missed you.

Thursday August 16, 2012 — 10:32 PM

I've been thinking a lot lately about what my guidance counselor said about writing it all down, and about that confessional site that the anonymous person posted. And thinking about Jagdish's death two months ago.

And it made me realize something. I've never spoken at all to a single person about what happened to my best friend Donnie when I was twelve. Yeah, I think I might have mentioned when I first started this blog about the fact that I lost my best friend.

But I don't think I talked about how it happened. And I know for sure that I've never let anyone know the exact details of what happened, or, more embarrassingly, how I'd reacted to it. And I don't think I can move on to deal with Jagdish's loss without going back and examining Donnie's tragic death and my involvement in it.

We were twelve and out hunting partridge with our .22s. Levack is pretty much surrounded by wilderness and so getting to the woods was easy, almost any direction that you walk. We headed into the woods down High Street, behind the school — behind what, at the time, used to be Levack District High School but is now Levack Public School.

Donnie and I were walking along with our rifles at our sides and pointed to the ground — sure, we followed at least one of the hunting safety guidelines, but we kept them loaded

I: The Online Journal of Peter O'Mallick / **193**

while we walked, eager not to miss the chance to shoot any partridge we stumbled across. We were walking down a trail when Donnie spotted a rabbit. It was a cute little white rabbit and it darted out on the trail in front of us. Donnie let out a startled laugh and raised his rifle towards it.

"No, Donnie," I suddenly blurted. For some reason it disturbed me that he was going to shoot the rabbit. I don't know why. Maybe it's because we were out looking for partridge, not rabbits. We weren't there to kill other animals. Something in my mind refused the idea. I wanted Donnie to stop.

Donnie glared at me, jumped off the trail and started running through the woods after the rabbit. He was laughing as he ran, and the entire time, I was hoping that he'd fall, stumble, and that the rabbit would get away. I watched as he ran, his head disappearing beneath the high growing ferns as he tried to duck and spot where the rabbit was heading.

I cringed when his head went down a final time and the rifle went off.

His head didn't pop up again. Instead, I heard a horrid, nasty wailing series of screams.

I dropped my own rifle and ran towards Donnie's screams. I found him laying on his back, looking up at me with one eye, his left. The other socket was a pool of flesh and blood and gunk, and a small trail of blood and fluid was leaking down his cheek. When he saw me, he stopped his screaming and reached toward me. "Peter," he said. "Help. My eye, my eye."

I just stared at him, my stomach pitching and rolling. I was afraid to touch him, even just his hand. Afraid that his blood, his gore, his death would get on me. I just stared at him, and then started to back away.

"Peter?" he said, sitting up, his one hand still reaching for me, his other hand starting to pawing madly at the side of his

194 / *I, Death*

face, as if it were merely a bug sitting there that he wanted desperately to be rid of, not some sort of permanent damage.

I turned and ran from him.

And I kept running, screaming, trying to banish the image of my best friend sitting there, helplessly reaching toward me, the messy gore running down the side of his face. Trying to block the sound of his continued cries for help.

I kept running away, away from him, away from the scene of the accident. I'm not sure how long I ran, but I ended up collapsing at some point where I could no longer hear him calling for help. I sat there in the woods, listening to see if I could still hear him (I couldn't) and crying.

I'm not sure how long I sat there, but when I finally got up and started walking back in his direction, I was cold and very numb. As I got closer to where the accident had happened, I had this strange feeling of calm. The forest was quiet, silent. Donnie was no longer calling for help, or crying or screaming in pain. I wondered for a moment if I'd come in the wrong direction. But no, I was in the right place. There was my gun on the path where I'd dropped it after I first heard his scream of pain.

The forest was completely silent. The ferns just above where Donnie had fallen were blowing gently in the breeze. I picked up my rifle and started heading back out of the forest, back home.

I'm told that some adults found me walking down a street with my rifle, heading in the direction of home, my head downcast and my face white as a ghost. They'd known that Donnie and I were out hunting, and when they asked where Donnie was, I'd just pointed back towards the woods, my jaw hanging open, my eyes wide, my tongue like a thick wool blanket in my mouth.

When I eventually spoke, I told people about the accident, but not about how I'd run away from Donnie. Everyone

I: The Online Journal of Peter O'Mallick / **195**

assumed that I was in shock from the accident — but I was in shock because of my reaction to my friend crying out for help — and the fact that if I'd actually helped him, not left him lying there, then perhaps things would have been different.

Donnie didn't die right away. But when they found him, he'd already dropped into a coma. The bullet had done some damage to his brain, an infection had already started to spread. There was nothing anyone could do. He never came out of his coma, I never ended-up going to see him, and by the end of the week he had died.

No, the last image I'd had of Donnie, the one that stays with me today, is the image of him sitting on the forest floor, reaching towards me, asking for help.

— 1 Comment —

Kim — said . . .
Shock and fear can have a strange effect on people.

When I was younger, I was playing with a friend's younger sister in her backyard on the Tarzan swing. I don't know how she got into the position, but somehow, she had managed to string herself up and hang by her feet. She was so frightened and was screaming that she was going to fall. I stood there and did nothing. Frozen in place.

Her father heard her screams, came running and got her down before she got hurt.

Then he yelled at me for not helping her and standing there like an idiot.

I've never forgotten that day. Or how angry that man was at me.

Shock affects us all in mysterious ways. Your reaction was normal.

Saturday August 18, 2012 — 7:28 PM

Couldn't sleep last night, or the night before that — the morbid memory was stuck in my head all night and I still can't get the image of Donnie out of my head. Every time I close my eyes he's sitting in the dirt, his face leaking eye pus and gore, looking up at me, pleading. Just wanting me to help.

In my dreams I keep seeing Donnie sitting there. Only instead of just some gore and pus running down his cheek from his eye, both of his eyes are hanging out on these long, crazy, fleshy strings, swaying back and forth, but still looking at me.

Jesus.

I spent a good part of the past month digging through Shakespeare, trying to read more of his stuff, you know, to see if there was something else like *Hamlet* that I could identify with. My aunt has this old, beat-up *Complete Works of Shakespeare* sitting on a book shelf in the den. I buried myself in it for days on end, reading from the time I got up until the time I went to bed, stopping only to eat when my aunt or uncle called me. I mean, I was fucking grounded, so there wasn't much else to do anyway. Focusing on imagined worlds was a far better option than thinking about what had just happened to Jagdish.

I: The Online Journal of Peter O'Mallick / **197**

Okay, fuck, I'm not ready to talk about that. Have to ease into that once I feel ready.

So last night when I couldn't sleep, since I'd finished reading Shakespeare, I started reading Sophocles: *Oedipus Rex*. I remember Miss Hamilton talking about how *Hamlet* included streams of plot from *Oedipus*, or something like that. I can kind of see a bit of that now that I've read it. But it's fucking freaky stuff. A guy who is left to die as a baby, ends up killing his father a couple of decades later without realizing it, then ends up marrying his mother. Geez.

Makes me wonder if maybe my Mom isn't dead after all — and, what if I end up getting it on with this older woman, and later find out that I'm sleeping with my Mom?

Fuck, what was it with these ancient writers? They came up with some wicked stuff.

I stopped reading when I got to the scene where, in his grief and rage, Oedipus plucks out his eyes. I couldn't get past it — that's when the images of Donnie started haunting me again.

Fucking Shakespeare.
Fucking Sophocles.

— *1 Comment* —

Kim — said . . .
They were masters of their times.

And their stories remain and sometimes haunt us to this day.

If *Oedipus* was bad — don't read *Antigone*.

Sunday August 19, 2012 — 7:44 PM

I think I'm starting to understand just what the hell is wrong with me.

Not in the grander sense. It'll likely take me my entire life to figure out why I'm surrounded by so much death, so much tragedy. Fuck, it feels like I'm at the centre of some sort of Shakespearean play.

What I mean is why I can't get my head out of this funk that I'm in.

It comes back to that damned guidance counselor.

Who would have thought that the overweight bastard with the coke bottle glasses and the obviously fake head of hair, sitting there at his desk and looking at me, his hands folded across the outcrop of his stomach, a smug look on his face, would have been so bang-on.

In order to clear my head of the endless images, the thoughts that are plaguing me, I need to either talk to someone or write it all down.

Well, since I don't have anyone to talk to — it's not like I can talk to Aunt Shelley or Uncle Bob any more — I need to write about it.

No, in fact, I'm blaming this funk I've been in these past two months on them.

I: The Online Journal of Peter O'Mallick / **199**

If I hadn't have been grounded, and cut off from this therapeutic activity that had been working well for me, I might not feel this way.

So I've got to try hard to focus, to go through the details of what happened that night to Jagdesh. Then maybe, just maybe, I can start to move on.

— 1 Comment —

Kim — said . . .
Don't blame them... they were only doing what they thought was best. Parents and guardians are like that. It sucks, but that's part of being a kid.

At least it's over and you can work through some stuff now.

Question is, if you were grounded from the computer and such, why didn't you write it out long hand — at least until you got your privileges back?

Tuesday August 21, 2012 — 10:47 PM

Damn, I've been sitting here for about half an hour, just staring at the damned keyboard and not able to get it out. It's not that there's nothing swirling around in my fucking head. I just can't seem to get it out. Being away from this journal for so many weeks seems to have put a stop to the rhythm I had fallen into.

It's funny. That Kim person left a comment on my last post asking why I didn't write it out long-hand, like I'd done before. But I guess I was so distraught when Jag died, especially following so closely after Robbie's demise, that I sank into a funk where I wasn't able to write. I just read, watched movies, and stared out the window. It's all I seemed capable of doing for so long. And it's taking me a while to get back into the habit I'd previously been in where I could just write out the things I'd been going through.

I have found one thing, though, a side-effect of all of this that is okay with me.

Sarah. I haven't thought about her in several weeks.

And when I think about her now, sure, it's with a pang, an emptiness, a sense of loss, but it's not the same obsessive compulsion that it used to be.

So thoughts of Sarah are still there, and it hurts to have lost her, still hurts to think about her, but it's not as bad as it was a few months ago.

I: The Online Journal of Peter O'Mallick

I think I'm getting over her.

Finally.

And it only took how many deaths to get to this point?

Wednesday August 22, 2012 — 7:47 PM

That night at the pit is starting to come back to me. No, it's not that it was never there; I mean, I never lost the memories of that night, well, most of them anyway. I did spend a long time trying not to think about it, trying to do anything *but* think about it. But now that I'm writing in my journal regularly, it's becoming easier to bring it all back.

I recall it being a pretty low-key party, just the four of us. But it was a relief, and it might have ranked up there as one of those "good times" memories that people say they look back on with fondness when they get older.

Just four friends, drunk, stoned, rocking along, goofing around, just letting ourselves relax and enjoy the moment.

I know, I must sound like one of those "Carpe Diem" poets that Robin Williams talks about in that movie where he plays a teacher at this private school, the one Robbie mimicked when he first arrived at our school. But, until the tragedy struck, it *was* a night like that. None of us had a clue what was going to happen.

No, that's not true.

Neil must have.

Yeah, now that I think about it, it's strange that Neil didn't smoke anything. He even seemed not to be drinking as much as the rest of us had been. It was almost as if he could sense that something bad was going to go down.

I: The Online Journal of Peter O'Mallick

At the time, though, I wasn't concerned with whether or not Neil was catching a good buzz. Jagdish and I were sharing a joint and a beer, doing air guitar and singing a song by a local bar band that Neil's older brother was a member of.

They were pretty cool. Called themselves the "Vicious Pigs" — we'd been to a lot of their shows, had all three of their CDs and one of our favorite songs was "Rock Me to Hell" — that's the one Jag and I were rocking down to.

"Hit it to me, baby!" I screamed, in an attempt to reach the high notes of the band's lead singer.

Jagdish finished off the can of beer, crushed it in his fist, tossed it in the fire, then started strumming the fingers of his right hand down near his hip and wiggling his left fingers in a half-closed fist at about mid-chest. He was mimicking the actions of Neil's brother, the lead guitarist for the band. With a higher-pitched voice than mine, he belted out the next lyrics. "Down on your knees."

We stepped closer to each other, leaning against each other's backs at a pretty steep angle the way we'd seen the lead guitarist and lead singer do on stage while performing this song.

"Rock me to Hell, baby!" we bellowed together, in much deeper voices.

Jag then moved away so fast that I fell onto the ground because I was still leaning on him. I landed hard and watched as he leapt onto a boulder beside the fire and started gyrating his hips to the unheard drumbeat of the song while his fingers moved along the invisible guitar in an effort that spoke to me like the awesome guitar riffs that always played during this part of the chorus of the song, and finished the song with: "Oh blow me a breeze."

Neil and Harley were sitting on a fallen tree, laughing their asses off. "Great show, you dumb fucks," Harley said.

"Yeah, nice fall, Peter!" Neil said.

204 / *I, Death*

I remember getting up to my feet, the sound of their laughter echoing in my head, and suddenly I was filled with a red-hot anger. I don't know why. It was an accident that I'd fallen when he leapt up onto the rock. But the fall, combined with him thrusting his crotch in my direction, and the laughter of our friends, just rolled into a burning anger that seemed to bubble up out of nowhere.

I glared at Jagdish and he started to shrug as if to say 'Hey man, sorry, but what can I do?' I was about to say something like: 'You dumb prick, you could have warned me you were going to move.' But I never got a chance to say a single word.

His eyes suddenly widened and he released a hot burst of puke, some of it hitting the side of my face, and he fell right off the rock, his arm and hand falling into the fire.

"Aw Christ," Harley said. "This just gets better and better. If you guys don't quit it, I'm going to fucking piss myself laughing."

I was wiping the puke off my face looking at how it seemed red in my hands in the strange firelight, when Neil let out a strange panicked yell.

I didn't hear what exactly he said because it was then I'd noticed that Jagdish was just laying there, his arm directly in the fire. He hadn't pulled it out at all. He was right out of it.

I grabbed at his other arm, dragged him out of the fire, the stench of burnt flesh and fabric suddenly filling the air.

Out of nowhere, Neil was down on the ground, his fingers pressed against the side of Jag's neck. Then his hand shot back, like he'd been stung, and he jumped up to stand beside me.

"Son of a bitch," Neil whispered and then, in a voice that kept getting louder and louder kept saying this over and over and over.

Sonofabitchsonofabitchsonofabitchsonofabitchsonofa…

Then, to the bizarre tune of Neil's endless stream of panic, I felt something welling up in my throat. Given the

I: The Online Journal of Peter O'Mallick / **205**

situation, how much I'd drank, the disgusting smell of Jag's burnt flesh, I bent over, ready to release the entire contents of my stomach.

But I didn't throw up, even though the feeling was exactly the same.

Instead, I released a deep and eerie laugh, which seemed to reverberate from the depths of my stomach and burned at my throat as it burst out of my mouth.

— 1 Comment —

Jane — said . . .

I came upon your blog only a few days ago. You made me cry! I have finished reading it. How come you are not posting anymore? Are you alright? Hang in there, Peter.

Friday August 24, 2012 — 10:52 PM

I see that someone named Jane has posted a comment asking me why I stopped. I've held the details of what happened the night that Jagdish died so deep down inside, that it's difficult for me to get it all out. I needed to take a break after writing in such detail about it the other night. But it's not only that. It's that I pretty much went blank immediately after what I'd described.

Laughing, my entire body shaking as the laughter forced its way past my lips, was the last thing I remember about that night.

The rest is just darkness.

Pitch black darkness.

Immediately after releasing the laughter from the depths of my bowels, I passed out and fell onto the ground immediately beside Jagdish.

Neil told me this. And this was just last week, because other than school and Jagdish's funeral, I hadn't seen either Neil or Harley because I'd been grounded. Anyways, Neil told me that as I fell down on the ground beside Jag, that they thought I was dead too.

Neil admitted that he thought maybe Harley had poisoned us in some sort of bizarre "end of school, end of friendship" death pact. I know it's something he would never tell Harley,

I: The Online Journal of Peter O'Mallick / **207**

likely because it's the crazy fucking kind of thing that Harley would come up with, and we both knew it.

Anyway, talking about all the mind-fuck kind of things that Harley is capable of is not the reason I'm keeping this journal.

No, I want to get on with remembering the sequence of events from that night.

Neil said that I'd fallen down right beside Jag.

When he checked for my pulse he could feel it. Said he'd only ever felt a pulse stronger once, actually. It was the pulse he'd felt on a wounded moose just moments before it bled to death. He said my pulse was something like that.

In any case, he knew that I was still alive.

He told me he hesitated again a moment before leaving for help, uncertain as to whether or not Harley could be trusted with our bodies — Jag's dead body and my unconscious one — with thoughts that perhaps he might come back to find Harley had rolled us both into the fire to see who might burn up first, or maybe dragged us over to the river to see if our bodies would float away or just sink into the murky depths. Yeah, Harley is that kind of strange fucker. I'll never forget the time that I came upon him when he had two poor frogs pinned down by the arms and was slowly pulling a single leg off of each of them. He'd been planning on seeing if there was any difference in the way that each frog hopped afterwards, claiming it was a scientific experiment.

No, Harley didn't do anything with our prone bodies. Neil ran to get help. When Neil returned with his older brother and father (and a quick 911 call put in) he said he found Harley sitting cross-legged in front of the fire and singing "Koom-Buy-Ya" or however the hell you spell it.

So help returned — I was rushed to emergency and treated for alcohol poisoning. It was later determined that that was what killed Jagdish.

208 / *I, Death*

But, dear reader, we both know by now that no matter what the medical report says Jag wasn't killed because he had too much to drink that night.

No.

Jag was killed because of me.

I did it. It's this fucking curse surrounding me.

Everyone who gets close to me dies.

And now Jagdish is dead.

And it's my fucking fault.

— 1 Comment —

Kim — said . . .

Curses are only true if you believe in them, Peter. It's possible that with all the unfortunate things that have been happening, you've begun to believe that you're the cause of all of this.

Stop believing in a curse. You're much too remorseful to be a killer.

You're just unlucky right now.

Tuesday August 28, 2012 — 3:18 AM

I had to stop writing the last time because it was becoming a little overwhelming for me. But I couldn't sleep for the longest time either. That night I just lay in bed, the events that followed going through my head.

But it was all going through my head too much to write them down.

And the same thing kept happening to me again every night.

Tonight, or this morning rather, I'd had enough. I finally just got out of bed and thought I'd try to slow those thoughts down, try to write it all down.

The weeks following Jagdish's death, the time at school, everything, is just a huge blur. Or at least, the images and memories of those weeks are mostly swirling around in my head so fast that I can't catch them, hold them down long enough to write about.

But I have been able to pick a few of them out of the air.

Yeah, I remember moments at the funeral, sitting there in the pew, looking up at the casket, then across the aisle at Neil. (He'd been sitting with his folks, me with Uncle Bob and Aunt Shelley) Like me, he'd been grounded as well, and, like me, it had been suggested to him that it would be best if he and Harley and I kept our distance from each other until the school year finished. So, perhaps under the fear that

210 / *I, Death*

others were watching us and would report our behaviour, we stayed away from each other during lunch or spare periods.

It was like being back in that exile I'd been under when I first broke up with Sarah. Only, this time, it wasn't self-imposed.

Damm it to Hell, though — and this is something that you'd think at least the guidance counselor would inject on our behalf — we needed to talk to each other, we needed to deal with our feelings of what happened when a friend of ours died. We needed that.

But we didn't get it.

Now, though I'm no longer grounded, I still haven't spoken much with Neil or with Harley — to be honest, I never did much with Harley one-on-one — we only hung around together as part of the larger group, actually. Neil or Jag were the only ones I'd ever had any deep or meaningful conversation with.

I'd always kind of shunned Harley, to be honest.

Perhaps in the way I'm convinced that Neil is now shunning me.

You see, Neil's a smart cookie — he doesn't know about my good friend Donnie, because his family didn't live in town when that happened. And I've never talked about it to anyone. But he knows about my parents, he knows about Sarah's dad and he witnessed the thing with Jagdish firsthand.

So he must have figured out the bizarre combination: that getting mixed up with me was an invitation to bring Death into someone's life.

He must have figured that out.

It's why he didn't call.

I get the feeling that he's shunning me, the way that we all used to shun Harley.

It has to be.

I: The Online Journal of Peter O'Mallick / **211**

Okay, I think I got most of whatever I could snag out of the air down. I actually feel better. I think I'm going to be able to sleep now.

Wednesday August 29, 2012 — 7:49 AM

I had some strange dreams last night.

I was walking through this field, wearing some sort of heavy fabric, but I couldn't see what it was. It was foggy, but just up ahead of me was someone that I was trying to catch up to. But I couldn't walk fast, because the heavy fabric on me was weighing me down, and I was also carrying something — something heavy that required both hands just to hold it.

The person ahead disappeared down a hill as I tried to pick up speed. Then, they appeared, even farther away atop of the next knoll.

Frustrated, I tried tossing the fabric off of me, but it wouldn't move, and I kept moving slower, but the stranger I was trying to reach kept moving farther and farther away.

Finally, as my walking slowed down, almost as if my feet were stuck in some sort of thick muck or quick-sand, the stranger crested the next hill and disappeared. So I gave up and just stood there.

I looked down in my hand. I was carrying a scythe.

I screamed, dropping the scythe, and tore at the fabric, doing whatever I could to get what I now knew was a shroud off of me. That's when I felt something hard pinching my leg. When I looked to see what it was, I could see these skeletal hands reaching up through the dirt and mud, grabbing at my

I: The Online Journal of Peter O'Mallick / **213**

legs, holding me in place. First there was one set of hands, then two, three, four. Then more. I lost count. The hands and skeletal arms were grabbing my feet, legs, my waist, pulling me down. I struggled to break free but I couldn't.

I struggled to yell out for help — maybe the stranger in the distance, the one who'd just disappeared out of view, would be able to hear me. But my mouth wouldn't work.

I struggled, helplessly, and then became aware that there was someone — no, not someone, there was a *group* of people coming up behind me.

"Peeeeeeter," their voices whispered in unison, the sound not unlike the quiet creaking of an old coffin lid being raised. "Peeeeeeeter."

I woke up as a hand came down on my shoulder.

Now what the fuck was that all about? Who was the stranger? Who was sneaking up behind me? The only thing I could tell for sure was that the hands coming out of the group were likely the people whose deaths I'd been responsible for over the years.

The freaky thing is that once I woke, I went for a quick piss, then got back into bed and slept like a baby. Not too sure about that. The fact that I could sleep after such a bizarre nightmare, well, that scares me more than the dream.

— 2 Comments —

Kim — said . . .
You've been through a lot, emotionally speaking. The body's first reaction to such things is sleep. It's the natural human healing process.

Rainy — said . . .
I think sleeping isn't freaky at all. Something like that can be pretty draining. It's just a dream after all.

Monday September 3, 2012 — 10:39 PM

School starts tomorrow. Not that that means anything for me. I won't be attending anywhere.

Aunt Shelly and Uncle Bob are pretty pissed off at me about it. But I honestly can't get my head into the thought of actually going to College or University. It's been way too difficult a summer, trying to get over the way that Jagdish died. Fuck. I still remember back to the long talks we had and all the worrying that I'd done when Sarah and I were together and she wanted to go to Carleton in Ottawa and I just wanted to stay here. Worrying because I didn't want to be apart from her.

It's pointless worrying, though. I have been kind of listening in on friends talking about Sarah and what she's been up to. I just can't help myself. And apparently, though Sarah was accepted into the journalism program at Carleton, she didn't end up going. She didn't end up going anywhere, in fact.

Just like me.

Funny that we should both be in the same boat and not be together.

— 1 Comment —

Rainy — said . . .

I: The Online Journal of Peter O'Mallick / **215**

I'm not too sure on the school thing. You probably could have used the diversion to take your mind off of the mess of the last year of school and this summer. I know sitting around and chewing it over and over could get to you after a while. You need to snag a job or a hobby to clear your head up a little. Plus the income might keep your aunt and uncle off your back.

Sunday September 9, 2012 — 12:09 AM

I had another one of those bizarre dreams last night.

Again, it was a foggy night and I was in this field, carrying a scythe and trying to catch up with this stranger who was walking quickly, moving faster than I was, and disappearing off in the distance.

Like before, there was this feeling that there was someone behind me. I could hear this noise, soft at first, then louder, perhaps as the wind shifted, or it got closer to me.

It was the unmistakable chaotic shouts of an angry mob.

When I turned to look, I could see them, about a hundred or so metres back, some of them carrying torches and too numerous to count. In the same way that I could tell the stranger ahead of me was getting away, I knew that they were gaining on me, and would be caught up to me in a matter of minutes.

I turned to look ahead for the stranger, but she was gone again. Yes, suddenly the stranger was a woman.

When I turned to look for the mob, they were suddenly gone too, but standing a few metres behind me were two of my friends.

One of them was holding a rifle and both of his eyes were hanging down on his cheeks by the thinnest of sinews, swaying as he walked as if they were trying to look at me. It was Donnie. That much I could tell. The other one's eyes

I: The Online Journal of Peter O'Mallick / **217**

were also popped out and his mouth was open, slowly leaking a steady flow of a thin red fluid. His hands were moving in a strange little dance, fingers wiggling. That, of course, was Jag, and I realized that he was doing air guitar and his mouth was moving to the lyrics of the Viscous Pigs song.

I froze in place, staring at them.

Then, as they stalked closer, I started crying for their forgiveness.

When I woke up this morning, I kept thinking about the mob moving towards me in the distance.

It reminded me of this scene from the old *Frankenstein* movie. No, not one of the versions that was true to the book, like the one where Robert De Niro played the monster, but the really old one with Boris Karlov.

Uncle Bob's being a movie buff can be a cool thing. He's shared many of his critiques about movies with me over the years — although I have to admit it's been a couple of years since we both sat down and watched one of his classic movies together.

I wonder if we might be able to do that soon.

I think that rather than try to sleep tonight I'll dig into his DVD collection and try to watch a movie. I'm kind of afraid to dream like that again.

Thursday September 13, 2012 — 11:19 AM

I just did something these past few days that I haven't done in ages.

I spent some time with Uncle Bob.

And it was great.

We watched movies. But we didn't just watch them, it was more than that. We were able to bring back a fun experience we'd had a few years ago, back when Uncle Bob had read in a movie magazine that a reboot of *Rise of the Planet of the Apes* was being worked on. When he'd read about it, we started chatting and he told me about the reboot of the original *Planet of the Apes* which had come out in 2001, and we watched it, and I loved it. But the next day my uncle showed me a DVD from his library — it was the original movie from something like 40 years ago. We watched the original then talked about it. It was really cool, the way they did the first movie. The special effects were pretty bland, but the apes looked pretty realistic and the ending was fuckin-A. At the end the main character, played by Charlton Heston, is on this beach and sees the arm from the Statue of Liberty sticking up out of the sand and realizes that they hadn't been on some alien planet at all, but had landed on Earth which had been taken over by apes. Gotta love those types of endings.

My uncle's a pretty cool guy when it comes to movies — I remember we'd talked about the fact that the newer version

I: The Online Journal of Peter O'Mallick / **219**

wasn't so much of a remake as it was taking a basic concept and doing a whole new thing with it. There are pros and cons for each, I think. But I love listening to my uncle go on about it. He really knows his stuff.

This past week we watched a few movies and their remakes. We saw the original *Flight of the Phoenix* as well as the one that came out half a dozen years ago. Kind of neat. We watched *Assault of Precinct 13* — the re-release and the one from the '70s. My uncle liked both of them as well, but for different reasons. We watched the *Star Trek* reboot, then went back and watched the first *Star Trek* movie and some of Uncle Bob's favourite episodes from the original TV series. Then we watched three different versions of *King Kong* which was really cool to do. We did those ones backwards, starting from the most recent to the original black-and-white.

We did the same thing with *The Karate Kid* movies. There was the original from the early 1980's with Ralph Macchio and Pat Morita and then the 2010 remake with Jaden Smith and Jackie Chan. We went back to watch Part II and III of the original *Karate Kid* series of movies, and even the one called *The Next Karate Kid*, the one in which Hilary Swank appeared as Miyagi's new student.

One of my favourite lines from the original series was a quote from one of the ruthless, evil *sensei* characters; a guy named Kreese. Sure, he's a douche, but I love how he put it. He said: "Mercy is for the weak. Here. On the street. In competition. A man confronts you, he is the enemy. An enemy deserves no mercy."

It's so simple, so pure. "Mercy is for the weak."

Last night we watched the original Alfred Hitchcock *Psycho* and the one they re-did a few years ago. It was neat to see the original, because I'd only seen the remake and thought it was pretty good. (Okay, I did see a clip from the black and white shower scene — I mean, who *hasn't* seen that part?). But in that case, the original was just more creepy, had a deeper type of atmosphere. My uncle was able to explain how Hitchcock was able to do that consistently in his movies, but I've forgotten most of the details he explained.

It was enough just to listen to him go on, so excitedly, about the movies.

I love when my uncle and I can spend time like that together.

It makes me wonder, though, why he didn't pursue a career in film-making. I haven't asked him that, yet, though.

— 2 Comments —

Rainy — said . . .
It's nice to reconnect with our family sometimes. I'm glad you guys could have that time together. I'm also glad he's trying to keep your interest in the older movies intact too. Most of what's out there today is remakes so it can be good to know where they came from.

MaliceAD — said . . .
If you really liked Hitchcock, you should check out *Rope* which is my favorite. It was actually shot in a series of continuous takes!

Saturday September 15, 2012 — 3:15 PM

I finally broke down today; maybe it has something to do with being back and writing in this journal regularly. Maybe it has something to do with the connection that I've rediscovered with Uncle Bob.

But I feel like I've been able to open up again, to life, to the experiences, to the idea of communication.

Yeah, sounds like flowery girly crap to me, too. But it's a powerful feeling. I haven't felt that way since Sarah and I last got together.

And I know that if anybody out there could possibly understand what I'm going through, what I'm dealing with, it'd be Sarah.

I'm pretty sure that enough time has passed now. I'm sure she's been able to finally come to terms with her father's terminal cancer. Maybe she'll come around if I just try again to speak with her — maybe she'd be able to see how much I need to have her back in my life, to help sort through this shit that I'm dealing with.

So I broke down today and left a message on Sarah's voice mail.

— 2 Comments —

Rainy — said . . .

That's taking a huge chance. I hope it all works out for you. I can tell you first-hand not to underestimate grief though. It has a strange tendency to carry on for much longer than you'd think.

Kim — said . . .
Agreed.
>Some things take awhile to come to terms with.
>Be patient, Peter.

Sunday September 16, 2012 — 10:14 PM

Okay, it's late enough that Sarah should have been home from wherever she was out doing. I mean how much is there to do on a Sunday night in Levack, or even in Sudbury? I didn't call her cell phone because that would be too intrusive. But I know she has her own private line and voice mail — so it's not like the message would have to be relayed to her — she could retrieve the message from her machine directly.

So she should have gotten the message I left today by now. When I called her place yesterday all I did was leave a message telling her that I was thinking about her. Pretty stupid, I know. But today, I left another message asking her to call me when she got home.

Of course, I'm a fool to think that she would actually phone me back.

Foolish, stupid, idiotic.

But I can't help myself.

I think I'll go try calling her again.

— 2 Comments —

Rainy — said . . .
You don't know what she's doing yet. Don't freak out until you know more. She could have gone away for

224 / *I, Death*

a few days. After all, you said she's not in school any more right?

Kim — said . . .
Don't panic. The more you call, even though you have the most innocent of intentions, the more freaked out she may get.

Trust me, I know from experience.

Sunday September 16, 2012 — 11:57 PM

No answer at Sarah's. Still.
I called about ten times, too.
Fuck.

— 1 Comment —

Kim — said . . .
Peter, calm down.

I once had a guy call me 41 times in 3 days.

I eventually unplugged my phone because it scared me. It made me NOT want to talk to him.

Patience is key. Sarah will call you when she feels she's ready to. You don't know what's going on in her life right now.

Just relax and breathe.

Monday September 17, 2012 — 5:52 AM

I just got back from Sarah's place. I snuck into the back yard, crept down by her window, just to, you know, peek in. There were plenty of times when we were dating that I would show up at the window and she'd stand on a chair, open up the window and the screen. We'd talk like that, her standing on the chair and me lying in the grass, sometimes holding hands through the window, through half of the night.

It kind of felt like *Romeo & Juliet*, doing that, although we'd never had the same issues with her parents hating Uncle Bob and Aunt Shelley. Fuck, what is it with this Shakespeare guy and the things in my life? Was he that fucking good at writing, or was he some kind of psychic?

We'd tried kissing like that once, but, even when she was standing on tiptoe, she couldn't quite reach.

So anyway, I snuck around the back of the house, to her basement window.

There was no light on that I could see immediately.

But there was a soft light coming in from the basement hallway, light coming from the bathroom — it didn't mean that someone was there, because I remember that they always left a light on in their bathrooms; both the one in the basement as well as the one upstairs. But I couldn't be sure. Sarah could have been in there, getting ready for bed.

So I laid there and waited.

I: The Online Journal of Peter O'Mallick / **227**

And fell asleep.

Not sure how long I slept — must have been at least an hour. Maybe two.

I woke up, the cold dew seeped into my clothes, my neck sore and stiff.

But her bedroom was still dark.

Still no sign of Sarah.

I gathered myself up and dragged my sorry ass home.

— 6 Comments —

Rainy — said . . .

That's almost touching. You want to take it easy hanging around windows uninvited these days though. People think less about *Romeo and Juliet* these days as they think about the likes of Paul Bernardo and other assorted freaky types when they see people hanging around at night like that!

Peter O'Mallick — said . . .

What, are you calling me Paul Bernardo? I'm not any kind of freaky sex pervert.

Rainy — said . . .

All I'm saying is that you want to be careful hanging around windows at night. People aren't near as naïve as they used to be. I'd hate to see you getting picked up for something you never intended to do. I can understand what it's like to feel like you're being brushed off, but you've been through enough lately, yes?

Peter O'Mallick — said . . .

Well, it sounded to me like you were comparing me to a fucking serial killer, which I don't appreciate.

228 / *I, Death*

Sarah and I are destined to be together, whether she realizes it or not. I'm not some sick fuck perv, and don't think that I look like one.

Rainy — said . . .
First off, sorry if I offended you. Second, how the hell would I know what you looked like? Besides, appearances can be deceiving. Most people said that freak looked like a nice guy.

I'm just trying to get you to see that some are not as open to things as others. Nosy neighbors who saw a guy hanging around a house after dark might call the cops. Cops have a funny way of not seeing things in a nice way. I hope you two can work it out and I'd hate to see any chance you have busted up because your uncle or her parents gets ticked off with you being picked up because of a misunderstanding. Good luck man… Sometimes love ain't easy.

Kim — said . . .
Oh, Peter…

Wednesday September 19, 2012 — 7:42 AM

I left Sarah half a dozen messages yesterday.

Still no answer.

Damn, why does this have to be so much work?

I have so much to say to her, so much to talk to her about, so much to explain. I know that she'd be able to see things clearly, help me deal with all this, put everything into perspective.

I just know it.

All I need is to get hold of her.

Well, after reading that comment by the Rainy person, I couldn't get the thought of them calling me Paul Bernardo out of my head. I wasn't all that familiar with what he'd done, other than some controversy I remember when some Karla chick that he conspired with was let out of prison several years ago. So I dug into the movie archives that my uncle has on DVD, and sure enough, I found a movie titled *Karla*. So I watched it.

Couple of sick fucks. That's all I can say. And I wish there was some way that I could get that freaking clown-nosed jerk named Rainy to understand that I'm not at all like this fucking Bernardo. I'm more like Romeo. And Sarah is my Juliet. I'm simply misunderstood, deeply in love.

And a note to Kim, I also saw your comments. I'm not scaring Sarah. I couldn't possibly scare Sarah. She knows me

230 / *I, Death*

too well. Sarah knows I love her. And I know exactly what's going on in her life right now, because I'm feeling it too. Her father is dying and she's terrified, just like me. Terrified of all the people around me who are dying. So where the fuck do you get off giving me advice? Are you and this Rainy person conspiring against me or something? I checked your online blogger profiles and you both live in the same city. I bet you are both gossiping and laughing your asses off at me. Wouldn't surprise me one bit.

I know exactly what Sarah's going through and exactly what she needs. She needs me.

My Uncle Bob said I could borrow the car today, that he wasn't planning on using it at all. I'm going to park just down the street from Sarah's house for the next 18 hours or so, see if I can catch her coming or going.

— 1 Comment —

Kim — said . . .
I have to say that I was really hurt by your comments, Peter. While we haven't met, I have never been anything but nice and understanding to you. It's unfair that you would dismiss my comments merely because they weren't what you wanted to hear.
But if you want to play mean...

If you love Sarah so much and know her so well, and she knows this... then why hasn't she called you back? Why haven't you seen her during your stakeouts? Could it possibly be that you have NO CLUE what's going on in her life? I mean, I've had a stalker more than once in my life (and that is what you have become by the way) and I know from personal experience that the LAST thing you want to do is talk to the guy hunting you. That is if Sarah's even living at home anymore. If she is, I'm surprised that neither she nor her parents have called the cops on you.

I: The Online Journal of Peter O'Mallick

Give yourself and her a little breathing space.

Back off. When she's ready to talk, she will.

But then again, I'm part of some "grand against Peter conspiracy" aren't I? Let's forget that I'm only trying to help. Let's forget that I still believe you have a good heart (when you're not being a jackass that is).

A friend tells you the truth, even when it isn't what you want to hear. That's what I'm doing, Peter. Why bother blowing sunshine up your ass when everyone else can see that it's raining?

And if you don't give a shit about what I have to say, well, when it all blows up in your face, don't say I didn't warn you.

Sunday September 23, 2012 — 2:58 PM

Fuck. I've been completely out of commission for several days now. I ended up spending half the day Wednesday parked outside of Sarah's house, but I fell asleep in the car only a couple of hours into my stake-out. I woke up all sweaty and feverish and it took all of my strength just to be able to drive the car home, walk from the garage to the house, then make it into my bedroom.

I've been laid-up in bed, sick for the past few days, mostly sleeping, without even the strength to watch television. It's only this morning that I started to feel better. Fuck. I must have caught something that night I fell asleep outside Sarah's bedroom window.

And if the cold that I caught wasn't bad enough, I had these freaky feverish dreams. Most of them involve waiting for Sarah outside her house or outside her bedroom window. The one that sticks strongest in my mind, of course is where I arrive at Sarah's window to find that Rainy guy there first, clown nose and all, laying in the grass looking through her window.

He stands up when I get there, all excited, telling me he can see *it*, and wants to get a picture of *it*. I have no idea what the hell he's talking about. He asks me to pose in front of Sarah's bedroom window so he can take my picture with *it*. For some reason I can't speak while he puts his hands

I: The Online Journal of Peter O'Mallick / **233**

on my shoulders and moves me into position, then tells me to crouch lower so he can get me and the window and *it* in the shot.

I'm finally able to speak and I say: "Get *what* in the shot? What is it that you see?"

"The skull," he says, pointing at the window.

And I turn and now I see it too. Hovering in her window in the dark, grinning at us with haunting vacant eyes. As I continue to stare at it, the eyes start to glow an eerie red and its jaw clacks open, saying something.

Then I turn back to look at Rainy, and he's taking off his clown nose. And, as soon as he takes it off, I can see that Rainy is actually Paul Bernardo. And, out of nowhere this chick shows up. Although I've never seen what she looks like I know that it's Kim. Except she looks like that chick Donna from *That 70's Show*, the one who played Karla Homolka in that movie.

"We've taken Sarah," they both say in unison. Then Rainy / Bernardo lifts up his camera and says. "Okay, now say cheese."

— *3 Comments* —

Rainy — said . . .
You want cheese, just make a movie out of that dream and run it on a loop. I can't decide what's funnier, the fact that your cocked up dream proves that you can't let go of a damn thing, or the fact that because you didn't listen to my advice to leave well enough alone and you got sick after sitting in the cold in your damn car all night.

Thanks for the laugh.

And since you don't seem to see the danger in what you're doing you should check out the listing for stalking on a site like *Wikipedia*.

Or maybe the Criminal Code?

Kim — said . . .

The subconscious loves to play tricks when you're vulnerable, but I think you've been watching too many cheesy horror flicks.

Take it easy, drink plenty of liquids and keep warm. I've had the cold that's going around myself, it's not nice.

(And if you're not gonna quit with the whole "stakeout/stalking" thing, at least take a blanket and thermos of hot coffee next time!)

Peter O'Mallick — said . . .

How dare you fucking laugh at me? How fucking dare you? And how do you know so much about stalking and the criminal code anyway? Is it perhaps that *you* have a problem?

You're from Hamilton — isn't that near where Bernardo committed those crimes? Maybe you're both made from the same mould. Maybe my dreams are trying to tell me something about you, Rainy.

Did you ever think about that?

Monday September 24, 2012 — 10:56 PM

I'm still not feeling all that better — haven't been able to leave the house, but at least today I got dressed, moved around the house a bit, watched a few movies, read almost an entire Richard Laymon novel (that made me think about Robbie — man do I ever miss him) and I watched some TV.

I started by checking out a few of the new shows — but there aren't enough decent shows with a plot, not the stupid reality crap or "everybody is good at singing or dancing or whatever talent" stage content show. Watching TV actually took my mind off of Sarah for a while.

Shit.

I stopped while writing this. Stopped for a few minutes to phone Sarah's place.

Her machine picked up after two rings, which means she hasn't retrieved and deleted her messages yet. Fuck. Where the hell is she? I wish I could be out there looking for her, waiting for her, instead of having been sick here. I know that she needs me.

Maybe I'm like one of those characters in that TV show *Heroes* from a few years back that I really liked. Each of them had this different uncanny super-power, some sort of supernatural ability. Yeah, I know, there's like this dark cloud of death surrounding me, but maybe it's the side-effect

236 / *I, Death*

from some really cool super-power that I have. Maybe it's just starting to show its ability.

Like maybe that Rainy character is actually some sort of freakoid pervert like Bernardo. Maybe my dream *was* trying to tell me something. Maybe that's what my dream was trying to tell me. Maybe he does have something to do Sarah. Maybe that's why he's been haunting this blog, because he's been stalking me and Sarah, waiting for a chance to get at her, now watching me to see what I know.

— 2 Comments —

Rainy — said . . .
Yeah, that's exactly how it happened. When I finish work each day I drive all the way up to Sudbury and unlock the crate I'm keeping her in to give her some food and water. Her parents are in the trunk of my car in tiny pieces. Sarah is mine, all mine!! MWA-HA-HA-HA-HAAAAA!

Get a grip, Speedy. If I was even remotely interested in your tragic little life in a deviant way, why would I be trying to help you out (which I've given up on, by the way)? Don't flatter yourself on that one. While I can't say the desire to drag my butt all the way north and warn her about you is overwhelming, I haven't been to Sudbury in years. Okay, so a generic email may or may not have been sent to warn the local police of what is happening with a person slinking around a house in their town, but I can't say as it was my doing.

Kim — said . . .
I've known Rainy for over ten years and I can confirm that he's not a stalker/kidnapper/psycho... a little on the odd side perhaps... but *not* a stalker/kidnapper/psycho...

You on the other hand...

Wednesday September 26, 2012 — 4:07 AM

Fuck. I can't believe the nightmare I just had. No, it's not just the dream. It's… ah shit, it's complicated. I've been lying here for almost two hours and can't figure things out. I had to get up and write about it. Maybe then I'll be able to close this off from my mind and get some sleep.

The dream was about Rainy. I know, I dreamed about him and Kim the other night. Some sort of combination of the lecturing and accusations they've both made about me, having watched that damn *Karla* movie, and anxiety over what has happened to Sarah. It all seemed to mix into a really bad few days of feverish dreams and paranoid delusions.

But this last dream, this was worse — far worse than any nightmare I've had before. But let me start at the beginning.

It was night time. I was sneaking up the side of Sarah's house, on my way to her bedroom window at the back of the house. Like before, Rainy was there, lying in the grass, looking in the basement window. And, like before, he jumped up, all excited, when I got there, telling me he had to take my picture. But this time, instead of letting him pose me, I stopped him by knocking the camera out of his hands.

"No." I said. "Tell me what you've done with Sarah, you sick fuck."

He smiled at me and shook his head. "You poor, stupid fool."

238 / *I, Death*

I grabbed for his throat. "Tell me!"

He knocked my hands down easily. "Get a grip, Speedy," he said. "If I had anything to do with Sarah's disappearance, why would I be hanging out here?"

"The criminal always returns to the scene of the crime."

"Okay, dimwit," he said. "Reality check. I've never been to the scene of the crime. The only reason I'm here is because it's your dream and I'm a part of your dream. End of story."

"That's not true," I said. "You're responsible for Sarah's disappearance. And you're trying to trick me. This is part of some elaborate scheme."

"Don't flatter yourself, tough guy. Why can't you just face the fact that Sarah is through with you, that the whole thing is over, and that you need to get a life? Why can't you accept the reality that you've turned into a creepy stalker? I've got half a mind to turn on my cell phone and call the cops right now."

I lunged at him at that point. "Sarah loves me!" I shouted. "I'm not a fucking stalker." I clenched my hands into tight balls and started flailing at him, my fists bouncing off his chest. I continued my useless assault. "Why don't you leave me and Sarah alone? Why don't you just get the fuck out of here?"

"Why don't you wake up and smell the damn coffee?" he chortled.

Tears of rage were burning in my eyes as I continued my feeble attack. *"Why don't you just fuck off and die!"* I screamed.

He suddenly stumbled backwards, as if my words had dug into him like so many sharp blades. "Oh shit," he said. "Now you've done it. I know where this is leading." He started to shake his head in pity again. "Peter, Peter, Peter. When will you learn?" Then a bright look flashed in his eyes. "Wait a second. Let's get a picture of this, capture the moment

I: The Online Journal of Peter O'Mallick / **239**

properly, shall we?" He reached down, retrieved his camera, then set it on a tripod, flicked a few switches and stood beside me.

"Oops," he said, reaching into his jacket pocket. "Almost forgot the final touch." He produced a red spongy clown nose that he affixed to his face. Then he put his arm around my shoulder and whispered. "Now we're ready."

At that instant, a red-green tentacle shot out of the camera lens, knocking me to the ground. I recovered, looking up to see that it held Rainy by the throat, completely lifting him off of the ground. "Gak," was all he managed to utter, before the tentacle closed around his wind pipe, then his clown nose fell off and rolled on the grass to rest directly beside me. As if instinctively, I picked it up, not taking my eyes off the action for more than a split second.

Rainy was struggling with the tentacle around his throat, his cheeks red and his eyes bugging out from lack of oxygen. But he managed to actually pull part of the tentacle free from his throat. A moment later, he pulled enough of the tentacle away that he was able to drop free from its grasp, and in three solid swift moves, he tore the tentacle out of the front of the camera, ripped it apart in two pieces, and threw them across the yard.

He fell to his knees, panting for breath and I remember looking at him, completely astonished. *He's done it*, I thought. *He has finally broken the death curse. It's finally over.*

He looked up at me and smiled. And then he shook his head, his lips pressed tightly together in a grimace as if to say, *No, Peter. I'm afraid not, my friend.* But he never had a chance to say anything else, because what happened next happened way too fast.

Out of the corner of my eye, I spotted the camera start to slide forward like one of those aliens in the remake of *War of*

240 / *I, Death*

the Worlds, the tripod legs suddenly as flexible and strong as the tentacle had been.

It moved forward quickly, and by the time I realized what was happening, one tentacle tripod leg shot forward and pierced through his left shoulder, pinning him against the wall. Then a second one stabbed into his upper leg. Then the camera pulled itself in for an attack, and I swear I saw a set of razor sharp teeth in place of the camera lens, as the camera collided with his face. It pulled away about a foot, a large chuck of his cheek in its mouth, then it swooped in to attack again, this time biting into his neck, and again coming back with a huge hunk of flesh.

Rainy didn't utter a single sound as the camera savagely and brutally attacked him. Stunned, I laid there in the grass, getting splattered with raindrop-like spacklings of blood, watching as it tore huge chucks of flesh off of his face, chest and neck.

There was a particularly chilling moment, when, in the midst of the piranha-like attack, Rainy looked over at me, his face consisting mostly of bits of sinew, muscle, and small pieces of meaty flesh, with a good portion of skeletal jaw showing. And I could tell he was smiling at me. And in my mind I could hear his voice. Not spoken aloud, but clearly audible within my head: *I was trying to help you, Peter. And look what you've done to me. Look what you've done.*

I woke up at that point. Completely freaked out.

But that wasn't the worst of it. By the time I calmed down enough to realize it was just a nightmare, I looked down into my hand.

And saw the spongy red clown nose.

— 2 Comments —

Kim — said . . .

I: The Online Journal of Peter O'Mallick / **241**

I just went to Rainy's blog to see if it was true… I can't believe it. I just can't believe it.

Rainy was a great guy. We went to high school together. He was always clowning around, making people laugh. He married his high school sweetheart… they have two beautiful little kids.

How could this happen, Peter?

You need to see someone about this. Please. For your sake as well as those who care.

Please.

Franny — said . . .

OMG, Peter! Rainy totally had it coming! You know what they say; you play with fire, you get brutally slaughtered by a camera.

By the way Peter, I have a few people I'd like you to get to know… people who deserve an "NC-17" rated death. Let me know and we can arrange a "blind-date."

Just, umm, stay the fuck away from *me*!

Thursday, September 27, 2012 — 5:25 PM

I can't fucking believe it. This isn't happening.

After reading Kim's comments, I went and looked at Rainy's blog. He'd stopped posting. But his wife left a notice thanking friends for their condolences. And a search online revealed the following article.

MYSTERIOUS DEATH HAS POLICE BAFFLED
Bill Williams — *The Hamilton Herald*

A local man was out taking night pictures of Hamilton when his life came to an abrupt and mysterious end on Tuesday night.

Local teenagers found Paul Rainy, 31, in a park along the escarpment while out for a walk last night.

The teenagers were visibly shaken when recalling their account of that night.

They wandered along the path at Sam Lawrence Park, a popular destination for local photographers with its panoramic view of the city. "We thought he was drunk or passed out or something" the shaken couple recapped. "It wasn't until we got closer and saw all the stuff we knew something was up." They used their cell phones and reported the incident to the police.

"We get all sorts of calls to the park but they are typically reports of mischief.

This is the first death we've had here," a stunned constable who wished to remain anonymous said.

I: The Online Journal of Peter O'Mallick / **243**

> "And I can honestly tell you that I've never seen anything so heinous in my life."
>
> The constable was referring to the fact that the victim, who had no criminal record, and had been reported to be a friendly person with no possible enemies, had been viciously stabbed multiple times in the shoulder and leg. Police refused to comment on further details, other than the fact that Rainy's wallet, complete with credit cards and cash, remained untouched, as well as his camera bag containing an obviously expensive collection of cameras and accessories.
>
> The police remarked, simply, that the murder seems to have not been the result of a robbery attempt gone astray, but rather some sort of obvious personal attack, and refused to comment further.
>
> But witnesses revealed two disturbing things.
>
> One, that the victim's face seemed to have been chewed away, as if by a wild animal.
>
> Two, that they could have sworn they saw a red foam ball clutched in his right hand. "Like a clown nose," the young man said.

It was the clown nose that freaked me out the most.

When I woke up with it in my hand, I knew. But reading that article, hearing about his wounds, I know it's true. He's dead, and it happened at about the same time I dreamed about his death.

But I was nowhere near him. I've never been to Hamilton. And it was only a dream that I had. A dream. My fucking death curse couldn't possibly work through the internet on someone who is six fucking hours away and whom I've never even met.

It's just a coincidence. Or maybe it was like I thought before: my dreams are somehow psychic, somehow trying to tell me something.

244 / *I, Death*

It couldn't have been me that killed Rainy. It couldn't be. Sure, I was pissed off at the guy, at the things he'd said to me lately. But I went back to his earlier comments, and I realize that he was listening, trying to offer words of advice of support.

And somehow, by getting close to me, emotionally, he was killed by my curse?

No, no, it wasn't me. How could my death curse possibly reach so far? What the hell am I talking about? I don't even understand what this curse really is. How the hell could I know its limits?

— 1 Comment —

Kim — said . . .
You couldn't... that's why you need to find out all you can... before it's too late.

Monday, October 1, 2012 — 10:14 PM

I've sat here for the past few days and thought about Rainy. A lot. I also went back and read his blog archives, looked at all of the really cool photographs that he'd taken. He was a pretty talented photographer and a funny guy. Strange, but funny in that way certain adults have.

I spent a lot of time getting to know him. I figured if I was responsible for his death, the least I could do was get to know him a bit.

But it doesn't make sense. How could I possibly have killed someone that I didn't even know; that I haven't even met? That suggests to me that it has to be a coincidence. A freaky, twisted coincidence. Either that, or my dream about his death was trying to tell me something.

I haven't been able to dismiss the thought that I kept dreaming about this Rainy guy hanging out in front of Sarah's window. It's as if my dreams were trying to tell me something — perhaps about Sarah.

I've called and called and called.

Still no luck hearing back from Sarah.

I'm planning on heading out and visiting her place again tonight. I know that Rainy would be rolling in his grave to learn that I plan on doing that again.

But I've simply got to figure out what has happened to her, and I'm sure that the only way I'll get an answer is to resume my post at her basement window and keep waiting for her.

Tuesday October 2, 2012 — 11:43 AM

Holy Fuck.
Sarah's gone.
She's fucking gone.
I can't believe it.

I'm sure I'm to blame for that too. See, I knew it. I knew that those dreams about Rainy at Sarah's window were trying to tell me something.

So there I was last night, laying in the grass, gazing into the darkness of Sarah's room, trying to make out the simple shape of the teddy bear that I knew sat in the chair closest to the door — with the light from the nearby bathroom, I could just determine the shape of its head, the tiniest glint off its one glass eye.

Then, all of a sudden, after what seemed hours of waiting, a shadow crossed the wall inside.

Sarah? Finally?

My heart leapt into my throat. I laid there, frozen, unable to move.

A light suddenly came on, filling the room with a bright, painful brilliance. I squinted as I looked in. But it wasn't Sarah standing there. It was some strange man. He slowly shuffled in to the room and sat down on the bed.

As my eyes slowly adjusted to the light and as I got a better look at him I realized it wasn't a stranger.

I: The Online Journal of Peter O'Mallick

It was Sarah's father.

Holy Christ, but did he ever look different.

He's always been a tall and powerfully built man, but the man I saw before me, though he seemed somewhat familiar in his facial features, was merely a ghost of the man I knew as Sarah's father.

This guy was like 100 pounds lighter than Sarah's father. He had this sucked-in face appearance, and moved slowly like he was in a great deal of pain or that it took every effort within himself just to move an arm or a leg. I guess he looked more like those photos you see of people in the Holocaust: starved, their eyes filled with horror, or else empty, completely spent, with no emotion or energy left to give.

And as he sat there and my eyes continued to adjust, I realized that his body was making a slight hitching movement. His hands went up to cover his eyes

He was crying. But there were no visible tears. Perhaps his cancer-filled body wasn't able to produce them any longer.

The sight made me want to cry, for Sarah, for him. I cringed and slunk away from the window and headed back home.

— 1 Comment —

Kim — said . . .
Don't think the worst. Maybe she's gone away to a family member's or a friend's out of town. Maybe she just took some time to get away from it all and her dad just misses her.

The worst thing you could do is jump to conclusions.

Friday October 5, 2012 — 9:58 PM

It took me a few days to find out about what happened to Sarah, but I spoke with Julie, a friend of hers who did return my call. And I just realized, after reading Kim's comment, that it looked like I'd thought Sarah was dead. Well, at the very least I knew that much, I just didn't know where she'd went — I mean, if she'd died I would have heard about it, I'm sure.

My Aunt Shelly and Uncle Bob read the obituaries in the newspaper every day, so I'm sure they would have told me.

So, no, Sarah wasn't dead. Or, at least, if she was, nobody knew about it. That's because she ran away.

Julie told me a few things that I hadn't realized. I wasn't the only person whom Sarah had shut out of her life. She'd shut out every single one of her friends by the time the school year had ended. I guess I'd been so overwhelmed in my own angst and grief over losing her, and with my obsession to speak with her I didn't realize that I wasn't the only one.

I wish I'd known that. I'm not sure what I would have done, but I just wish I'd known that. Maybe because it means it had more to do with Sarah, rather than with Sarah and me. I don't know if that even makes sense.

According to Julie, Sarah disappeared a couple of weeks ago. Around the same time I was having those freaky dreams

I: The Online Journal of Peter O'Mallick / **249**

about Rainy being at her bedroom window and seeing the skull hovering there.

Sarah had been on a trip with her cousin, out of town. Her cousin lives in one of the suburbs just west of Toronto. Burlington, I think. As the story goes, they'd been planning on seeing a concert or something and were both in downtown Toronto. Then nobody heard from them all night, and they never returned home to her cousin's. Instead, her cousin was found, dead, in an alley. She'd died from an overdose of some sort of narcotic. And Sarah was nowhere to be found.

And nobody has seen her since.

There has been a lot of speculation about what happened to Sarah — that she must be somewhere, strung out on drugs, or maybe even being held against her will by some Paul Bernardo-like character. But not a single person has reported seeing her.

It's like she disappeared off the face of the planet.

And I can't help thinking back to the fact that Burlington and Hamilton are so close to one another, and that I was dreaming about someone from Hamilton being at Sarah's window at about the same time this whole freaky thing was going down near Toronto.

I just don't know what to make of it all.

Saturday October 13, 2012 — 9:41 PM

I was in Sudbury yesterday, like I've been almost every day for the past week. I'd hitch-hike in, go shoot pool with Harley and a bunch of the Sudbury guys that he would hang out with, drink, smoke a bit of pot, then head back home. I've found it much easier to spend my days like that than to try to figure out what happened to Sarah.

I mean, I went so far as to actually log onto this Toronto website where they have these cameras you can control for up to a minute, zoom in, pan across, up and down. I spent over twelve hours one day going from camera to camera trying to see if I could spot Sarah. How fucking pathetic is that? I want to believe that she's still alive somewhere, that she's still okay, but what the hell are the chances she'd be anywhere near where these cameras can look? Fuck.

Anyway, after a full day of doing that I'd started to hang out with Harley and some of his pals. They're pretty fuckin' creepy, some of them a lot more strange than Harley is, but it was a useful distraction for me.

So we'd sometimes hitch-hike in to Sudbury in the morning together, particularly if we couldn't catch a lift with someone we knew, and we'd hitch-hike back. When I say together, I didn't mean we actually went at the same time in a group. No, it's easier to catch a ride when there's only one of you, so we'd split up then connect once we got there.

I: The Online Journal of Peter O'Mallick / **251**

Anyway, Friday, yesterday, I got picked up while hitching by this older chick. She was pretty friendly and had an interesting sense of humour, really dry, and I can't believe the things that happened in our short drive. But I'm getting ahead of myself now.

So she picks me up, not even a few minutes outside of Sudbury, and we exchange names and start chatting. Her name is Gwen, she tells me, and she works for the company that runs Chapters, but not the store in Sudbury, at their head office in Toronto. It's called *Indigo*. She's some sort of corporate sales rep and is in town working on a deal with Falconbridge or Inco, I can't remember which one, but that's why she's heading up Highway 144. So we're chatting, and actually exchanging jokes about city people (she grew up in North Bay, so she's a Northerner like me, which is pretty cool) and she's telling me stories about these dumb ass people that she has met or worked with in Toronto, and we're laughing through all these hilarious stories. It's one of the best rides I'd had in a long time, because usually we just sit there in silence, make a bit of small talk about the weather and a half an hour ride seems like fucking eternity. But this chick is pretty cool.

Then, somewhere in the laughter, it hits me. She's from Toronto. That's where Sarah was last seen. I then start to turn the conversation into questions about where she lives, what neighbourhoods she visits. And, I guess I didn't realize it, but she must have been getting a bit creeped-out by me. But I kept pushing.

Then I start asking if I can ride back with her when she returns to Toronto, and she gets this horrified look on her face. She starts acting all freaky, or at least I begin to notice, and I realize that she's freaked out, maybe thinking I'm some sort of perv, or one of those dumb asses she was telling me stories about.

252 / *I, Death*

"Look," I say. "I just want a ride down south. And maybe someone to show me around. I'll give you money for the gas. I need to find my girl."

But she's not listening, she starts talking about not knowing how long this business trip is going to take, how long she'll be staying in Sudbury, and the fact that she's a new driver, not all that used to highway driving, and is uncomfortable with a stranger in her car. As she's saying this, I'm starting to get really angry. Angry with myself for ruining a fun conversation and spoiling an opportunity so easily, angry with her for her reaction in thinking I'm some sort of freaky pervert.

She tells me she's going to let me out now, and I unbuckle my seat-belt, the fury slowly building inside of me.

The anger barely begins to build when suddenly the car goes out of control. She was pulling over near the side of the highway near the cut-off from Highway 144 to Regional Road 8 that leads to Onaping and Levack. She must have slipped and her foot presses down on the accelerator and the wheel hits the ditch and the car starts moving, fast, off the road and toward the lake. It bumps down across the wild grass, over a few rocks and is airborne, pitching down. The front of the car slams into the lake, keeling on the passenger's side. I get tossed out the open passenger window and dive headfirst into the lake. I don't even hear her scream as the car splashes down in the water. I swim over to the shore and watch the car slowly sink, upside down, to the bottom of the lake. She never surfaces, never appears.

There's not another car or soul around besides me, to witness this woman's watery grave. After a few minutes of sitting there, completely chilled to the bone, watching the fresh flakes of snow land on the lake, I get up and start walking home. It's only a twenty minute walk from there,

I: The Online Journal of Peter O'Mallick / **253**

but it's fucking freezing, and I'm worried about catching my death of cold.

I laugh at that thought. At least I think that's where the uncontrollable laughter that rumbles up from my gut has come from.

Wednesday October 17, 2012 — 11:29 PM

I've checked *The Sudbury Star* and *The Northern Life* for the past several days and there's still no mention of a car crashing in Clear Lake on Friday. Still no sign of the car being discovered.

Of course, the road was pretty deserted, I can't recall seeing any traffic around when the car headed into the water, so it's entirely possible that nobody witnessed it, nobody heard anything.

And since this Gwen chick was from Toronto, nobody has started looking for her yet.

I popped down to Clear Lake today to see if I could see anything, see tire tracks leading off the road and towards the drop into the lake, or even part of the car, but I couldn't see anything even in the murky depths.

She's dead. Yet another helpless victim — and this time, nobody even knows that she is dead.

Except me.

Sunday October 21 2012 — 9:37 PM

It's gotten worse. This curse of mine.

And unlike before, it's gotten a whole lot worse rather quickly.

This morning, before I left the house for the day, when I was sitting at the kitchen table eating the bacon and eggs that Aunt Shelly had made for me, she asked me why I was looking so glum.

Actually, these past several months she'd asked me that a lot. I mean, sure, I'd been moping around here a lot when Sara and I first broke up. I'd be the first to admit it. But this morning was the first time that I paid attention to it, that I actually heard her words. It made me wonder about the last time that Aunt Shelly and I had actually exchanged words in a conversation. Not a simple question and answer type of thing, but a conversation.

I remember it clearly. It was last week. During supper, after one of the recurring back to back movie marathons Uncle Bob and I had sat through. Aunt Shelly wasn't much for movies, but she enjoyed listening to the both of us talk about it — she usually sat there, her napkin crumpled into her hand which would be cupped into her other palm with her chin propped up on it, smiling as the two of us went on and on. But that time, she'd been an active participant.

256 / *I, Death*

And I'd been pretty chipper. Instead of what I realized had been a usual stance for me lately at dinner — my head down, uttering single syllable responses to questions from either of them — I'd been animated, eager to listen to and share ideas about the movies we'd just spent the afternoon watching. It's funny, neither Uncle Bob nor I were all that hungry, having scarfed down at least three bowls of popcorn and half a dozen colas earlier, but we sat there, enjoying Aunt Shelly's lasagna and enjoying the conversation.

I actually felt like an adult. For the first time.

And maybe that's why I actually heard Aunt Shelly's words this morning.

And why I answered her. I wish I hadn't.

I told her that Sara had gone missing — had disappeared when on a trip to Toronto.

She told me that she knew, that Sara's parents had phoned here a few weeks ago, asking if Sara had been in contact with me at all. "I told them that you hadn't," Aunt Shelly said, still standing at the kitchen sink, dropping the frying pan into the sudsy water.

"How would you know?"

"Pardon?"

"You're not with me every moment of the day. How would you know?"

She lifted the frying pan out of the sink, started scrubbing it with a cleaning brush. "If Sara had been in contact with you at all, I would have seen it in your eyes, my son." Aunt Shelly had this special way of letting me know how much she knew me, how easy it was for her to be able to understand me, and it normally made me feel better to know that, at least subconsciously. But not this morning. This morning, I was a white hot ball of fury.

I: The Online Journal of Peter O'Mallick / **257**

"But you didn't even ask me!" I screamed, slamming my fork and knife down on the table. "You didn't even let me know that they'd called."

"Peter, calm yourself down. Sara hasn't been in contact with you, has she?"

I paused. "No."

"So why are you so angry?"

"I just wanted to know, okay."

"I'm sorry, Peter. I wasn't sure how you'd be able to handle the news. Especially with what happened with Jagdish and everything. I didn't know how to tell you."

"It's not like Sara is dead, Aunt Shelly. She's just run away."

She carefully put the frying pan down on the counter and wiped her hands on her apron. "Peter," she said in a very gentle voice. "Oh, Peter."

"What?"

"Stella Stanwick told me she'd heard about how Sara disappeared. About her cousin. You know about that, don't you?"

"Yeah," I said. "Julie told me about it."

"Then you can't believe that Sara is actually still alive, can you?"

That completely shocked me. Aunt Shelly had never come across as a stupid woman, as someone who didn't pay attention — nothing like that. But I'd never heard her speak in such a way. I'd never heard her say something with such simplicity, as if she understood the inner workings of the universe. She was saying, based on the evidence, that it was likely that some sort of harm had come to Sara. She was saying it the way I imagine you might try to convince someone who just couldn't see it that the world was round, not flat.

258 / *I, Death*

But I would have none of it. I refused to believe that anything bad had happened to Sara, and I was furious with her for suggesting otherwise.

"She's okay, Aunt Shelly!" I said, my voice rising again as I pushed away from the table. "She's fine. She's just run away!"

"Peter..." she stood there, a concerned look in her eyes, and pursed her lips together, still wiping her hands on her apron, though they must have been dry already.

I didn't say anything more, just glared at her, and walked out.

That was this morning.

I stormed out of the kitchen, leaving Aunt Shelly behind, still standing at the sink, wringing her hands in her apron, and headed down to a pool hall. I ended up spending the day hanging around with Harley.

I didn't care that Harley was a sick fuck; that he was a strange, odd bird. It didn't matter the things he'd done to frogs or other animals, or the bizarre stuff we always thought he was capable of. None of it did.

Harley was a "good times" friend — a guy who knows how to fuckin' party, how to let loose. How to just let it all hang out, unwind.

Did I ever need that.

We shot pool, played video games and pinball, told dirty jokes and stories, and drank most of the day away.

It was after dark when I got home a couple of hours ago.

The house was completely empty. And dark.

There was also a message on the answering machine. The single red indicator lit up the entire room like a cry for help in the dark. There was a sick feeling in the pit of my stomach as I looked at it. And for the longest time I just started at it, not wanting to push the button, not wanting to hear what the message said. But I finally did.

The message was from Uncle Bob.

I: The Online Journal of Peter O'Mallick / **259**

He was at the hospital. Aunt Shelly had had a heart attack.

— 1 Comment —

Kim — said . . .
I'm sorry Peter.

Monday October 22, 2012 — 4:04 AM

I moped around the house for hours, waiting for Uncle Bob to either return home or call. At first, I'd wondered why he hadn't called my cell phone, but then I remembered that they'd taken away my cell phone and canceled my service plan when I'd been grounded. And it hadn't been reinstated. And in his message, Uncle Bob hadn't mentioned what hospital they were at.

I stood in the kitchen for a long time, staring at the phone and the sink, which was still filled with water. It was dirty water, no longer sudsy, and the frying pan that Aunt Shelly had been cleaning when I'd left was still sitting on the counter.

I wanted to pick up the phone, start calling hospitals, find out where they were, but I kept looking at that frying pan, at the sink full of water. Aunt Shelly must have had her heart attack very shortly after I'd left. I mean, my breakfast dish, half-eaten eggs covered with ketchup and a few curly pieces of bacon, still sat on the table, the fork and knife not even moved an inch from where I'd slammed them down in anger.

I kept looking back at the phone.

But I couldn't bring myself to call the hospitals. To find them.

I couldn't stand to face Uncle Bob.

Not after what I'd done to Aunt Shelly.

I: The Online Journal of Peter O'Mallick | **261**

When he finally returned home, not even an hour after midnight, I'd been standing in the living room in front of the television, a picture of Aunt Shelly and Uncle Bob in my hands. I'd don't remember picking it up, this picture that had sat, for as long as I could remember, on top of the television set in the living room, but I was holding it my hands when Uncle Bob arrived.

It was a black and white picture of Uncle Bob and Aunt Shelly. They were standing in front of a Christmas tree. A real one, not an artificial one. And they were young, really young. Perhaps it was a picture taken before they were even married. I certainly couldn't tell where the picture was taken, but it didn't look at all like the house we were in now.

When Uncle Bob came in, I'd been studying their young faces which had been so full of love. The same type of open and eager love that they'd given me for as long as I'd known them — love that I had never truly acknowledged or even properly returned to them.

The pain in my heart grew as I realized that I'd never told Aunt Shelly, not in recent years at least, how much I loved her. The pain of that knowledge was intense, difficult to come to terms with.

It was when I was looking at that picture that Uncle Bob came in.

I was standing in the living room and he was standing in the kitchen — and, across both rooms, we looked at each other. Without him having to say a thing, I knew that Aunt Shelly was dead. And I knew that a part of his heart had died.

His wife — his best friend, his whole life — was gone.

He looked deeply into my eyes, searching for something, perhaps for hope, for pity, for comfort.

Instead, he found terror.

Because he suddenly backed away, his blood-shot eyes widening dramatically.

262 / *I, Death*

The look on his face were as if he was staring at the devil himself rather than his nephew, the buddy he'd recently spent so much time enjoying movies with.

He backed into the refrigerator, his hand suddenly clutching his chest, and he fell to one knee. The crunch of his nose on the kitchen floor tile as he pitched forward sent shivers down my spine, and I screamed at the top of my voice, but knowing I was too late, too damn late.

"Uncle Bob — I love you!"

Tuesday October 23, 2012 — 1:17 AM

I've been mostly sitting in my room. All day I waited for the sun to go down. Since it went down, I've still just been sitting here, waiting for it to come up.

But I know that the sun coming up again won't make a difference. It won't change a single God-damned thing.

Because I am finally to beginning to understand what I am.

I am death.

And the death has to end.

These nightmares I call 'life' have to end.

Maybe if Sarah was still around, if she hadn't run off (and I can't believe that anything worse has happened to her — she's merely run away, that's all), if she was still here, maybe we could talk, and she could make things better.

But I know that isn't going to happen.

And even if it did, what would keep her safe from me, from my essence of death?

I've been thinking, again, about Hamlet's soliloquy, thinking about how wonderfully he put the whole situation, the debate about suicide. I've been trying to come up with my own way of putting it, a way that someone else can appreciate.

But I can't.

I keep falling back on Shakespeare's words.

264 / *I, Death*

To be, or not to be.

There is no question in my mind, now. I don't care if it's nobler to suffer the slings and arrows of outrageous fortune. I need to take arms against this sea of troubles, and by opposing end them.

> *To die — to sleep no more.*
> *And to end the thousand natural shocks and*
> *heartaches that flesh is heir to.*

I've been heir to many heartaches, many shocks. From my mother, who died during my childbirth, to my father who died when I was very young, from Donnie to Jagdish, Robbie, Rainy and Gwen, from Sarah's father to Aunt Shelly and Uncle Bob.

Over time, my power, this death I give others, has gotten stronger as I've aged. It's taken all kinds of guises, too: from a slow rotting cancer to a sudden accident. But lately, as I saw with Jag, and especially with the last death, Uncle Bob's death, and even, partially, with Aunt Shelly's, it can be sudden.

And it seems as if the death can be conveyed through a simple stare.

Through my eyes.

I've known for several hours now that I'm going to end it, here, before the sun comes up. I just wanted to leave something, this last journal entry, as a way of explaining to people who come here and find Uncle Bob's dead body in the kitchen and mine in the bedroom.

I want people to understand that I had no choice.

Because, when I finish typing this last entry and posting it, I'm going to walk over to my bedroom mirror and stare at my reflection intently.

For as long as it takes.

Part II:

Brecht's Story

1

The kid's journal just ended.

The way he'd gone on and on for so long, writing almost every single thing he did, jotting down every thought that had occurred to him, it was shocking the way it just ended.

And if Bryan Brecht didn't know any better, didn't know the actual truth, he would have believed the kid had actually succeeded in killing himself during the face-off with the mirror.

But he'd seen the kid once since that last blog entry — about a week later. And one of his street soldiers — that's what Brecht liked to call the goons who worked for him — had spotted him hitch-hiking on Highway 69. Heading south.

At that point, Brecht had put out the word through his contacts in the Greater Toronto area that he wanted to be called immediately if anybody spotted Peter O'Mallick. He'd even faxed a picture of and emailed a link to the single online photo the kid had placed online — his profile picture for his blog.

So the word was out. And though it had been well over a year since Brecht had received any update on his whereabouts — the last update placed O'Mallick living on the streets in Toronto — it was just a matter of time before

II: Brecht's Story / **269**

someone found him again and Brecht would be able to catch up with the kid.

Of course, the trick still remained on how he would survive a face-to-face meeting with the kid.

And based on some things he'd picked up in the journal, as well as his own two encounters with the kid, Brecht had a theory.

The only issue, of course, had been that if the theory didn't hold out, it could be fatal.

Though he'd only seen the kid twice in person, Brecht had crossed paths with the kid indirectly prior to that. Of course he didn't realize there had been a connection to him back then, through either the teacher or that young slut he'd been with that one night and whom Brecht had fucked six ways from last Thursday.

His pecker started to get hard just thinking about that night.

‡   ‡   ‡

That night Brecht had been sitting in the passenger seat of the car. He'd been the one to discover Robinson's vehicle on the side of the road in the little parking nook near the slag dump site. Fitz had been driving. Dillon had been in the back seat.

Brecht respected Dillon tremendously — always had, and not just because while Dillon was the leader of Sudbury's most powerful gang he still did a lot of the face time and dirty work that he sent his men to take care of. No, it was mostly because Dillon also could look deep into the heart of the men he kept close to him. People like Brecht and Fitz. Brecht, a tall gangly albino wore thick pop bottle glasses and looked more like a bookworm or college nerd than a henchman. But Dillon knew that Brecht was right for the role, that he was a loyal and reliable right hand man. He also knew Brecht was a

270 / *I, Death*

black belt in Tae Kwan Do and not only had the ability to kill a man in a heartbeat, but would do so whenever necessary and that his deceptively innocent looks and lethal skill made for a powerfully deadly combination.

Fitz, Dillon's driver, possessed similar abilities.

If Brecht was Dillon's right hand man, then Fitz would be his left hand man.

Fitz was a tall black man who looked like a linebacker. He had a perpetually stupid look on his face at all times. Looking at him, you'd believe the only thing he was capable of giving any deep thought to would be his next meal or most recent bowel movement. But that's where people went wrong with him. Fitz was a fucking genius. Sure, he looked like a bargain basement goon, like so much dumb muscle, but he had a Ph.D. in physics, read a dozen books a week, spoke four languages fluently and was simultaneously teaching himself a fifth and sixth. Several of the gang members referred to him as 'MacGyver' because of his keen ability to make anything work that he put his mind to. But nobody dared call him that to his face, because he had the patience of a gnat and tolerated nobody except for Dillon.

Fitz and Brecht sat silently in the car watching as Dillon approached on the passenger side. They didn't say anything to each other as Dillon started talking with Robinson and the chick with him.

They didn't say anything when Dillon opened the door, pulled down his zipper, pulled his cock out and forced the girl to start sucking on it.

They didn't need to say anything. That's why Dillon trusted them. Though Dillon was the leader, they all had each other's back and worked together as though they were capable of psychic communication. Most of the time, Dillon didn't need to issue an order, the other two just stepped in and did his unspoken bidding. Fitz had made a comment

II: Brecht's Story / **271**

once that they were like Dillon's ants, but when the others in the room didn't understand the meaning, he dropped it. Brecht knew what he'd meant though, because he felt the same way too.

Brecht and Fitz were out of the car and immediately beside the car just as Dillon was spewing his load into the chick's mouth. Brecht grinned at the thought that they knew their boss so well they could tell when he was going to orgasm.

As Dillon pulled the chick out of the car, holding his switch-blade to her throat, Brecht had the driver's door open and Fitz dragged Robinson out by one arm. Once the teacher was half out of the car, Brecht placed two quick kicks to Robinson's throat and stomach.

"Leave him alone!" the chick yelled, trying to break free of Dillon's grasp. Dillon pushed her around to face him as she squirmed out of his grasp and then kneed her in the stomach, knocking the wind and the fight out of her.

Fitz lifted the man to his feet and Brecht took his other arm as Dillon held the chick from behind again and called across the top of the car. "Now listen up, and listen good," Dillon said. "I was planning on making you hurt in new ways just to show you I mean business and want my fucking cash already. But this lady friend of yours gives me a much better idea." Then he started cutting off the chick's clothes using the knife.

"She's going to learn a new definition of pain." Dillon said as he finished cutting off her shirt and bra. "When we're done with her, she'll be sorry she ever made your acquaintance." He then slipped his knife into the waist of her pants and started slicing down. "And maybe, just maybe, you'll think twice about trying to stiff me out of a payment."

With her pants completely cut off, Dillon dragged the chick, who was now standing there in just her panties, toward their car and shoved her into the back seat. Brecht

272 / *I, Death*

entered the back seat through the opposite side and held onto the chick with both of his hands. She was still wheezing heavily from having the wind knocked out of her, and Brecht could tell that she was trying to say something even as she struggled and attempted to squirm out of his grasp.

Just remembering seeing the thin line of blood produced by the tip of the blade against the girl's skin on the side of her throat, and recalling the sour sweet smell of her sweat and fear caused Brecht's cock to throb painfully the same way it had done that night. He couldn't take it any longer. He unzipped his pants, freed his aching cock and started pumping it furiously in his fist, re-living the scene.

Within mere seconds, Dillon had been in the back seat on the other side of the chick and Fitz was pulling the car out of the lot. Not saying anything more, Dillon punched the broad in the side of the head and ribs a few times, then hauled her body completely onto the seat and mounted her from behind. By then Brecht had his own cock out and had started jabbing it against her closed lips. When she refused to take him in her mouth he grabbed her head and stabbed his cock into her eye then squeezed her throat.

Gasping for breath, she opened her mouth and he shoved his dick in.

The memory of her sweet lips finally parting and the way she choked as he thrust himself in sent Brecht over the edge and he came in spastic waves.

Fitz had driven around for a good hour while Dillon and Brecht alternated between trying different positions and hitting, squeezing and choking her. After that first hour, when she had eventually stopped groaning or shrieking in pain and fear, the fun died off and they dumped her in an alley.

Of course, even that hadn't gotten to Robinson. Not completely. Sure, he came around a few days later with a hefty

II: Brecht's Story / **273**

payment, still not the full funds that he owed, but enough of it that they could lay off of him for a while.

But then, as is inevitable, he bought more stuff a few weeks later. On credit, of course. A few days after that he was back for more. Within the space of three weeks, the teacher owed almost twice as much as he had the first time.

By then, Brecht had discovered the kid's blog. And it was funny how that happened.

2

Fitz and Brecht were sitting in the alley having a smoke outside of the downtown club where Dillon did most of his operations from. In that offhand way Fitz had, he started talking about the internet and how he was fascinated by the possibilities held there — he mentioned things like Facebook and blogs as ways of connecting with kids, infiltrating their world. The discussion didn't really go anywhere beyond a few initial thoughts from Fitz because Dillon had beckoned them inside to head out on a collection run. And they never talked about it again. But the ideas had really sunk home and Brecht thought about them all night while they did their work.

Early the next morning, when their work was done and they'd headed off to their respective homes for sleep, Brecht went online and did a Google search using Robinson's name, the words 'teacher' and 'high school.' And that's when he discovered O'Mallick's online web log, and the constant, almost obsessive mention of his teacher.

Brecht stayed up all night reading about the kid, and he knew immediately that he wasn't going to share any of the details with either Fitz or Dillon. He wasn't sure why at the time, but he wanted to keep the detailed knowledge of the kid in his back pocket. It was enough that Fitz and he were equally second-in-command and always covertly looking for

II: Brecht's Story / **275**

that additional edge over each other with respect to their usefulness to Dillon. And there was something nagging him — yes, even back then, though he didn't actually believe the kid's claim that he held some sort of death curse — so that Brecht felt this should be his jewel alone.

A few days later, when O'Mallick posted about the book event and that he would be attending with Robinson, Brecht mentioned it to Dillon, making it seem like he'd gotten the information from one of their usual street sources. Again, he kept the kid's blog a complete secret.

The night of the bookstore event had been the first time Brecht had encountered the kid in person. In retrospect, until the events that lead to Dillon's death, the stalking and capture of the teacher and kid had worked out beautifully.

Dillon, Fitz and Brecht had arrived at the store in the mid-afternoon. The event was slated to run from 2 until 4PM and they got there just about mid-way through it. The author table was set up in an open space near the front of the store just off the main aisle that went up the middle of the store. They spotted Robinson immediately, and guessed correctly that the scrawny, dark-haired kid beside him was O'Mallick. The two of them were standing amid a crowd of people, listening to that Sudbury doctor and author recite some sort of engaging story that held not only the crowd, but several of the bookstore staff members in rapt suspense.

They split-up and wandered the store for a while. Fitz hung around in the magazine section near the front of the store, Dillon sat in the Starbucks past that at a table beside the only other public exit to the building, and Brecht wandered through the elevated Fiction section on the far side of the store. Though they did shuffle and move themselves around a fair bit in the several hours they were there, occasionally trading areas for a few minutes, they kept mostly within

276 / *I, Death*

a certain radius of those stations and at least one of them had an eye on Robinson or the kid at all times.

And the great thing about the big box stores was that they could wander around the store for hours and, just like their prey, not seem conspicuous. It was the culture of such places that people would enter through the front doors and spend as much as half of a day wandering the stacks of books, magazines, CDs and other book-related items.

Twice during the late-afternoon and evening, either Robinson or the kid headed to the washroom located at the very back of the store. That was closest to Brecht's area, and he'd made eye contact with Dillon across the store both times, inquiring to see if it was the right time to make their move, but each time Dillon had just shook his head. Brecht always respected the man's absolute patience. He never made a move until the timing was absolutely perfect and execution of a plan allowed for very little surprises.

In his browsing and without losing track of where Robinson or O'Mallick had been, Brecht had been able to check out a good number of books in the fiction section. He hadn't read a book in years, and spending time in the bookstore brought back a keen sense of nostalgia for his younger years, and the countless hours he had spent with his nose buried in either comic books or the pile of books he used to borrow from the library over the course of the summer.

Until he left high school, books had always been his only real friend, and he'd lost himself in them constantly.

Looking the way he did — skinny, tall, whitish blond hair and thick round glasses — hadn't earned him a lot of friends in elementary school. But it had earned him nicknames such as "nerd" or "Beaker" despite the fact that Brecht had never been all that good at school. He was the popular kid to pick on, almost from Grade 1, and over the years he'd suffered countless teasing, name-calling, as well as physical bullying.

II: Brecht's Story / **277**

It had been some time in Grade 7 after being beaten up for the third time in a month by the biggest kid in his class, Bruce Higgins, when Brecht started doing something about it. Sure, over the years, Higgins would fire a quick punch to the back of Brecht's head when he wasn't looking, breaking his glasses on more than one occasion which, more often than not, led to Brecht receiving a second beating from his old man when he got home. Constantly drunk, and off on worker's compensation for back pain and stresses he'd supposedly suffered from his work at the Inco mine, Brecht's old man constantly took out his frustration on his two kids. Brecht, being the uglier one of the two, seemed to be the recipient more often. But he'd never hated the old man for his actions. On the contrary, the slaps and punches and spankings were virtually the only physical contact Brecht ever had with anyone, and he'd grown to look forward to them as a sign that the old man loved him.

After all, Brecht's brother, being a bit meatier and more capable of defending himself, received half the beatings that Brecht did. And in the back of his mind, Brecht told himself it was because the old man loved his brother Charlie a lot less. Even to this day, when Brecht tasted blood, he often thought about the old man, and those glorious early years of his childhood, of looking at the old man, the taste of blood strong in his mouth and hearing him tell Brecht through a series of cries and sobs how much he loved him.

In any case, it was after a pretty severe beating by Bruce Higgins — this time, more publicly during recess in the school yard, with a large group of kids from their class standing around and laughing, and even blocking the spectacle from the teacher patrolling the school yard grounds — that had pushed Brecht over the edge. Though the group was chanting "beat Beaker, beat Beaker" over and over, they kept the chant low enough not to attract attention

278 / *I, Death*

as Higgins railed punch-after-punch and kick-after-kick to Brecht's head, chest and stomach.

Brecht had never mistaken the beatings from Higgins as love. There was a difference between the beatings from Brecht's old man and from Higgins. Brecht's father loved him — he never called Brecht names while striking him. On the contrary, he often cried while hitting him, and sometimes, depending on how drunk he was when it was happening, he'd tell Brecht how much he loved him with each blow, and how it hurt him far more than Brecht every time he had to do this to teach his son a lesson.

No, for some reason, Higgins hated Bryan Brecht — hated him with a passion.

When the teacher, Miss Murphy, finally got close enough to investigate the growing crowd gathered around, Higgins had finished with his beating and blended back in with the crowd. By the time the teacher got there, it was simply a crowd of kids, laughing and looking down at Brecht as he laid there on the pavement, his face slick with tears, blood and snot, his glasses broken, his bag of books torn and strewn all over.

As the teacher knelt down, asking Brecht if he was okay, and tried to help him up, Brecht caught a quick flicker of disgust in the woman's eyes — disgust not at what had been done to him, but disgust at Brecht himself. He recognized the fact that she was mortified to be so close to this ostracized kid. For some reason, up until that point, Brecht had always believed that though the kids weren't on his side, at least the teachers were; even though, in retrospect, they'd given him no real reason to believe that, other than the fact that they called him by his name rather than some insulting nickname. But at that moment, he knew the truth. The adults, the teachers, they weren't at all on his side. In fact, they were worse. They didn't call you names to your face, despite the

II: Brecht's Story / **279**

fact that they were repulsed by you, despite the fact they didn't care at all. That was when he firmly decided that he wasn't going to take the bullying and teasing any longer, that he would do something about it.

Being a bookworm, he'd naturally sought out books on self-defense, books on judo and karate and other martial arts. And, slowly, in the following years, he taught himself some of the moves. When he entered high school in Grade 9, he joined the judo club at school, and that's when he really started to learn. Practicing moves and training himself on his own was one thing, but being able to practice with other students made the difference.

By the time he was in Grade 11, Brecht had mastered his way to a brown belt, and was confident enough to strike back. Of course, by the time he entered high school, the blatant name-calling and bullying had ceased. Higgins had actually gone to a different high school, which helped. But by then Brecht knew the truth — that even though the other students still hated him, were still repulsed by him, they were just better at hiding it from him, at keeping it to themselves and laughing at him behind his back. Just like Miss Murphy.

The fact that Higgins went to a different high school and that so many years had passed since the last time he'd beaten Brecht to a bloody pulp made it easier for Brecht to get away with his plan of revenge. He laid in wait outside of Higgins' school for several weeks, waiting for the opportune moment. When the moment finally came — when Higgins was alone, it was dark, and there were no witnesses — Brecht struck, fast and hard.

Within five minutes, Higgins was lying on the ground, his right arm broken, his nose smashed in, and his body covered in as many bruises as Brecht felt he'd received from Higgins in all those elementary school beatings over the years.

280 / *I, Death*

As Brecht stood and looked down at his fallen adversary, he'd felt a huge sense of pride in his achievement, a tremendous feeling of power. As he turned and walked away, he'd realized one other thing: it was exciting. Overwhelmingly exciting. So much, in fact, that he'd gotten hard while administering the beating to Higgins and that when he got home that night, he kept growing a boner just thinking about it, and no matter how many times he beat off, his cock kept getting hard at the thought of seeing Higgins lying there, covered in the dirt and blood.

Higgins, of course, still had a reputation as a bully, and so despite the fact he'd been hospitalized from the beating he'd received, Brecht wasn't even one of the suspects questioned. He doubted he even made it to the long list. There was no shortage of people on the list of who wanted to do such a thing to Higgins. Brecht was never in any sort of schoolyard fight except for when he was on the receiving end of a beating and was still considered the weak scrawny nerd in all the circles he hung around in — except maybe for the few students and the one teacher in the judo club who knew him. That, and the years between his last encounter with Higgins helped secure Brecht's ability to get away with it.

Again, another reason why patience was a virtue.

Brecht was certain that if he'd tried to exact his revenge on Higgins back in Grade 7, he'd have been a more likely suspect.

That lesson taught him to bide his time, wait for the perfect moment, even if it was years away. Back then Brecht had often wondered when he might do the same thing to his father. He considered waiting until he was old enough to move out of the house. But though he thought about it from time-to-time, he never seriously planned on getting revenge on his father. On the contrary, he still held fast to the notion that the beatings equaled love; that his father expressed his love through physical abuse. When the old man stopped hitting

II: Brecht's Story / **281**

Brecht when he was in Grade 9, that's when Brecht started feeling less loved. He missed those cherished moments of feeling so close to the old man; missed them severely.

It was around the same time that Brecht's younger brother Charlie started to become more withdrawn, started talking less, and occasionally appeared with a shiner or strange bruises on his body.

When Brecht had inquired about it the one time, Charlie said it was their father who had done that to him. He also started to ask Brecht *if Dad had ever pulled off his pants and fucked him in the ass or if he ever stuck things like the neck of the beer bottle up his behind.*

But he clammed-up when Brecht freaked and told him to *shut up* that he *didn't want to hear about it.*

The old man hadn't delivered so much as a single punch to Brecht in well over half a year.

It meant, of course, that his father no longer loved him. And that he had more love for Charlie. Much more, in fact, because he was doing things to Charlie that he'd never done to Brecht.

That incensed him.

That was why he finally intended to seek his revenge on the old man. But not then. He planned on waiting several years to do it, intended on developing a plan, and waiting patiently to execute it. To wait for just the right moment.

Only, he never got that chance.

A few days after Charlie had confessed to Brecht about what their father was doing to him, Charlie had snuck into the old man's bedroom in the middle of the night, blown the back of his head off with a shotgun, then loaded the gun again, put it in his mouth and blew a matching hole out the back of his own head.

Brecht had awoken to the explosive sound of the first blast of the gun, and made it to the bedroom in time to

282 / *I, Death*

see Charlie sucking on the barrel of the gun. He didn't say anything — completely pissed at his brother for taking away the revenge he'd already decided he would take out on the old man — and watched as his brother pulled the trigger.

Disappointment raced through Brecht as he watched his brother's body crumple to the floor beside the old man's bed. But something else ran through him: that same strange excitement he'd felt looking down at a defeated Higgins. As he looked at the splattered blood in the room, he felt his dick growing rigid as a rod iron. Without pause, he headed back to his room to whack off before going to the kitchen and calling 911.

3

When he bumped into another customer, Brecht snapped out of the detailed memories of his childhood and focused again on the task at hand. It couldn't have been more than a minute that his mind had wandered, but O'Mallick had moved closer and was browsing in the row directly beside him. Brecht had been able to avoid being that close to him all night — not that he thought the kid would recognize him, but there was always a chance that Robinson might. Even though Brecht had been within the teacher's line of sight a handful of times in the past year, he'd always been focused on Dillon and on the fix. Brecht was certain Robinson wouldn't be able to recognize him out of context — but he still wasn't taking any chances. When Robinson walked down the aisle toward O'Mallick, Brecht pretended to change his browsing direction and slowly made his way down a couple of rows and around to the side until he was at Robinson's back.

He watched Robinson pour some Bailey's Irish Cream into two coffee cups, and couldn't help smiling. He hadn't noticed they'd been drinking earlier, but any amount of alcohol they consumed would just help deaden their reflexes and reaction time when the action went down.

O'Mallick was laughing at something the teacher had told him when his eyes landed on Brecht. But, unlike the

284 / *I, Death*

other times his eyes had crossed over Brecht, this time they stopped on him. And stayed there for an uncomfortable amount of time.

Brecht felt his heart start to race. He was trying to understand where the anxiety was coming from, when it came to him.

It was the kid's death curse.

Brecht had subconsciously believed the curse was real.

Now the kid was staring at him.

Now his heart was racing.

Was he having a heart attack?

Was this the kid's death curse having an effect on him?

The sharply rising anxious feeling grew strong.

It was all Brecht could do to turn and dart behind a tall set of bookshelves. Once out of sight of the teacher and student, Brecht let out a breath of air, put a hand on his chest and sank into one of the many armchairs that peppered the bookstore.

After a few minutes, the tension racing through his body started to ease.

Brecht took in another long, deep, slow breath of air and let it out just as slowly.

No. He was fine.

Everything was fine.

He got back out of the chair and was able to locate the two, still standing in the same spot. He kept an eye on them from a much larger perimeter this time, continuing to move so that Robinson's back was to him. The teenager seemed more anxious than before, his eyes darting around the bookstore a bit more often since he'd stared Brecht down.

Brecht took that as a sign that the visual encounter they'd had a few moments ago had put the boy at some sort of unease. He began to wonder if, with the kid's alleged death curse there might also exist some sort of additional extra sensory perception — like a strong sense of danger. Brecht

II: Brecht's Story / **285**

had read no evidence of that through O'Mallick's journal, but he figured once you opened up the possibility of some supernatural ability in a person, where did you draw the line? And if the kid was just discovering some innate death ability, maybe there were other abilities he possessed, like an additional perceptive ability that he didn't have a handle on.

In any case, Brecht felt he couldn't be too careful in that regard.

Brecht ducked behind a tall set of bookshelves when, for a second time, the boy's eyes lingered a bit too long in his direction. He glanced across the vast bookstore's floor area, able to spot Dillon easily sitting in his chair by the door. Dillon was far enough away that Brecht couldn't make out his facial expression, nor establish eye contact, so he had no way of passing along his fear that the boy might be on to the fact that they were being followed.

He decided it would be a good idea to yet again increase the perimeter he'd kept around the two of them and work his way closer to Dillon so that at least some sense of communication could be established. If not with Dillon, then with Fitz, whom Brecht hadn't seen for at least the past ten minutes, but whom Brecht knew must still be lurking somewhere in the front northwest section of the store.

When Brecht stepped out from the shelves, he walked directly into Robinson's line of sight. The teacher's eyes immediately widened, his mouth open in mid-sentence. Brecht knew he'd been made and the two would be leaving the store immediately. He quickly headed across the store toward Dillon.

Walking across the main center aisle, Brecht caught Dillon's attention and pointed at the teacher and teen as they headed out the front door. Within another half dozen steps, Brecht made eye contact with Fitz who'd been lurking in the greeting card aisle, and gestured to him that they'd been made by quickly putting the tips of his fingers together with each hand in a half circle shape.

Fitz headed out the main entrance while Brecht made a quick rendezvous with Dillon, letting him know that the teacher had spotted and recognized him. Dillon and Brecht headed out the Starbucks entrance and almost immediately spotted Robinson's blue Honda Accord at the far end of the parking lot. It peeled away just as Fitz pulled up to them in their car.

They got in and began the chase.

Fitz was a good driver and an expert at tailing someone without being detected.

They followed the Accord as it raced down the Kingsway toward the downtown area, then darted back and forth along several of the downtown streets before shooting out through a residential section and took the road that led to both the University as well as the Science Center which was now closed for the evening.

Fitz slowed the car down as they watched Robinson's car turn into the Science North entrance instead of heading straight down the road that led to more residential neighborhoods and the Laurentian University campus.

"Dead end," Fitz said. "He has no idea we're still behind him."

Dillon laughed. "The perfect place to corner them. We've got a nice deep body of water to drop a body into without having to go all that far." The three of them quickly discussed their strategy.

Since the Accord could only leave through the single entrance — the science center grounds were bordered on the far side by Ramsey Lake — they decided Fitz would park the car just down the road from the entrance. Brecht and Dillon would quickly scout out the perimeter of the parking

II: Brecht's Story / **287**

lot to ensure there was nobody else around. Then, they'd reconvene and teach Robinson yet another lesson.

And maybe this time it would sink in.

It took a little more than half-an-hour to ensure the area was secure. Fitz, Brecht and Dillon then briefly discussed their strategy. Dillon liked doing his work alone, asserting his strength and fearlessness over his clients. Brecht and Fitz thus usually hung around just out of the mêlée, but ready to jump in when the time came. So it would be normal for them to just hang out in the car, like they'd done the last time Dillon had to teach Robinson a lesson. But since Dillon was planning on taking Robinson and O'Mallick down the pathway to the waterfront to kill the teen, far from view of the parking lot, Brecht insisted that one of them go as backup. Dillon, of course, refused. It was important to him to convey a strong, lone wolf atmosphere. With a bad feeling in his gut — which he realized was due to the way he'd felt when O'Mallick had been staring at him in the bookstore — Brecht was leery about Dillon doing this one completely alone, and offered to circle around and wait out of sight of the path that led to the waterfront.

Despite Dillon's desire of going it alone, he gave up after Brecht continually insisted that it would be best to bring backup.

"Fine," he'd said. "But keep your lanky ass out of my way unless I call for help."

Brecht started walking back in the direction of Ramsey Lake through the treed area out of sight of the Accord and watched as Fitz raced the car into the parking lot and over to where Robinson's car sat.

He could only catch some of the words, but watched as Dillon pulled Robinson out of the car, kicked him and yelled for O'Mallick to get out of the car. Brecht started laughing when he saw Dillon gesture toward his crotch and beckon

288 / *I, Death*

the boy forward. Then, when Robinson did something completely out of character and actually tried to get the knife from Dillon, Brecht almost bolted from the trees. Even though he knew Fitz was much closer to the action and could get to them in one tenth the time it would take Brecht, he was ready to dash over if needed.

Dillon easily regained control of the situation. It looked like he might have even stabbed Robinson in the shoulder. Yes, it was likely he did, because he ended up grabbing the teacher by the same shoulder — a strategy Dillon often employed — and gesturing to the teen to start walking toward the waterfront.

Since the small treed area converged at the end of the parking lot, Brecht was able to get closer to them yet still stay out of sight as they made their way down the mostly dark path to the boardwalk on the shore of the lake.

Brecht was still making his way forward when he heard Dillon order the boy to his knees in front of him. When O'Mallick didn't move immediately, Dillon planted a foot between his legs and then easily forced him down with one hand.

Dillon had pulled down his zipper and was pulling out his cock when Robinson again did something Brecht hadn't thought was in the normally meek teacher. He attacked.

Amazingly, the teacher had been able to wrestle the knife from Dillon and stab him with it in the space of about five seconds. Brecht didn't react — partially because he was so stunned that Robinson attacked, and partially because he was afraid to get involved in the mêlée. The back of his mind gnawed at him about the teenager's death curse. The thought that perhaps there was also an aura of curse about the boy and that was why Robinson was able to gain the upper hand so quickly held him at bay.

II: Brecht's Story / **289**

Brecht stood dumbfounded and watched the rest of the very short fight go down without raising a single finger or taking a single step forward.

Robinson lunged at Dillon with the knife extended, and, while Brecht couldn't be sure if he'd been successful in sinking the knife into his chest, he did see Dillon snap out of his own shock to dodge back, dropping to the ground, rolling, and coming up with the pistol in his hand and firing it.

The teacher stumbled backwards, clutching at his stomach, as Dillon turned the gun and pointed it at the teenager, who still remained in a mostly motionless crumpled position on the dock.

That's when Robinson surprised his foe for a third time by rushing Dillon while letting out a hoarse and mournful cry. Despite the fact he was fighting a man that Brecht respected and had learned so much from, he was impressed with the teacher's spirit and determination.

Dillon was able to retrain the gun back on Robinson and fire. But Robinson was already moving, and the momentum carried him forward in a tackling move. They stumbled backward, and Brecht spotted a glint of steel coming out of Dillon's throat as they both tumbled into the water.

O'Mallick was still a motionless lump on the dock when Brecht heard Fitz rushing up the path. Brecht ran over to meet him.

"Dillon's dead," Brecht said matter-of-factly in a low voice. "Let's get out of here."

Fitz was incredulous. "That's not possible." And for what seemed like a dozen times that night, someone again reacted in a way that surprised Brecht. Fitz just stood there, a dumbfounded look on his face, his posture completely deflated like a rag doll somehow just able to stand without swaying over.

290 / *I, Death*

Brecht took Fitz by the arm and started to lead him back to the car. "Robinson's dead too."

"What happened?"

"I'll tell you once we get out of here," Brecht said. "I'll drive."

They were getting into the car when Fitz finally seemed to be coming back around. He turned in the passenger seat to look at Brecht, his eyes no longer glassy or with the thousand yard stare they held just moments ago.

"What about the boy?" Fitz asked.

Brecht didn't answer as the car sped out of the Science North parking lot; the sound of sirens echoing off the nearby lake. The two of them remained silent until they saw that it was an ambulance on its way to the hospital across the road from the Science North parking lot.

But by then the silence in the car, resulting from Brecht not having answered that simple question, grew heavy and pronounced between them.

4

Fitz never made it a secret that he suspected something else had gone down on the waterfront that night; that Brecht might in fact be responsible for Dillon's death. Towards the end of the drive home, he plainly stated that to Brecht.

"Dillon never would have gone down like that," Fitz said.

Brecht shook his head, not taking his eyes off the road. "The teacher and the student got the jump on him. It happened quickly."

"Nobody gets the jump on Dillon," Fitz mumbled looking out the side window. "I think you had something to do with this."

"For what purpose?"

"So you could take over the gang. I know you've had your mind on the top spot for a while now."

"Oh?" Brecht said, slamming on the brakes and stopping the car dead in the middle of the Kingsway, one of the city's main roads. "Like you haven't?"

"Move the car, Brecht."

"The only reason you would notice something like that is because you had your eye on the very same thing."

"Move. The. Car."

"Admit it."

292 / *I, Death*

Although it was still several hours before traffic would begin to become thick with morning commuters, they were sitting at a dead stop on one of Sudbury's main roads. The Kingsway was a four lane roadway and one of the two main thoroughfares that linked New Sudbury and the downtown core together. A few cars passed them on both sides.

"C'mon. You're attracting attention to us."

"I'll move the car as soon as you admit it, Mister *Holier-than-Thou*."

Fitz tried to press on Brecht's leg, grab the wheel, but Brecht pulled away.

"Fuck sakes," Fitz said. "Let's get out of here and we can discuss this later."

"You're the one who fucking started it."

"You're the one who let Dillon down. Now c'mon, get this car moving. Let me drive, for fuck sakes."

Brecht turned off the car, pulled the keys from the ignition and got out of the car. "You want the keys?" he said, pitching them across the road. "Go get them."

"You stupid fuck!" Fitz scrambled out of the car and raced for the keys.

Brecht started walking away.

"You're going down!" Fitz yelled out to him. "You're fucking going down."

"We'll see about that."

5

It didn't take long for Dillon's gang to split into two factions. The schism occurred the very next day, in fact.

Word quickly spread through the gang about Dillon's death and the rift between his two second-in-command men.

Fitz ensured that Brecht's apparent disloyalty to the gang's leader also spread; about how the power hungry gang member allowed their leader to be taken down by a single client and a young teen.

By the time the sun came up, every single immediate member of Dillon's gang were already split in their loyalties between Fitz and Brecht. The word Fitz had been spreading seemed to hold more credence with the majority of the gang members and of the two dozen gathered in the back room of the closed bar on Durham street in downtown Sudbury the next morning at 8:00AM, eighteen of them were against Brecht and only six of them were with him.

The division was immediate and quickly turned violent.

Heated argument and discussion about who the next leader should be didn't take long to degenerate into a fist fight.

By the end of the fight, seven gang members — two from Brecht's camp and four from Fitz's group — were dead. The members supporting Brecht fled the aborted meeting after determining they were outnumbered and didn't stand a chance of lasting any longer.

294 / *I, Death*

The four remaining gang members that supported Brecht reported to him later that morning, bruised, bloody, and two of them suffering near fatal stab wounds.

That was when Brecht knew Fitz had succeeded in taking over Dillon's gang. He held the majority of the gang members under his control. The dozen or so immediate members each had a half dozen lower level contacts and peons, which left Brecht with a substantially smaller group than Fitz had and with only a handful of peons working in the downtown core of Sudbury.

It didn't take long for the newly rejuvenated gang Fitz led to undermine and thwart any efforts of Brecht's gang in gaining any purchase in the downtown core, the most profitable concentrated area of operation. This had a ripple effect through the supply chain as well, with contacts in Toronto and larger urban centres neatly severed. The word of Fitz and his gang held more punch, more substance than word of any of the members of Brecht's gang, and it was difficult for Brecht to maintain any operations with his existing contacts. He was forced to pretty much sever ties with all but two of his existing supply chain contacts in Toronto, and had to forge new ones from scratch.

The whole effort was made doubly difficult for two reasons. The word Fitz had been spreading about Brecht's betrayal of Dillon was wide-spread and had planted seeds of doubt about Brecht in the minds of many people planning on associating with him; plus the men in Fitz's gang were also poised to destroy any operations that Brecht and his gang were planning. It was often the case that when Brecht was able to secure a new artery in his supply chain, an attack from a group of Fitz's gang took it down and out of operation.

The attacks were swift, brutal and had a dual effect. They not only put an entire arm of Brecht's gang out of commission, but they also served as a warning to others who

II: Brecht's Story / **295**

might be considering going into business with anyone from Brecht's gang. The message was clear: Join up with Brecht and face annihilation from Fitz's gang.

The four men who had stuck with Brecht from the beginning of the rift remained loyal and dedicated to the cause. Brecht was appreciative of them, and for their own contacts, because they were what kept him focused and believing that they could return to their former glory, that they could be victorious over the other gang.

Brecht was determined to claw his way back to the top and overthrow the gang Fitz led. In order to ensure a flow of money and the ability to maintain his few loyal close gang members, Brecht focused a good portion of their operations on the areas not controlled by Fitz. They worked more on the outlying, lesser communities which meant harder work, longer hours for less of a return on investment. They required longer channels and more hands exchanging money down the chain which took a larger cut out of profits before it flowed back to the top. But Brecht was able to make it work, following a model of quantity over quality as well as diversification. If the profit made on the sale of drugs was cut down to a third of what he would normally be making, then it just meant Brecht needed to have three times as many transactions to make up the difference.

And unlike the operation that Dillon used to run, Brecht wasn't above using a few of the arms of his organization to accept cheap and easy contracts on people. He allowed Marko and Martin, two of Brecht's right hand men, to offer hit contracts — while the gang operated in Sudbury, North Bay, Timmins and Sault Ste. Marie, their main income came via channels in the Toronto and Hamilton area. And Marko and Martin, who traveled to each area as needed, didn't just take kill orders; they worked lesser contracts like kidnapping and warning beatings. The amount of income brought in

296 / *I, Death*

from that was quite substantial, and in many ways more rewarding for Brecht.

That particular operation was known simply as MarMar — a short code standing for the particular services offered by Martin and Marko. Word quickly spread through the underworld that if you needed someone taken out, or at least taken down a few pegs, the quickest and most cost effective way was hiring a MarMar attack.

One had only to whisper the word "MarMar" in the right bar to the right person to be contacted about their required details.

Fitz's gang and some others made fun of the name for the operation, saying it sounded like a candy bar. They also looked down their nose at that particular task as being beneath them. Fitz was of the mentality that torture and beating deaths should be reserved for those who crossed him and his gang.

But Brecht knew, when he heard these things through the grapevine, that Fitz was actually jealous of the new line of business he'd established.

No, it wasn't as clean and the money wasn't as easy flowing as the drug operation. But at least they kept Brecht and his gang in business.

So consumed was he with his drive to overthrow Fitz's gang, Brecht had all but forgotten about the teenager O'Mallick who had escaped the night Dillon died.

But it was due to following the *modus operandi* of his former boss that led Brecht back to the teen.

He was working a reconnaissance mission in Levack, looking at recruiting some lower-level fresh blood into his drug operations, when he spotted the kid coming out of the local beer store.

Finding these contacts was as easy as hanging out in a car down the street and around the corner from the beer store.

II: Brecht's Story / **297**

Small towns were easy pickings for such activities — Brecht had seen enough of it to know it could be like a decent fishing trip: if you sat there long enough, you were likely to catch something.

When under-age teens approached with cash in hand asking if he'd be willing to help them out, buy them a case of beer and make a quick buck, he'd size them up in a quick exchange. If they seemed to have the right stuff, he'd uncover the cases of beer sitting in his back seat and make a counter offer.

"Tell you what," he'd say, "I'll *give* you a case of beer if you'd be willing to help me out." He'd hand them a small package of hash and ask them to wait in front of the bar down the street for a middle-aged guy in a red ball cap to walk past. They were to ask him if they could bum a smoke off him. He would respond by saying he didn't smoke, but could give them a light. At that point, he would hand them an envelope in exchange for the little package. They were to return the envelope to Brecht's car, and if they did, the beer would be theirs.

About half the time, Brecht was able to entice new recruits to join into the chain. They'd start small, with simple tasks, in exchange for cases of beer or small amounts of the drugs themselves. If it worked out, usually after trial runs over a month or two, the payments would turn into serious cash for the kids.

Brecht liked doing this sort of recruiting personally so he could maintain a direct feel for the people at the lowest end of the drug supply he was feeding. He didn't want to give Fitz any sort of way to slip dissenters into his own ranks.

Parked down the street on the opposite side, facing the beer store, Brecht spotted Peter O'Mallick walking out the front of the beer store with a case of cheap beer and a bag of

298 / *I, Death*

what must have been plastic litre sized beer bottles — more of the dime store priced brand.

As O'Mallick walked toward him, Brecht noticed his bloodshot eyes immediately and the fact that his clothes looked as if he'd slept in them for more than a few days. The wind shifted as the teen approached and even though he was still half a dozen paces away, Brecht could smell the sour reek of stale beer and vomit off of him.

It was enough to make Brecht cough.

O'Mallick slowly turned his head toward the car and made direct eye contact with Brecht through the windshield. His eyes lingered there a moment, and there was the twinge of recognition in his face — as if he thought he might know Brecht from somewhere — but it was subtle. Sure, he knew the face, but wasn't able to place how he knew him.

It was a good sign, but within a split second, Brecht felt his blood run cold within his veins.

O'Mallick slowed his pace and his eyes remained on Brecht. But his stare was glassy and blank, and after a couple of steps, his lazy gaze drifted onward, and he walked past.

6

Brecht still got chills thinking about that last encounter with O'Mallick.

After it, he'd gone back and re-read the teen's blog, studied it intently.

Previously, he'd been convinced that the death curse was somehow channeled through the teen's eyes. Some further studies and intense research he'd done about eyesight and the brain, led him to the conclusion that Brecht's own albinism, and the resulting side effects of crossing optical nerve fibers combined with the mild Nystagmus, which causes very subtle rapid movement of the eyes, might both be factors preventing O'Mallick's death stare from working on him. Hell, for all Brecht knew, it could even have just been the pop-bottle thick glasses he wore.

And he was pretty convinced that the boy's high blood alcohol level during that face-off through the windshield had been preventing the boy from properly focusing and was likely also a diluting factor.

It took about a month for Brecht to put these facts together after doing a bit more reading about his own afflictions. And by then, of course, the teen had disappeared. His disappearance was in conjunction with police having found his uncle's dead body lying on the floor in the house where the teen had been drinking himself into oblivion.

300 / *I, Death*

Following news stories and word on the street, mostly through his low level contacts from the small town of Levack, Brecht learned that the police believed O'Mallick was on the run down south in Toronto and they were desperate to talk to him about his uncle's death. The police tried to make it clear that they didn't suspect him for the death of his uncle and failed to understand why he would run from them. A spokesperson for the department speculated at length in one newspaper article that the boy must have cracked over the stacked-up deaths of both of his guardians as well as the classmates and teacher whose lives were tragically cut short. She made it clear that Peter O'Mallick was not to be considered a danger to anyone other than himself and pleaded for any information that would lead the police to find him.

Brecht knew that O'Mallick was hurt, angry and confused. He also knew this was the best possible frame of mind within which to bring the teen under his control.

II: Brecht's Story / **301**

7

The call came at about four o'clock one Sunday afternoon from one of Brecht's Toronto area contacts. A teenager vaguely matching O'Mallick's description had been repeatedly spotted in the same neighborhood over the course of a single week.

The next call came from Jordan, one of his higher ranking members, stating that two members of Brecht's gang had turned up dead.

"Is this likely the work of Fitz and his crew?" Brecht said to the phone.

"It doesn't look like any targeted hit I've ever seen," Jordan said. "Sorry boss, but I've never seen anything like it. The one guy was bleeding from the eyeballs as if some sort of poison had been shot into them. The other guy's head seems to have exploded. Yet there was no entrance wound and no gunshot residue on him."

Brecht was silent.

Jordan went on. "The Fitz gang usually slices their throat, and, you know, they like to leave their calling card." Jordan was referring to the Fitz Root Beer labels Fitz's gang were known to leave, particularly whenever taking out someone in Brecht's gang.

Back when they were working together, Fitz got his nickname from a soda he had been obsessed with and was

302 / *I, Death*

constantly drinking. Though he had to import it at quite an expense, the premium root beer made in St. Louis was the only root beer — hell, the only soda pop — he drank. And about the only other obsession he could remember about Fitz, one that drove Brecht nuts, was the way Fitz would carefully peel the label off the bottles of root beer and carefully stow them in an envelope he kept handy at all times.

Brecht remembered asking him how many of those fucking things he had. Fitz only laughed. The labels, of course, made the perfect calling card, the perfect statement — particularly since Brecht knew where the labels came from — that the hit was personal.

"Yeah, I know." Brecht said, more to himself than to Jordan.

He looked across the room at the suitcase he had lying on the couch, already packed when he first started devising his plan. "Okay, make arrangements for me," he said. "I'm coming down."

He hung up the phone then he said them once more.

"I'm coming down."

Part III

Sin Eater

1

"You think I'm just a stupid punk?" Richard Yale shouted, advancing across the storage room of Johnnie's Bar & Grill at the teenager with his fists held in front of him. He wore a classy designer shirt and slacks, but there was no mistaking the blatant street fighting stance he moved with.

"No, Richie, no," Allan said, backing away. "I d-don't."

"Why did you have to start cheating me, Allan? Did you think I wouldn't have found out about this?"

Allan had backed all the way to the end of the aisle and moved around to the other side of the eight foot length of shelving that split the storage room into two areas.

"I never cheated you, Richie. Never."

"The fuck you didn't," Richard spat, rounding the shelves, moving in closer and grabbing Allan by the front of his golf shirt, "and we had such a good relationship, didn't we?"

"W-we still do, Richie."

"You made some drops for me, you got a pretty decent cut. And it was a damn good percentage, too. You made thousands from me in the past two weeks alone. You had it pretty fucking good. But then you had to take me for some sort of stupid punk and start cheating me." Richard easily lifted Allan off the floor and bounced the side of his head and

III: Sin Eater / **307**

shoulder off the shelving unit. The shelf swayed precariously, but neither of them noticed.

"I n-never cheated you, Richie," Allan said, his face turning red.

"The fuck you didn't."

Richard noticed how the redness of the teenager's face started to overshadow the pale red freckles and liked it. He hefted Allan again, this time twisting him so that his nose connected with the edge of the shelf. There was a satisfying crunch as Allan's nose broke, and a smattering of blood coated his left cheek. Richard liked how the crimson smear completely covered the kid's freckles.

He'd never liked freckles, and hated anyone who had them. He also hated red hair; hated it with a passion. Allan had red hair. But he'd been professional enough to ignore all that back when Allan was working deals for him — back when the relationship had been going smoothly. Allan was a Business Administration student at George Brown College and nicely covered a decent-sized physical and demographic area for Richard's drug trade business.

Because he was studying in the marketing area, Richard found the kid very successful in moving supply for him. Allan not only had a large clientele among his fellow students and faculty members at the college, but he actually applied some of the marketing techniques he was taking in school. Richard was delighted to see how it increased the flow of goods tenfold.

The relationship had been more than good, it had been one of the most profitable operations that Richard oversaw.

But then Allan had decided that Richard was just a stupid, uneducated punk.

That had been the youth's first mistake.

It was just a few weeks ago, when the business took a slight dip after steadily rising for months, that Richard first

308 / *I, Death*

suspected something was amiss. He'd experienced this type of thing before. Hell, Richard had done it himself when he first started out — it was one of the ways he proved what he was capable of and eventually awarded the position he currently held. He had called Allan on it, asking him if he'd been skimming some of the supply, keeping it for himself and doing his own private sales.

Allan had denied it.

Which was his second mistake.

Despite Allan's denials, Richard warned him not to skim the supply. He made it quite clear what would happen if he ever caught the kid cheating him. But again, Allan had denied it.

Allan's third mistake had been not realizing that Richard would plant someone as a customer to test him out. It was a simple matter of measuring the weight of the product before handing it over to Allan, then measuring it again after the purchase. And it was a damn good skim, too. Barely a sixteenth of an ounce — something that might be attributed to humidity.

But Richard knew better. After all, he might look and talk like some uneducated punk, but in order to stay ahead of the law, in order to stay on top of the low-lives working for him, Richard had to be quite a bit sharper than he appeared.

"I gave you a chance," Richard said, lifting Allan off his feet again and smashing the other side of his head against the door leading to the alley. "And you blew it."

"I dever cheated dou, Richie," Allan sputtered, blood continuing to flow from his broken nose.

Richard punched Allan in the left eye and threw him against the shelving unit.

This time it toppled to the floor with a resounding crash, with boxes, tins of sauce and meat, bags of sugar and flour all clattering and spilling to the floor.

III: Sin Eater / **309**

Richard stood over Allan's thin body watching the teen try to get up, try to push himself up on one of the uprooted shelves that collapsed under his weight.

On the other side of the shelving unit, the door from the kitchen area opened and Johnnie stuck his head in. "The fuck is going on in here?" His head bobbed around like one of those turtles you find in a Caribbean souvenir shop as he surveyed the damage to the room. Then he spotted Richard and grimaced.

Richard just smiled at him. "A little business, Johnnie. If you don't mind. Now fuck off."

"Sorry Ritchie," Johnnie said and closed the door again.

"Damn right you're sorry," Richard muttered, enjoying how frightened Johnnie was of offending Richard; or, more specifically, the organization Richard represented. While Richard didn't know what exactly the Brecht organization held over Johnnie, he was glad to have the restaurant and bar as one of his convenient main operation locations.

During the minor distraction, Allan had managed to crawl backwards off the fallen shelving and was on his knees on the floor. He was holding his swollen left eye with one hand and had a can of tomatoes in his right hand.

Richard laughed. "I can't fucking believe you, man. First you take me for some stupid punk who you think isn't going to notice that you're skimming from me. Now, you've got ahold of this can. What, you going to attack me with it, going to try to bust my head with it? You're fucking pathetic."

"D-oh, Richie. D-oh, I wasn't."

Richard kicked the can out of Allan's hand.

"I've wasted enough time here." Richard pulled the knife from the sheath on the back of his belt. "You know, I was going to just beat you, teach you a lesson and give you another chance. But you won't simply admit what you've done."

310 / *I, Death*

"I dibn't do adything," Allan blubbered, finally able to move up into a crouch and then stand.

"See, that's what pisses me off more than anything," Richard said, bringing the knife down into the side of Allan's neck. He pulled the blade out and watched a stream of blood shoot in a fine arch onto the room's small window. "You still just won't admit it."

He brought the knife down again on the opposite side, this time striking closer to the front of Allan's throat. His throat and mouth made a strange hissing, wheezing sound and this time the blood splattered up and across his right cheek, covering even more of those ugly damn freckles.

Richard felt a warm moment of satisfaction as he watched Allan's hands clawing frantically at both sides of his throat.

He stepped back enough to ensure the blood splatter didn't hit the white Green Shag Classic dress shirt he was wearing and was enjoying the moment of the teen's panic, when a shadow crossed the dirty blood splattered window.

Someone is outside, Richard thought, and stepped over to peek out the window.

As he brought his face close to the window, he was startled to see a thin, boney face, no more than an inch away on the other side of the glass. The face was covered in a strange looking patch of whiskers and a pair of blue eyes framed in a road-map havoc of bloodshot lines. The face of this street bum wore an expression of utter surprise, and, as Richard felt a strange bolt — as if something was striking and puncturing him on the right side of his head — he thought about how comical the expression on the bum's face looked.

Then he dropped dead to lie on the floor beside Allan.

The student's blood spurted out all over Richard's Green Shag Classic shirt.

2

Peter O'Mallick closed his eyes in a reflexive gesture, but he knew the damage had already been done. He had looked directly into the eyes of another man — something he hadn't done for nearly six months — and that man had died.

Instantly.

The rumbling pain that had been a constant background noise in his head increased dramatically, washing across his conscious mind. Only, it wasn't like before. Peter crumbled to the alley floor, his throat starting to issue forth a heavy stream of giggles as he fell. On his hands and knees, his body hitched as if he was vomiting and he let the laughter flow out of him in huge uncontrollable waves as he thought about what had just happened.

Before, with the other ones, each death seemed to have some sort of natural cause or naturally occurring accident. Like Uncle Bob's heart attack, or Jagdish's alcohol poisoning.

Sure, Uncle Bob's heart attack occurred suddenly and without warning. Unlike most of the others, it seemed to happen immediately. Peter had taken it for a sign that his death curse was growing in strength, like a cancer inside, taking over, growing more powerful and altering him further.

But this latest victim was dramatically different.

The side of the man's head had exploded outward.

Had the power he was harnessing within grown that much in the intervening months? Or could this be a side-effect of the fact he had been keeping his death curse in check all these months — like the contents of a soda can being opened under intense pressure?

When the uncontrollable bout of laughter stopped, Peter noticed a large droplet of fresh blood on the pavement. He brought his hand to his top lip and felt the thick line of blood that had leaked from his nostril. Then he touched his nose.

Nothing hurt. In fact, the massive migraine he'd been walking around with was gone. And despite the fact he hadn't eaten a single scrap of food since the day before, he felt a newly acquired sense of energy.

He got to his feet, moving more quickly than he'd been able to for weeks.

Reflexively squinting his eyes, he moved along the alley and carefully made his way to the door. That is what he had been originally doing in the alley, after all. Peter had often found that during the day restaurants and bars kept their back doors either unlocked or cracked open. And if he was careful enough, he could slip in and nip a little something to eat, or to drink, depending on what was stored there.

But the crashing noise from inside the room had stopped him just as he was about to open the door. Instead of going inside, he had ducked to the side of the door, afraid that someone might come out. When nobody did, curiosity had gotten the better of him and he had then peeked into the window to see what was going on. That's when the man's face had appeared directly on the other side and a quick glance directly into Peter's eyes killed him.

Peter reminded himself the man's death was an accident. With that in mind, he was no longer disgusted with what he was about to do. He had accepted the fact he could kill people at a glance and eventually also came to accept the necessity

III: Sin Eater / **313**

of having to steal from their dead bodies. He justified the act by reminding himself that he hadn't intentionally killed any of the people he stole from. It had been almost four months since the last accidental death, after all. In the intervening months between that last death and this, Peter had survived on the pocket change and hand-outs people offered him where he sat crumpled and not making eye contact with anyone on various street corners during morning and afternoon rush hours.

He had pretty much avoided staying in shelters or anywhere that other homeless people congregated for a sense of community and security. He moved around a lot, not wanting to become known anywhere, hoping he was able to stay incognito, even amongst the homeless.

The door in front of him was unlocked. That would make the process easier. His first thought of what he was going to do with any money he found on the body of the man he'd just killed was not to purchase food or some sort of drink to take the pain away. First, he would purchase a pair of sunglasses. A nice dark shade that completely blocked out his eyes. He had found that keeping his eyes squinted or wearing dark shades seemed to reduce the effect of his death glance, as if they somehow blocked the ability of his eyes to penetrate those of his victims.

When he walked through the door, Peter was stunned to see two bodies crumpled together on the floor. Closest to him lay the man with half of the side of his head missing. But beside him, there was another man, a younger one, blood still pouring from his neck.

Peter was a bit taken aback, trying to figure out what had been going on in here.

He realized, though, that he didn't have much time, so knelt down and started going through the man's pants' pockets. His designer shirt and fancy trousers suggested to

314 / *I, Death*

Peter that he'd find more than a few measly dollars. He pulled a wallet from the man's back pocket and a thick billfold from the front left pocket. When he moved the man's arm to check his other pocket, a bloody knife clattered to the floor from the clenched fist.

The young man lying on the floor next to fancy pants moaned.

Peter started and dropped the billfold.

"Holy shit!" he muttered.

The young man was still alive. Peter looked more closely at him. The young man's eyes were barely open, his nose was smashed in, and he was bleeding from the side of his neck as well as a gash across his throat.

Peter glanced at the knife on the floor.

Then back at the young man.

"Holy shit," he repeated, louder, starting to piece together what must have been happening in this room a few minutes earlier.

"H-help," the young man managed to say, and his eyelids opened and he looked up at Peter.

Peter didn't know much about stab wounds or how much blood loss a body could survive, but the steadily growing pool of blood gushing out of the man suggested to him that there was nothing he could do to help.

Well, Peter corrected himself, there was nothing he could do to help the man *live*. But there was one thing he could do to help him.

Peter leaned forward, took the young man's head between both of his hands and stared deeply into his eyes.

Blood started pooling in the man's eyes, then started pouring down his cheeks.

He wasn't sure how much suffering he was able to prevent by taking the man's life — if it was a mere few seconds he'd spared him, or minutes, or perhaps even another hour — but

III: Sin Eater / **315**

all the same, an orgasmic shiver rolled down his spine and a deep guttural laugh forced its way up as he felt the man's life force leaving the body.

And Peter felt a renewed strength and energy — even stronger than before.

He wasn't sure how much of it was the effect of releasing the power and how much of it was the satisfaction that he had been able to put it to a good use twice within a matter of minutes.

First to kill a killer.

Then an act of euthanasia.

Peter smiled in the dimly lit room as he considered this.

The sun was setting somewhere far beyond the tall buildings of downtown Toronto. Dark shadows crept out from the corners, growing longer and larger, while everywhere lights were being turned on in an attempt to hold off that darkness until the sun reappeared the next morning.

Just a few blocks away, the Blue Jays were halfway through a home game at the Rogers Centre. They were beating the Red Sox by three runs, evident from the distant roar of the crowd on the wind heard even above the steady song of cars passing by on the Gardiner Expressway.

As always, the city was alive with change, alive with light, alive with sound and with life.

But, getting to his feet in the back room of Johnnie's Bar and Grill, Peter smiled and let out a laugh. This time a normal, mirth-filled laugh.

For the first in a long time, Peter too felt alive.

Alive with the power of death cursing through his veins.

He had never really considered it before; but his curse could be put to good use. Peter O'Mallick — who had killed his parents as an unknowing baby and child, who had killed his guardians, several friends, classmates and even strangers — had spent most of the past year wandering the

316 / *I, Death*

streets as a derelict, avoiding looking at people, avoiding eye contact. That same nineteen-year-old who had spent the better part of each day trying to deaden the pain and guilt of all the people whose lives he had taken had just discovered a way to redeem himself.

3

Charlie Watkins felt the strangest band of pain around his frontal temporal lobes just shortly after his encounter with the guy with the thick grey whiskers on his chin and the long ugly scars on his wrists. But he had made twenty dollars out of the deal, and that was the quickest cash he'd ever made in five minutes without having to blow anyone.

All he had to do was go into the corner store and purchase a pair of sunglasses with money the guy had given him. It was the strangest request he'd ever filled — and he'd had plenty of bizarre requests in the years he had been living on the street and selling himself for sexual favors.

But if only that pain would go away.

He rubbed at his forehead, closing his eyes. That made the pain worse.

The newly formed tumor in his brain was growing at an incredible rate.

Charlie would be dead before he would be able to turn his next trick.

4

Peter walked down a bright and sunny Yonge Street, actually enjoying himself for the first time in over a year. He wore the sunglasses proudly, aware of the simple freedom that wearing them granted. Nobody could look into his eyes and then die while he wore those sunglasses.

Of course, he was concerned for the young male prostitute he'd asked to go into the store and pick up the sunglasses for him. He'd been careful to keep his eyes squinted and not to make eye contact with him, and he'd been positive the kid would just walk away with the money. But sure enough, he came back with the requested sunglasses. Peter was surprised at this and momentarily opened his eyes as the kid handed them over. Peter averted his eyes quickly as he passed the kid a twenty dollar bill.

He beat a hasty retreat as soon as Peter handed over the money, so Peter figured he would be fine. He was still worried though. After all, now that he had figured out a use for the power surging within him, he was hoping he wouldn't have to kill any more innocent people.

The sunglasses gave him not only freedom, but confidence. He could kill at his own pleasure now — it no longer had to be an unavoidable accident.

III: Sin Eater | **319**

It was all clear now, or at least as clear as things had seemed for the longest time. There was at least some sort of light in his future now. Things were looking up.

Except for Sarah, he reminded himself, and his thoughts turned, as they often did, to the one lost love that he still couldn't get over. No amount of drink, no amount of time passed, was able to take that pain away.

His original plan — besides running from the authorities when they'd found he'd been living in the house with Uncle Bob's dead body — had been to flee to Toronto, to the last place that Sarah had been spotted before her cousin had turned up dead.

He'd known it was going to be virtually impossible to find her; if she was even still alive. But what else was there for him?

And he had nothing left to lose, after all.

After deciding to give it all up, after staring at himself in the mirror to self-apply his death curse having failed, Peter tried slashing his wrists, taking a hand-full of Uncle Bob's heart medication, and tried overdosing himself with booze.

None of them worked.

Sure, his wrists bled, and hurt like hell. He passed out from the pain and from the blood loss. But he woke up a day later. It hadn't killed him, and his wrists were all hacked up and burned with the pain. But they eventually healed over, leaving nasty scars there.

Then he'd tried the pills. The same thing happened — he fell into a dark bliss, but awoke a day later in a pool of his own vomit, his head splitting in pain.

He did the same thing with drink. He consumed more than he knew he should be able to survive. But again, it didn't work, it didn't kill him.

The only benefit of having consumed so much alcohol was the numbing sensation that seemed to help. So he kept

320 / *I, Death*

at it, kept drinking as much as he could, and while he knew it wouldn't kill him, it did help to numb the pain.

The one pain he'd not been able to dull was the memory of Sarah.

Peter barely acknowledged almost being hit by a car as he jay-walked across the street because his mind was suddenly filled with memories of Sarah. Memories of a happier time. He caught a clear vision of her from his memory of almost three years earlier and clung to it desperately.

Sarah. Her black hair, green eyes and the slightly twisted smile on her face. Beautiful Sarah as he held her in Uncle Bob's pickup truck in the parking lot by the Levack ski hill, far from the city, far from the evil and corruption, far from any thought of a death curse. Innocent and sexy Sarah, the look of excitement in her eyes that first night he touched the exposed flesh, fingered the kidney shaped mole on her breast. Her cute squirm and the sparkle in those green eyes. It had been the first time they'd gotten to that point, and was one of the fondest memories he had of her. They had just finished talking for several hours, sharing with each other their worst fears, their greatest insecurities. That's what had made the physical moment which had come later more intimate and why it stuck in Peter's mind so clearly.

Peter never understood why the death curse had never affected Sarah. Particularly when they'd spent so much time together, when he'd spent so much time gazing into and being lost in her eyes. He'd always suspected that perhaps, like Sarah's father, she had been dying from some cancer he'd caused in her — likely some sort of undetected cancer.

Perhaps she was dead by now.

But he clung to the thought that she might still be alive, and that he might still have one more chance to just talk with her.

III: Sin Eater / **321**

Because Sarah was the only person who had completely understood him.

And since she'd also lost several people close to her — her father and her cousin and Miss Hamilton — she was possibly able to understand the unending waves of grief that flooded his heart.

5

A piercing shriek came from the alley to the right.

It cut through the night with a suddenness that brought chills to Arny's spine. It wasn't the volume that had gotten to him. It was what the rising pitch of the shriek actually reminded him of: laughter.

Arny threw the car into drive and merged into the light flow of evening traffic, rolling up his power window. He was married with three chubby kids who would probably grow up to be lazy and disgustingly obese like he was now, with his belly pressed against the lower part of the steering wheel. The last thing he needed was to be found slashed open by some homicidal maniac leaping from the alley where he was parked waiting for some sleazy skank to walk past and offer to blow him for twenty bucks.

It was a ritual that he chickened out from performing each Friday night for the past six months. His wife, that bitch, hadn't gone down on him in over a decade, and he was longing for nothing more than the sweet feeling of lips on his cock.

So every Friday night he cruised around, thinking that this would be the night he would do it, he would be in the right place at the right time and pay some stranger to blow him to high heaven.

III: Sin Eater / **323**

Then his wife, that bitch, would really have something to storm and whine about. Not that he'd ever tell her, of course.

He thought of her lower lip trembling as she growled at him through a spray of spit; her course brown hair would slip over her forehead and in front of her eyes and she wouldn't brush it away — that bothered him the most — because she was too busy cranking out her unending list of complaints. That he was too lazy, too fat, didn't spend enough time with the kids, didn't do enough around the house, never picked up after himself, ate like a slob and chewed with his mouth open.

As Arny drove away, he wasn't sure he would ever have the courage to pay for sex from some sexy young chick. But it was the mere thought of it that allowed him to keep going, to put up with his wife's bitchy complaining. He actually smiled thinking about the pouty look on her face as she cursed at him.

Because thinking about her unpleasant disposition and endless whining was certainly better than thinking about that high pitched cackle he'd just heard echoing through that alley.

6

Moments after Arny drove off, Peter O'Mallick stumbled out of the alley, fumbling to get his sunglasses back on. The deep pounding in his head was so severe that his nose bled in a thick stream from his left nostril. And some damn fool was tilting the street on him, making it difficult to walk straight or completely upright.

As the pain faded slightly to a low dull throb, he regained more of his balance.

He closed his eyes for a moment but all he could see was the fresh coat of crimson and brain matter splattered on the alley wall behind him, the startled look on the face of the mugger as the back of his head exploded like he'd just been sucking on the barrel of a shotgun.

Peter had been startled to see the dramatic effect of his death stare hadn't faded even though he'd used it three times in the last 24 hours. His original thought had been that the power had been pent-up within him for a long time and that was what caused the man's head to explode back in Johnnie's Bar and Grill. But that didn't seem to be the case now that he let the power of his curse out again.

His power seemed just as strong.

And, strangely enough, Peter himself felt stronger, had more energy than he'd had in years. Part of him wanted to attribute it to the fact that he finally felt in control of

III: Sin Eater / 325

himself, in control of this curse he'd lived with his entire life. But another part of him knew that there was more to it. Something preternatural about the way each death provided him with an energy, a power that seemed to pulse through his veins.

7

It hadn't taken Brecht long to find the teen. Not with the string of bodies the kid carelessly left in his wake.

But the first thing Brecht knew was that O'Mallick hadn't been purposely hitting his gang members. He might have been responsible for a few of them, but, following the kid, observing his random pattern of vigilante killings, Brecht knew the teen had not been specifically targeting his gang.

That was a good thing.

The bad thing, of course, was it meant someone else was out there knocking his gang members off slowly, one by one.

And the fact they weren't leaving the Fitz root beer labels at the scene meant one of two things: either Fitz was orchestrating the hits but for some reason didn't want them to be attributed to him, or that Fitz's gang wasn't responsible for the killings at all, and that meant some new player had arrived on the scene.

Either way, Brecht had to take someone down.

And to do that, he needed O'Mallick under his control.

8

The ambush on Peter started off as a regular mugging.

A man in a business suit was walking down the street after dark and a tall blond thug about six feet tall and with shoulders at least three feet wide jumped out from the shadows with a knife in hand and forced him to duck into a nearby alley with him.

Peter, watching from across the street, an apparent homeless bum sitting in a pile of filth, and looking oblivious to the rest of the world, had become quite proficient with this scenario. He waited until the blond meaty mugger pushed the guy into the alley before he rose to his feet and quickly ran across the street.

He figured it would be only fair to give the bad guy a chance to live before taking him out, so he shouted as he ran.

"Hey, leave him alone!"

In following to the standard script Peter had become used to, the mugger reacted surprised to see the prone bum from across the street that he'd thought was not going to be a problem witness suddenly on the attack, and turned the knife toward Peter.

Again, Peter thought it only fair to give him one last chance.

"Drop the knife and I'll let you live!"

328 / *I, Death*

The large blond man with the knife kept the blade trained on Peter and let out a short laugh. *"Let me live?* Fuck off and die!" Large gobs of spittle flew through the air as he shouted.

"That's where you're wrong," Peter laughed. "You're the only one who'll be dying tonight."

As Peter reached up to pull his sunglasses off and deliver quick death to this man, something hit him fast and hard from the left side. His sunglasses flew through the air as Peter was tackled sideways and bounced off the brick wall to his right. Peter couldn't believe it. Someone else had been lurking in the alley and had attacked *him.*

He whirled to face the attacker who was still close to his body, but he couldn't make eye contact with him. The man's shoulder pressed up under Peter's armpit as he rained multiple punches to his ribs and stomach. Peter folded into the punches.

While he was still being pummeled, a third man joined from out of nowhere, landing a few punches to the right side of Peter's head and face. Lashing out with his right hand, Peter was able to ward off at least one punch while the blond mugger stepped forward and thrust his knife into Peter's shoulder. Peter looked back toward him, eyes glaring and meeting his gaze full on. The man's head flipped back as if being punched by an invisible fist. Blood poured from his nose and mouth as he staggered back, dropping the knife.

Peter saw the man in the suit scramble for the knife before another punch stuck him in the right eye and a white burst of pain clouded his vision.

He felt himself stumble as fists, knees and feet repeatedly hit him from both sides. The two unseen assailants delivered piercing blows to his face, stomach and sides. Peter felt his ribs break from a well-delivered series of kicks, and blood poured from a gash in his forehead. The blood ran down his face and mostly obscured the vision from his left eye. By that

III: Sin Eater / **329**

point, his right cheek and brow were swollen from repeated blows to the side of his head. Surrounded in a growing whirlpool of pain, he managed to watch as the man in the suit picked up the knife the blond mugger had dropped and a brief sense of hope filled him.

Funny, he thought, that the man Peter had been about to save from a mugging might actually turn out to save Peter's life.

The unseen assailant who'd first surprised Peter grabbed both of Peter's arms and pulled them tight across his back while lifting Peter up to his feet. The move was startling, because, through the explosions of pain Peter hadn't even been aware that he'd stumbled and fallen to his knees. The intensity of the pain, of the sudden assault prevented him from even realizing that fact. The man on his right grabbed him roughly by the hair and yanked his head up, exposing his throat.

Through blurred vision, Peter managed to spot the man in the suit approaching, holding the knife. But he wasn't looking at the attackers, he was looking directly at Peter — and grinning an evil, twisted grin.

This was a complete ambush, Peter realized, as the knife carved an arc through the air toward his throat.

The blade was halfway toward Peter's exposed flesh when a high pitched cry boomed through the alley and a blur knocked the knife out of the man's hand. Peter couldn't really see what was happening, but felt his arms being released.

No longer supported, Peter toppled forward, heard the sound of flesh striking flesh, of bones cracking, cries of pain, shouts of alarm, and, more than anything, the victorious battle cry of some additional unseen person who appeared out of nowhere.

The whole thing was surreal.

330 / *I, Death*

Supporting himself on hands and knees, Peter tried to get up but the throbbing pain in his head and body were too much. He kept listening, helplessly, while the sounds of a ruthless and vicious fight raged all around him.

His consciousness winked in and out several times during the scuffle, but the only thing that remained constant was the high pitched cry echoing off the alley walls. As the fight continued, his arms finally gave way and Peter crumpled to his side on the alley floor.

When Peter cracked his one eye not swollen completely shut, he looked up to see, through a thin film of blood, a figure standing above him, silhouetted from behind by a single street light. He appeared to Peter like an angel.

"It's okay, Peter," a voice said, as a hand reached out and took his. "You're safe now. I'll take care of you."

9

Deciding to sacrifice four of his gang members hadn't been easy, But Brecht marvelled at how beautifully it had worked.

The kid might have matured a great deal in the last half of a year, learned some appropriate defensive and offensive tactics to stay alive on the street. But that essence of "naïve Northern Ontario bumpkin" still seemed to reign in his blood.

That and the fact the kid was desperate for a strong father figure. The same way he had fallen into the role of protégé under his teacher Kyle Robinson, he would similarly slip into the same role with Brecht as his master.

Brecht, of course, used all this knowledge of the kid's psyche and previous history to his advantage. He summoned up the style and manner that Robinson had used in the classroom to win O'Mallick over. And he spoke a strange mix of philosophical quotes that he gathered from literature as well as the some of the movies the kid had cherished watching with his uncle.

Over the course of several weeks, O'Mallick — whom Brecht had checked into a small private hotel suite — would anxiously await the arrival of Brecht, who appeared between doctor visits (a medical resident who was indebted to Brecht and working to pay it off), sweeping in and out of the young

332 / *I, Death*

man's room with a cloak and dagger mystique like some sort of secret "Deep Throat" type character.

During these visits, Brecht would toss out obscure yet tantalizing references to the fact that, as O'Mallick himself had begun to understand on his own, the innate powers he was born with weren't a curse, but rather a blessing.

10

It was always after the painkiller was injected that Peter's angel-like mystery benefactor would appear.

The young doctor or nurse — Peter wasn't sure the man's actual role, nor even his name — didn't speak to him about anything other than his health, how he felt, or offering an update on how he seemed to be doing. The only conversation or even human contact Peter had was with the tall dark figure.

Peter wasn't sure how much time had passed; whether it had been a few days or even a week. But when he finally was able to speak through the pain and drug-induced haze, his first words were to the mystery man.

"Thank you,"

The man simply smiled down at Peter, the light from the window behind him casting him in the same angelic haze Peter remembered from the alley.

"Rest, my son," he said gently, and Peter dripped back off into the darkness.

The next time Peter saw him and was starting to heal, his words were inquisitive rather than appreciative.

"Who are you?"

"I am your destiny, Peter," the man said.

Again, Peter slipped back into the darkness.

334 / *I, Death*

The next time he awoke, the man was still standing above him, looking down on him with an affectionate grin.

Peter again asked the question.

"My name is Bryan," the man said. "And you need not do this alone any longer."

Again, the darkness consumed Peter, despite his struggle against it.

‡   ‡   ‡

Bryan explained to Peter that he too had been living on the street, confused, hurt and alone; unsure of where his next meal was coming from or where he could find shelter and remain safe from the elements and those who sought to harm others.

Over the course of an entire afternoon, broken by brief passages of Peter's loss of consciousness, Bryan shared his tale of the stranger who took him under his wing and taught him basic martial art skills in order to survive.

"This man, whose name I never learned, somehow found me every day, no matter where I wandered," Bryan said. "He brought me food, clean clothing. He taught me simple moves of self-defense.

"I never understood why he was helping me; but I knew, I just knew he was there to protect me. I could sense it in him. Whenever I asked why he was so kind to me, why he was being so generous, he would shake his head and say that the fates had guided him my way. He said when the time was right, the fates would speak to me too, and reveal my destined path.

"Months passed; I still never learned his name. But he continued to find me, and explained the need for people to clean up the ills of society.

"He said that people like us were destined to live among the down-trodden, that we became stronger from helping

*III: Sin Eater / **335**

others; our goal was to protect the weak, defend the innocent and use our powers for good."

"P-powers?" Peter asked.

Bryan nodded his head, closing his eyes, seeming to struggle with what he was about to reveal.

"I seem to have been born with a bizarre affliction."

His ribs protesting in pain, Peter tried to sit up, get closer to this man.

"You were?"

"Yes. Since I was a youth I have been able to *know* things that I shouldn't know. About someone. About their intensions, their desires; what turned them on, what frightened them.

"It was something which was difficult to explain. Nobody believed me when I told them. Sure, some of my friends offered sympathy, some professed to empathize. But nobody really understood what it meant.

"When I meet people, I can see right through them. I can understand their nature, see the brightness and blemishes of their very soul. I can detect the evil in some men; and it reeks terribly in some."

Stunned, Peter stared at Brecht with his mouth hung open.

"My mentor told me he understood what my destiny was; and his goal was to help me. So he trained me in martial arts, explained the necessity for me to use my powers for good — to acquire enough wealth that I could help others.

"But he also explained the difficult nature of my true destiny to help detect and wipe out the evil that runs through society, that I should continue to fight and overcome evil whenever I could.

"He explained that nobody would ever truly understand what I was; the power I possess, the good I was meant to play. I should, thus, keep my powers secret, until I met the person I was destined to take under my own wing.

336 / *I, Death*

"When I came upon you and the men who were attacking you in the alleyway, Peter, I immediately knew.

"Your name came to me, your special ability and your goodness shone through. They were beating you, crowding around you and there was an incredible stench of hatred, anger and fear surrounding them.

"But within that, your light, your goodness, your purity shone through.

"I saved you because, looking at you, even through the murk of their dirty souls, I could see it. And I knew.

"You were the one.

"The voice within my own soul told me the power you possessed, the one causing you so much conflict and pain, was the complementary element I had been seeking.

"It told me that I have been called to guide you on your Path."

Fighting against the haze and pain, Peter smiled and a tear leaked from his eye. For the first time since this madness began it felt as if someone else finally understood him. Without questioning, without suspicion. This man, Bryan — Peter's savior, understood him.

Peter finally spoke again. "My Path?"

"Yes, the Path you had already begun to take. Likely because there was a part of you that already knew."

"Knew?"

"Yes. Your destiny, Peter. You were put here to help me clean up the ills of society. I can detect them, I can sense in my very nature, those who are so evil that there is no redemption; where the only answer, the best answer is death."

"You detect them with your power?" Peter asked, an overwhelming sensation of relief flooding through him. "And I kill them with mine?"

Bryan smiled, placed a hand on Peter's shoulder.

III: Sin Eater / **337**

"Assassination of the truly evil. It is the highest form of public service."

11

Brecht marvelled at how easy it was, given the right mixture of drugs and of leveraging O'Mallick's desire for a strong father figure, merging in concepts from the hero movies O'Mallick had enjoyed.

Given that the young man had already begun to use his death power in that way, it was a simple path to convince him to continue on, but in a guided fashion.

Brecht continued to paraphrase and steal quotes from various movies, explaining to O'Mallick how he had amassed his wealth and resources by taking from those he purged from society; that he operated like a modern day Robin Hood.

O'Mallick embraced the concept that Brecht headed up an organized gang of vigilantes to assist him in this quest. But Brecht kept Peter from interacting with any of the others, explaining how nobody else would understand him.

Brecht also described to Peter the necessity that the men who worked for him weren't always of the same breed as Peter. Their souls were 'grey, extremely grey;' but dealing with them, and keeping them close was a strategy Brecht needed to employ.

"The best way to properly infiltrate the underworld and to do what we need to do to purge them from our society," Brecht had explained, "is to infuse ourselves within their culture, gain their trust by operating within their circles."

III: Sin Eater / **339**

Peter felt that he understood. "You need to cross through the gates of Hell in order to slay some demons."

Brecht nodded. "Exactly. But that doesn't mean I want you to be sleeping next to those demons. I still need to keep you protected from them as much as I can."

Through this special type of isolation, Brecht was able to completely control the young man's perspective, and use him to strategically take out rival gang members.

‡   ‡   ‡

As the days rolled to weeks and the weeks to months, Peter's loyalty to Brecht grew to such an extent that there was never a question as to the good he was playing.

Simply, to Peter, it felt as if he finally belonged, he finally fit in; he could finally do some good to make up for all the mistakes he had made.

12

As the diarrhea-like flow of laughter finally subsided, Peter was able to again get control of his balance. He wiped the tears from his eyes and looked down at the crumpled figure lying at his feet.

He let out a deep breath.

The man he had just killed was one of the few people who worked within Brecht's organization that Peter had gotten to know, and even considered a friend.

‡   ‡   ‡

His name was Jacob Hailey.

He had been the first friend, other than Bryan Brecht, that Peter had made since his trek south from his small Northern Ontario town.

Of course, though Peter respected, looked up to and depended upon Brecht, he didn't count him as a friend. Brecht was more of a mentor, a teacher. He was someone to be revered, followed.

Which is why, when Jacob offered that first small sign of friendship — the extended package of cigarettes as they both sat in silence on a shadowed park bench — it meant so much to Peter.

III: Sin Eater / **341**

None of Brecht's other men would even speak a word to Peter. But Jacob's offer was an outreach he felt deep in his heart.

The two of them were on the bench in the wee hours of the morning, just sitting and watching a club across the park and on the other side of the street.

The club was supposedly operated in conjunction with a major gang affiliation. But, like most endeavors Peter went on, he knew nothing about it. Peter wasn't supposed to be out on this type of mission, but he had expressed to Brecht a desire to get out, to work on a task other than an outright kill mission.

He said he needed to do something a little different in order to gain a bit of balance.

Brecht had been hesitant, but finally gave in and told Peter he could accompany one of his closest trusted men on an observation mission.

On the way out, Jacob hadn't even glanced at Peter — he barely said more than the words necessary to convey where they were going next or to utter simple instructions or orders such as "keep quiet" or gesture at something and say "over there."

But the offer of cigarette felt different.

"Thanks," Peter said, taking the proffered cigarette. "Do you think we'll see anything?"

Jacob didn't immediately answer, and Peter thought they would go right back into the silent routine.

"You know the boss doesn't want us making small talk with you."

Those were the first words Peter had ever spoken with one of Brecht's men, other than simple questions or direct orders.

"So I've heard."

"Why is that?" Jacob asked. "The boss explained that you're something special, but never explained what or how

342 / *I, Death*

your assassination technique works. All he kept saying is that it would be dangerous to get close to you. And that, when necessary, you should be defended at any cost. But you don't look all that dangerous to me."

"I am."

They sat in silence for another minute.

"The boss might very likely get rid of me for this, you know."

"For what?"

"For speaking with you so openly."

"So I've heard."

Silence again.

"I still don't think you look that dangerous."

"That's a mistake too many people have made," Peter said. "You're likely best to not get too close. That's another mistake people make."

Their simple conversation evolved from there. Without revealing too much about his secrets or his curse, Peter had gotten to know Jacob a bit better.

Peter learned that the man had two children; a boy aged nine, and a four year old girl. That he was estranged from his wife and one of the few pleasures in life was when he got to spend time with their kids on alternating weekends.

Peter and Jacob kept their friendship from Brecht; and though Peter had felt guilty for this minor betrayal, he didn't see any harm in getting to know someone that he could just speak with.

The friendship had continued for almost two weeks; the occasional shared cigarette and brief chit-chat when nobody else was around.

When Brecht informed Peter of his latest mission — to take out Jacob Hailey, who was suspected as being an infiltrator into Brecht's ranks — Peter thought it was possible his mentor knew of the friendship they had developed.

III: Sin Eater / **343**

But he never doubted Brecht.

Though it was hard, he did what he was asked.

He went into Jacob's room in the downtown townhouse headquarters, said he had something to ask the man.

Jacob smiled at him. "Sure. What?"

"Did you ever wonder why I never made eye contact with you?"

Jacob grinned. "I always thought it was because you were shy."

"No," Peter said, grasping the man's head between his hands and staring him dead in the eyes. "Not shy. Just... *this*."

And that was all it took.

Tears streamed down Peter's face as if in a bizarre mirror response to the blood pouring down Jacob's.

That was when the uncontrollable laughter began.

‡   ‡   ‡

Peter stood over the crumpled body, thinking about how it seemed his fate that he could not have a single friend.

Brecht stepped up behind Peter and placed an arm around his shoulder. Peter felt himself melt into the comforting embrace.

"You done good, kid," Brecht whispered.

"I still don't like it," Peter said, letting out another long breath and feeling the strange tickle in his throat that sometimes came as an after-effect of the use of his power.

"I know. I know. It's not easy doing the right thing, Peter." Brecht patted Peter on the shoulder. "But Jacob was very likely behind the infiltration into my... family. He needed to be stopped before more damage could be done. Maybe now that you've taken care of him, the surprise killings of those working for me will stop.

344 / *I, Death*

"You did the right thing, Peter. You did the right thing. Some lessons can't be taught, Peter. They must be lived to be understood."

13

I t took a long time for Peter to fall asleep that night. Thoughts of Jacob, the man he was very nearly friends with — as well as all of the other friends he had killed — came back to him, flooding his mind.

Donnie, Jagdish, Robbie, Rainy, Gwen. Chad, Sarah's father, Miss Hamilton, Aunt Shelly, Uncle Bob.

All of them dead.

Because of Peter.

Their faces swirled in his mind.

But he must have fallen asleep, because a muted thump woke Peter some time later.

He sat up in his bed. The clock radio on his night table read 2:13 AM.

He heard the muted thump again. It was coming from down the hall. He got out of the bed and, wearing only his briefs and a t-shirt, the standard clothes he normally slept in, he slowly crept to the door.

Inching the door open, he saw a shadow moving along the hall, accompanied by quiet footsteps.

Whoever it was, they were coming closer, he would be able to see them in another second or two.

Then she appeared.

Peter almost fell on his ass.

346 / *I, Death*

Because the woman creeping down the hall was the spitting image of Sarah.

Okay, not necessarily the spitting image.

But she looked uncannily like the girl who still held his heart captive.

Sure, she was older looking, and her hair was the wrong colour: it was a golden wheat, where Sarah's was a raven black. And this woman's face was weathered, worn and tanned; even in the faint light of the hall the crow's feet around her eyes were pronounced.

So, yes, she looked remarkably like Sarah, but it couldn't be her.

It couldn't.

Particularly since this woman was dressed unmistakably like a hooker in a black dress that barely ended at her ass cheeks and cross-thatch stockings held by a thick black garter strap at the front.

She moved through his line of vision quickly, but Peter's head was swimming with thoughts of Sarah.

Who was this woman?

He had to keep watching her.

It was like getting a dose of Sarah.

He opened the door a little more and stuck his head out, watching her move down the hall.

She walked like Sarah.

Yes, even though she was wearing heels higher than Peter had ever seen Sarah wear, she moved so much like the girl he loved that, from behind, if he didn't know any better, Peter would have sworn it was her.

His heart swirled with an intense pang of longing and, strangely, comfort.

Peter's life had seemed to be like riding a sea of pain while forging through a fog of horror. But through the murkiness

III: Sin Eater / **347**

of it all, there was always Sarah, with fond memories of her cutting like a beacon through the murk.

If Sarah were truly here, and if she still loved him, then maybe all of it, all of the death, all of the suffering, all of the needless pain would be all right. All the death in the world would be all right if only Sarah loved him.

As he watched, she stopped three doors down from Peter's, the door belonging to a guy Peter knew only as 'Dave,' and rapped quietly on it.

The door opened, Dave muttered a few words under his breath, then Sarah quietly slipped into the room and the door closed behind her.

Peter shook his head. He'd just thought of this woman as Sarah, as if she were Sarah, the woman he loved.

What if she was?

What if it were her?

Peter stepped out into the hall and took a few tentative steps down the hall.

What if it were her?

"Sarah?" he whispered very quietly under his breath.

What if?

Placing his hand on the door handle, Peter slowly turned it and pushed the door in a crack. He saw Dave, wearing nothing but a pair of boxers, sitting on the bed, leaning back on his elbows and grinning.

In front of him, the woman, Sarah, gyrated in a dance to some unheard music, and then began to peel her top off slowly; the start of a sensual strip tease.

No!

Peter stumbled back, shaking his head, trying to tear the vision out of his eyes.

This isn't Sarah. It's a hooker.

Plain and simple.

348 / *I, Death*

He had to keep telling himself this. This isn't what Sarah has reduced herself to. Not his Sarah, not the love of his life; not his one and only true love.

He turned and headed back down the hall toward his bedroom.

That was when a cold deep laughter from Dave's bedroom stopped him dead in his tracks.

He would recognize the laughter anywhere; in particular because it sounded so very much like his own when killing.

He stood in the hall, waiting for more. But there was no other sound.

Suddenly, the door opened, and the woman came out, seeing Peter.

She stopped.

Looked him dead in the eyes.

"Peter? What are you doing here?"

14

"Sarah? Is that really you?"

A startled look of realization came across Sarah's face as she looked at the way he was dressed. Then she closed her eyes and nodded. "You were in one of these rooms. Sleeping here. I get it. You're one of them."

She turned away from him and quickly stalked down the hall.

"Sarah?" Peter called after her. "Wait."

She stormed down the hall and descended the stairs.

Peter ran back to his room, quickly pulled his pants on, then threw on a button-down shirt. He didn't bother grabbing shoes, but paused long enough to grab the pair of sunglasses from his nightstand.

He raced down the stairs and out the front door.

Sarah was a full block ahead of him.

His bare feet slapping on the cold concrete of the sidewalk he raced to catch up with her.

"Sarah," he called. "Please don't leave. Please. Not again."

She still didn't turn, just kept walking away.

"Sarah! Please!"

Out of breath, he finally caught up to her, reached out for her arm.

350 / *I, Death*

"Sarah!" he said, pulling on her arm, managing to stop her from going forward any more. "Please. I just want to talk. I just want to understand."

Keeping her eyes closed, she shook her head.

"I thought I already told you a long time ago, Peter."

"I-I know. But a lot more has happened. I have so much to explain."

"I don't want to hurt you, Peter."

"Then please. Come back with me. Come back and talk."

"No," she said firmly.

"Y-you don't want to talk?"

"Not there." Sarah said. "Come with me. My place."

15

Sarah hailed a cab and they both got in. After she gave the address to the driver, they remained quiet for the rest of the trip.

It wasn't until they entered her apartment that they began to talk.

Peter was the first to speak.

And when he started to talk, he couldn't seem to stop himself. It all came out as natural as anything he'd ever felt. Even though it has been almost two years since he and Sarah had spoken, Peter felt just as he had when they had been close; back when he could tell her anything and he knew she would understand.

Sarah had always been a good listener; she'd been the first person he had ever been able to open up to. Going back through his story, explaining what had happened from his point of view since their breakup just after the Christmas of 2011, he skipped many of the minor details, but expressed a good deal about how the various circumstances had made him feel.

Ultimately, he expressed his regret for the pain he had caused her, for the grief he had put into her heart; for the death curse he had placed on her father, the curse that landed Miss Hamilton in the hospital; the one that had killed Chad and Robbie.

352 / *I, Death*

Sarah sat back and listened — mostly quietly, occasionally nodding and offered brief verbal cues that she was paying rapt attention to his words.

There were many moments while he spoke that she had seemed eager to interrupt him. But, as she had always been, she maintained her consistency as a good listener and waited until he was finished.

About the only thing that Sarah did, other than her active listening, was she guided Peter to a couch and she sat across from him in an armchair. And once, during his story, she got up to get them both a glass of water, hearing his voice starting to break in his mad rush to get everything out.

He ended his tale explaining how he learned, by accident — and then, again, through Brecht — that his curse could be used for good, and told the story of how he had been putting his powers to use these past several months.

He ended with the tale of having to kill Jacob, the one friend he had made, and coming to realize he could never get close to anybody again.

Finally, exhausted, he crumpled against the back of the couch and laid his head back.

"Oh, Peter. You poor thing."

Sarah slid from the chair across the way and sat beside him on the couch. She slipped an arm over his shoulder as if it were still the Christmas of 2011, they were still best friends and lovers, and he melted into her embrace, burying his head in her shoulder, breathing in the fine scent of her hair, amazed that she still used the Rainforest scented Herbal Essence shampoo, and let himself cry.

"Peter, there's so much for me to explain."

"I shouldn't even be here, Sarah. I'm putting you in danger by being here, by being with you. I've been here too long already."

III: Sin Eater / **353**

He started to stand up, but she held onto his arm and rose with him, preventing him from stepping away.

"Peter," she said, placing a gentle hand on the side of his face. "Listen to me."

He looked at her and couldn't control his emotions any longer.

"Sarah, I still love you. I never stopped loving you. That's why I have to leave right now. That's why I…"

She startled him by leaning in and pressing her lips against his.

Her lips prodded and pushed against him and her tongue pressed against his lips, pushing them open, exploring inside.

The pain, the confusion, the torture he'd been living with, slipped away as he felt himself falling completely into Sarah's kiss.

His left arm went around her body, pulling her closer; his right ran along the side of her face, his fingers swirling through the curls of her hair.

Sarah moved one hand around his back while the other rubbed his chest, then quickly moved down, across his stomach and to the growing bulge in his pants.

Peter moaned as Sarah rubbed him through his jeans, and he brought the hand from her hair, down along her face, her neck, and gently massaged her breast through the black silky fabric.

She found his zipper and tugged down on it, pushed aside his briefs and freed his aching erection. As her fingers wrapped around him, his body shuddered and he let out a gasp of ecstasy; hot sticky fluid erupting from him and coating the black fabric of her stomach.

Peter broke the kiss.

"S-sorry. It's been a long time."

They both then laughed and Sarah stepped back shaking her head. "Now I'm going to have to get out of this dress."

354 / *I, Death*

"I'm sorry, Sarah. I... it's... I..."

She pressed a finger to his lips, slowly peeled her dress off, then sank to her knees. "I'm sure I can bring you back."

It didn't take her long at all.

When she did, she stood, again they kissed, and slid onto the couch together. Peter took his time exploring every curve of her body with his fingers and lips, gently kissing the kidney shaped mole on her breast and feeling, for the first time in what seemed like forever, that he was home.

His exploration of her body and the homecoming complete, Sarah then guided him inside of her, and, grinding in perfect rhythm, their bodies arched together. The impassioned dance of their sweaty naked bodies took away so much pain, so many difficult memories, that it seemed neither one of them would ever let it end.

But it did.

Eventually, their passion grew in intensity and ferocity. The gentle rhythmic movements became more urgent, more hurried. It seemed to be a mad race to the finish, but neither one of them was pushing ahead. Instead, they were pulling one another along, urging each other towards the finish.

As they climaxed, the sunglasses slid from Peter's face and for the first time he looked Sarah directly in the eyes.

"Sarah. I'm so sorry. I love you." Was all he could say, hoping she would hear the words before the violent finish.

16

"You're sorry?" Sarah said, laughing. "Oh, Peter, don't be. That was the best orgasm I've ever had. I love you."

Peter shook his head, the tears that had been streaming down his face shaking off like water droplets off of a dog that had just gotten out of the water.

"I... I don't understand," he said. "How can you still be alive?"

"Oh honey," Sarah said. "You still don't get it, do you?"

"Get it?"

"I think," she said, "that it's time for me to tell you my side of the story. Perhaps then you'll understand."

"Understand?"

"There's nothing more to understand than how this lying cunt has tricked you, me, and everyone!"

Peter and Sarah turned to see Brecht standing in the doorway of Sarah's apartment.

"This woman is the assassin we've been looking for, Peter," Brecht said. "She is the one who has been taking out the members of our family."

"What?" Peter said, getting up from the couch. "What is going on?"

"Kill her, Peter!"

356 / *I, Death*

"Don't listen to him," Sarah said, standing naked in front of him, one hand gently placed on Peter's chest. "Brecht is a liar and a cold blooded killer. He is pretending to be a vigilante seeking justice, but he is nothing more than a low life drug dealer who needs to be stopped."

"Lies from this despicable whore!" Brecht yelled. "I can see it all over her, just as plain as day. Her soul is black with it.

"She has used the power of temptation to lure men in, and then kill them. You saw it yourself earlier this evening with Dave. That was what awaited you, Peter. She was about to kill you before I burst in. I can read that in her lying face. Step away from her, quick!"

Peter immediately took a step back, noting the look of horror on Sarah's face when he did so. He looked from Sarah and over to Brecht, then stood stunned, suddenly confused over what to do.

He took another step back, away from the two of them. Then another, and another, until he was a full six feet from Sarah, and eight feet away from Brecht.

Brecht was the one person Peter had come to count on, to depend on — someone who knew about the strange power he possessed; who held his own unique power to see through deception.

But he was asking Peter to kill the only woman he had ever loved; and she had just told him she loved him.

She'd meant it, hadn't she?

She did love him.

But it did seem strange, all of a sudden, for her to behave like that — particularly when, for the longest time, Peter had tried continually to reach out to her and she had simply turned him away.

Perhaps her words, her actions, were another trick, a simple yet horrible lie.

III: Sin Eater / **357**

"You need to kill her, Peter. Show her no mercy. Mercy is for the weak. She is an enemy. An enemy deserves no mercy."

Something about the words Brecht had just spoken struck Peter as strangely familiar. He shook his head, trying to push away the feeling of why they sounded so familiar; why they seemed to poke at his memory.

Mercy is for the weak.

There was something about those words.

An enemy deserves no mercy.

Brecht lurched forward, brandishing a knife that he produced from out of nowhere.

His right arm arched quickly through the air, the silver blade glistening in the light, towards Sarah.

She was looking at Peter still, turning her head only at the last second to see the blade coming toward her.

Sarah dodged to the right, too late to avoid the blow completely so that the knife sank into the soft space between her left shoulder and her chest.

She fell to her knees, the blade sticking out of her, and Brecht kicked her in the stomach, ripping the knife out.

A rainbow-like arc of blood sprayed as he pulled the knife out and booted her once more in the ribs. She fell against the couch, then to the floor on her stomach.

An enemy deserves no mercy.

The words came to Peter suddenly, in a flash-memory scene from a movie he'd seen.

An enemy deserves no Mercy. What is the problem, Mr. Lawrence?

358 / *I, Death*

The Karate Kid: Daniel and Mr. Miyagi are visiting a karate dojo and witness John Kreese training his students. He is ragging on them about competition, confronting an enemy, then turns to see them standing there.

Another movie line, again from Brecht's mouth, rushed into Peter's mind.

> *Assassination: it is the highest form of public service.*

Also from a movie. Chiun in *Remo Williams, The Adventures Begins*.

Another warrior, sensei / trainee type movie.

> *Some lessons can't be taught, Elektra. They must be lived to be understood.*

So many of the things Brecht had said to Peter were snippets from movies he'd watched and enjoyed.

And blogged about.

Had Brecht been playing him?

These thoughts and memory-snippets all came to Peter as he watched Brecht kick Sarah in the stomach, then slam his foot into her ribs, then repeat the process.

As he was realizing their sources, his vision suddenly cleared so that he saw Sarah getting to her hands and knees and Brecht swinging the blade down towards the middle of her back.

Peter dove at Brecht, knocking the blade from his hand.

They stumbled together towards the armchair, Brecht falling against it, but then grabbing Peter by the hair with his left hand and by the scrotum with his right. Pulling and twisting, he easily lifted Peter over his head and sent him flying through the air, landing, upside down against

III: Sin Eater / **359**

the fireplace mantle, sending a sharp pain through his lower back.

Peter crumpled to the floor as Brecht advanced on him, stepped down hard on his back with his boots, then placed several kicks into the exact spots of his old wounds. Then he struck him with three kicks in rapid succession: his left eye, his forehead, his nose.

As Brecht walked away, Peter cradled his broken ribs, his vision clouded by the blood leaking down his face, and tried to get to his hands and knees as Brecht grabbed Sarah by the hair and pulled her to her feet.

She swung at him, her fist bouncing with little effect off the side of his head and he threw her down on the couch.

He jumped onto her, pinning her arms above her head and straddling her. Sarah struggled beneath him, but was unable to break free.

"Are you watching, Peter? Are you watching your little whore?"

Brecht laughed madly.

"You moaned and cried and whined about her nonstop on that stupid blog. She abandoned you, tossed you aside like scraps on a plate. And still you longed for her, begged.

"I came along, offered you everything, trained you, taught you to become a true warrior, took you under my care. Showed you how to be strong.

"And she returns, and is able so easily to turn you away from me. You chose *her* over me?"

Brecht moved so that he was pinning Sarah with a single hand. With his free left hand he began to fumble with his belt and zipper. His cock poked out, solid, hard, every inch a weapon as the knife he'd held just moments earlier was.

"I was going to kill her outright. But this betrayal, your choice of her over me says you need to be taught a lesson about loyalty.

"She is a looker, I'll give her that." With his free hand he swatted at her breast. Droplets of blood from the wound just above her breast spattered through the air. Brecht's cock bobbed in eager anticipation at the pain he was causing, and the sight of her blood. "For that, I'm going to throw one hell of a fuck into her. I'm going to rape every possible orifice while you watch.

"And then, I'll do it again. And you'll watch again.

"And *then* I'll kill the cunt."

"Noooooo!" Peter yelled, struggling to get to his knees. He moved forward about a foot before the pain sent him sprawling back to the floor. He started inching his way toward the couch.

"Go ahead. Fuck me. Do whatever." Sarah said, fixing her eyes on Brecht. "Just let Peter go. Stop using him in your twisted way."

Brecht slapped her breast again, then her face.

"Shut up, bitch!"

"Go ahead. Hit me. Beat me. Have me. Have all of me. I won't struggle. I won't fight you. In fact, I'll make it good for you, better than you could ever imagine, if you just let Peter go."

Sarah licked her lips and pursed them.

"I'll make it really good."

Brecht leaned forward and tentatively released her left arm.

"Go ahead, bitch. You know you want it."

Sarah reached down, wrapped her fingers around his cock and started stroking him. She squirmed on the couch as if in eager anticipation.

"That's it," Brecht breathed. "Nice..."

Brecht slapped her breast again, relished the splatter of blood across it, then leaned down and licked a droplet of blood from her nipple.

III: Sin Eater / **361**

Peter tried again to get to his knees. This time he was successful and had moved another two inches forward before he fell to the floor again. He still had three feet to go. He wasn't sure if he'd be able to do more than pull at Brecht's ankle, but he was putting everything he could into moving forward, inch by inch.

"Kiss me," Sarah moaned. "I want to taste my own blood."

Brecht's cock visibly throbbed again at these words, and he lifted his face to hers, pressed his lips against hers.

Peter was on his knees one more time, within reaching distance of the couch. He reached out, his fingers inches away from Brecht's ankle.

That's when Sarah, in the middle of their open mouthed kiss, suddenly sucked in.

Brecht's eyes opened wide, as if she had yanked on his tongue.

Then the top of his head imploded, and his eyes burst out in a climactic-like explosion of fluid.

Sarah turned her head to the side and let out a bone-chilling deep guttural laugh that seemed to go on without end.

It was the last thing Peter heard before he blacked out.

EPILOGUE

Sarah and Peter stalked the city together.

Like Peter, Sarah was born with the death curse. But, as she explained to him, it *wasn't* a curse. Brecht — in his twisted manner of using Peter — almost had it right. Sarah quoted the old Lewis Carroll line about even a stopped clock being right twice per day.

When she first realized she was affected by this power, she pulled away from Peter. Sarah had blamed herself, not Peter, for her father's cancer. She attempted to remove herself from those she loved the most, so as not to have them fall victim to the power coursing within her blood.

She had confided in Miss Hamilton about how she felt, and the two of them had researched the concept that Sarah came to understand as *Sin Eater*. Their research was revealing a lot when the accident happened. That sent Sarah further into reclusion, fearful of harming anyone else.

She explained that people like Peter and herself were born with a unique power and responsibility of vanquishing evil souls and sending them back to the void.

It wasn't until she was in Toronto with her cousin and they were surrounded by the biker gang that Sarah realized she could be in full control of her innate nature.

It had something to do with the manner by which women matured more aggressively than men. Peter's bouts

Epilogue / **363**

of uncontrolled death were the side effect of a hyperactive pubescent period, something which again often occurred earlier for girls than for boys. She explained that the sunglasses trick Peter had used worked as a type of placebo. Because he believed it held his power in check, it worked.

Sarah also explained that the visions she had, the dreams she experienced, often twisted, nightmarish and grim, were likely the result of the consumption of souls, a side effect of the nature of their purative power.

Peter simply couldn't believe it.

After all this time, after all the angst and suffering, this curse was a blessing.

Because it meant he would spend the rest of his days, side-by-side with the one person he truly loved, the only person he could trust.

Brecht was gone, but Fitz was still out there, as were countless others, willing to take their place.

It was another natural cycle of the universe.

Holding hands, Sarah and Peter embraced their role, pleased to be able to do it together.

They still had a lot of catching up to do.

And there was a lot of work ahead of them.

About the Author

Mark Leslie lives in Hamilton, Ontario and has been writing since he first discovered his mother's Underwood typewriter in the spare bedroom closet of the family home at the age of thirteen.

His first published short story "The Progressive Sidetrack" (1992) was a Young Adult humor story, and his first published horror story "Phantom Mitch" (1993) received Honorable Mention in Ellen Datlow's *The Year's Best Fantasy & Horror*.

Mark's first book was a short story collection entitled *One Hand Screaming*, which he released in 2004. Since then, he has edited science fiction and horror anthologies such as *North of Infinity II* (2006), *Campus Chills* (2009), and *Tesseracts Sixteen: Parnassus Unbound* (2012). Curious about the paranormal (and still frightened by the monster under his bed), Mark also writes a series of true ghost story books for Dundurn which include *Haunted Hamilton: The Ghosts of Dundurn Castle & Other Steeltown Shivers* (2012), *Spooky Sudbury: True Tales of the Eerie & Unexplained* (2013), and *Tomes of Terror: Haunted Bookstores & Libraries* (2014).

When he is not writing, Mark Leslie tacks "Lefebvre" back onto his name and works for Kobo (www.Kobo.com) as Director of Kobo Writing Life (www.KoboWritingLife.com), a platform that allows authors and smaller publishers direct access to publish to Kobo's global company. He divides his free time between playing LEGO and video games with his son, Alexander, tasting regional crafts beers, and getting lost in bookstores and libraries.

Here's some we made earlier...

TERRIBILIS
A novel by Carol Weekes

Witty, charming, handsome and a skilled conversationalist, Alison Mornay's ex-husband is also a biology prof at Ottawa U. His specialty is a rare breed of frog found primarily on the east coast of Colombia. His colleagues and students love him; one of them even married him. But when a string of apparent heroin overdoses leads to the death of a very odd assortment of people — including Lee-Ann Boudreaux, a human resources specialist at the university, and two Byward Market prostitutes; one male, one female — Detective Constables Morrow and Crowther start looking a little more deeply into Dr. Gerry Scott's field of study, and the Ottawa U biology lab.

Other than cause of death, there doesn't seem to be any connection between the victims, which makes Morrow and Crowther think they're dealing with a serial killer who's both highly intelligent and absolutely ruthless. But will they be able to cover the distance between Eastern Ontario and Muskoka fast enough to prevent a fourth murder? And will they get enough evidence to arrest their serial killer before he outwits them yet again?

They looked at each other, sickened in the pale rind of the street lamp.

"That woman doesn't deserve to die," Morrow told them. "Not that way. Not any way."

Mystery, thriller, and medical drama, *Terribilis* is an uncomfortable journey into a 21st century heart of darkness.

RECOMMENDED RETAIL PRICES

Paperback: \$19^{99}/£12^{99} ‡ ISBN: 978-0-9866424-1-8
Hardback: \$39^{99}/£22^{99} ‡ ISBN: 978-0-9866424-4-9
E-Book: \$14^{95}/£9^{75} ‡ ISBN: 978-0-9866424-0-1

SLEEPLESS KNIGHTS

Mark H. Williams

Sleepless Knights *is, quite simply, a cracking good read.*
— Toby Whithouse, writer for *Doctor Who*, creator of *Being Human*

Sir Lucas is butler to King Arthur and the Knights of the Round Table — the person who managed every quest from behind the scenes. He's a man whose average working day involved defeating witches and banishing werewolves, while ensuring the Royal pot of tea never crossed the thin line separating 'brewed' from 'stewed.' What's more, 1,500 years after that golden age, he's still doing it — here in the modern world, right under our noses.

When King Arthur and six of his knights are exposed as living among us, Merlin is unleashed and a grim apocalypse unfolds, uncovering secrets from the past that King Arthur would rather stay buried. When Lucas is forced to confront his own peculiar destiny, will he choose to sacrifice his true love and lay down his life in the service of his master?

Sleepless Knights is a tale of high adventure and warm humour, with a spring in its step, a twinkle in its eye and, at its heart, the *ultimate* butler.

A cross between The Remains of the Day, Le Morte d'Arthur *and* Harry Potter, *it's packed with charming characters, thrilling chases, intrigue and mystery. A glorious modern chapter of an age-old legend,* **Sleepless Knights** *introduces us to a distinctive and sympathetic new voice in fantasy writing.*

— *Toby Whithouse*

RECOMMENDED RETAIL PRICES
Paperback: $17^{95}/£12^{95} ‡ ISBN: 978-1-927609-01-9
E-Book: $14^{95}/£9^{75} ‡ ISBN: 978-1-927609-02-6

ATOMIC FEZ PUBLISHING

Eclectic, Genre-Busting Fiction

www.AtomicFez.com

CPSIA information can be obtained at www.ICGtesting.com
Printed in the USA
LVOW04s1242230914

405430LV00006B/13/P